Milo's Scale

Jane Chipperfield read Classical Civilisation at Warwick University, going on to enjoy a twenty-year career as a Primary School teacher. She left teaching to explore other opportunities, initially studying at Sotheby's Institute in London.

Her novel, *Milo's Scale*, is the first in a trilogy of thrillers featuring Rick Devan.

Jane Chipperfield

Milo's Scale

VTP

Published in 2013 by Village Times Productions
Avebury House, St Peter Street, Winchester, SO23 8BN

Copyright Jane Chipperfield 2013

ISBN 978-0-9576497-0-5

A CIP catalogue record for this book is available from the British Library

Acknowledgements

Much appreciation and many thanks to
Adella Lithman, Nicholas Young and Edward Matthews.
Their technical expertise was invaluable.

For Kay

Prologue

Geoffrey Bolt emerged from the florist twenty yards from High Street Kensington Tube. He was carrying his briefcase in one hand and clutching a bunch of red roses in the other, holding it far enough away to prevent any drips landing on his Crombie overcoat or his lace-ups whose shine had the reflective properties of a chrome kettle.

It was seven fifteen on Friday evening and cold. He'd been lucky to get away from the office even at this hour but pissing off Jessica by being late for a second time on their anniversary, was not an option. Geoffrey had the roses,

"I don't want flowers from a supermarket or a garage forecourt," she'd warned – she was very particular about that kind of thing, "But most of all, don't be late; I don't want to be entertaining the Harringtons alone while I wait for you."

Bill Harrington worked in his department but was his junior and never late for anything – a bloody saint in Jessica's eyes.

The streets were busy and there were still a fair number of going-homers entering the station. Taking the steps down to the platforms, Geoffrey checked the time at his wrist. 'Home in half an hour', he thought. Dinner was to be at eight. There'd be time to spare.

A train pulled out just as he walked onto the relatively empty platform ….. but, it was Friday; Geoffrey had no doubt it would fill again before the train, predicted in two minutes by the digital notice board, screeched in.

He sat on a metal bench seat two thirds down and watched the numbers swell as he polished his glasses with his tie. At the sound of an approaching rumble and a warm breeze from the darkness, he stood and ambled to the yellow line at the platform edge only to be suddenly knocked backward, as a man in his forties carrying a rucksack, rushed past him and, to the gasps of others on the platform, jumped into the path of the train as it emerged from the tunnel at speed – dropping his rucksack on the platform as he leapt. The man's head hit the driver's window with a sickening smack, sending a crimson spray onto the platform and over those closest to the impact before his lifeless body fell beneath the wheels.

Geoffrey's expression turned from surprise to horror as he staggered back to his seat. He sat down, looking up the platform. The train had come to a halt half-way. A scrum surrounded the cab as the driver stepped unsteadily out, his face drained of all colour. Geoffrey stared at the scene for a moment through spattered lenses and then looked down at the sleeve of his coat. Dark red globules were settling into the fibres.The bouquet he'd bought for Jessica lay at the platform edge – dropped at the moment of impact. No point in picking it up. Despite his good intentions, he was going to be late again and a bunch of roses would be no defence.

1

The shop was five minutes' walk from Rick's front door; he'd buy a newspaper and spend the rest of the morning lazing around on the sofa. Max had made himself comfortable on an armchair, purring and inspecting the underside of his paw, searching for whatever it is that cats search for with such focused concentration. Rick scooped him up, tucked him under his arm and made his way out of the flat. After a brief struggle with the deadlock – Max was wriggling – he started up the stairs to return the cat to his owner.

At the door, Max jumped to the floor, pushing his nose impatiently at the wood. Rick knocked and waited. Milo was either out or in a deep sleep. He knocked again; there was still no response. Maybe the Professor had gone away without telling him. The key Milo had given him was in his pocket; he'd leave a note telling the Prof. Max was fed and warning him not be tricked into feeding him again today.

Mail scuffed on the mat behind the door. Rick picked up the letters and piled them on the shelf above the radiator. The door at the end of the hall was open and Max ran off into the main room. Rick followed. The curtains were open and the room brightly lit with morning sunlight lating a scene of carnage. Drawers were pulled out, their contents strewn about the carpet. The sofa and armchairs were upturned and slashed open, springs and stuffing spewing. The grandfather clock lay on its side, winding door open, pendulum askew. The day/date windows showed Saturday 21st March. The hands had come to rest at twenty minutes past twelve. Books, wrenched from the bookcase, lay in disordered heaps. Nothing had been spared in the frenzied attack. Max perched himself on the corner of the overturned sofa looking around him for a moment then suddenly, leapt off, heading for the bedroom.

The door was slightly open and the cat didn't break step as he shot through the crack into darkness. Rick picked his way across the room cautiously, stepping over the Professor's scattered possessions. He reached the bedroom door and pushed. The curtains were shut tight and it took a moment for his eyes to adjust to the gloom as he stepped in, fumbling for the light switch.

A second picture of chaos greeted him when the lights came on. The Professor's elegant clothes and shoes were torn from the wardrobe and flung about the floor. Every drawer was open and the contents spilled. Rick stood in shock for a moment, wondering if the perpetrator was still hiding somewhere or long gone. He snapped out of it and reached for his phone. Milo needed to know there'd been a break-in. Max had disappeared somewhere but as Rick was scrolling his phonebook, the cat's echoing cries were coming from the bathroom. The Professor's number came up and he hit the speed dial. The ring tone of a mobile phone broke the silence almost immediately; it was coming from the bathroom.

The door was open half-way and Max's piteous calls were continuous from within. With a sense of foreboding, Rick stepped in and stiffened at the sight of a blood-soaked Milo staring at him with unseeing eyes from the bath. Milo was naked, head propped against the wall with his arm over the side of the bath. The wrist was cut and a penknife lay where it had fallen almost covered by congealing blood spread across the tiled floor. Next to the knife, Milo's mobile jiggled in a still soft crimson puddle as it vibrated and shrilled simultaneously. Milo's other arm was inside the bath; also cut at the wrist. It lay across his thighs next to an almost empty Vodka bottle. Rick cancelled the call and everything was silence again save Max's mournful cries.

Feline paw-prints of blood trailed along the ledge that ran across the wall at the back of the bath. Max was sitting there, eyeing his master's lifeless body. Rick was sure Milo was dead but summoning up courage, reached over, searching for a pulse in the Professor's neck. There was none and Milo's head lolled forward as Rick snatched back his hand with an equal mix of horror and nausea. He picked up Max and went into the lounge, careful not to disturb anything, flipping open his phone and this time, dialling the Police.

It could have been the slap of the letter box flap that had woken Rick that Saturday morning or maybe it had been the sound of Max, whining in the passage outside; either way, his lie-in had been interrupted and there was no going back to sleep. He'd pulled on his boxers and hurried to the door barefoot, scooping up the letters from the mat and making it back to bed in quick strides, instinct hunching his naked torso to stave off the chill air in some imagined way.

The monthly missive from his mother in its blue air-mail envelope, stood out from the assortment of college updates and dross from junk mailers who were gradually getting his number. Despite being more than able to use a computer, she steadfastly refused to use email, insisting he maintain a written correspondence with her.

"If a fuse blows or something breaks in the electronic world," she would say, "there'll be no record of our words to each other. Writing will be good exercise for you, besides, you'll think of me longer than the few seconds it takes to send an email."

She hadn't always been like this and he knew the reason for the change – his accident. The letter was a monthly update of life back home with the sub-text of 'we're here if you need us'. It was also a regular, if fleeting, reminder to him of how his world had been turned upside-down in the literal sense when his car flipped on the Interstate, skidding at speed, wheels in the air, down an embankment and halted with devastating effect by the unyielding trunk of an ancient oak. One week in a coma and two years of physiotherapy had put a hold on his fledgling career as a journalist as well as killing a budding relationship with Juliet Laskey. Two summers on and she was the rising star at *The Seattle Times*, not him.

Juliet Laskey – they'd got talking on the day of his interview – both up for a junior position at the *Times*. It was between Rick and the dazzling Juliet. They were the final two pitching for the post, whittled from a hungry pack of graduates. Waiting in the outer office to be called for the final session, she sat opposite him in a smart suit – her blonde hair tied back in a French pleat away from her porcelain smooth features and soft, clear blue eyes. A man could drown there, Rick thought, and, if she was as competent as the way she looked – and why wouldn't she be – she'd made it to the final cut after all, he'd better be at the top of his game when he was called through that door at the corner of the room. He studied her as she flicked through her notes. She gave an appearance of confidence but he thought he caught a glimpse of apprehension in those blue eyes; maybe she wasn't quite as sure of herself as the sharp suit implied. Maybe he still had a shot.

The vending machine in the corner caught Rick's eye.

"Coffee?" he offered, breaking the nervous tension in the room.

She looked up, catching his eyes in hers, saying nothing for a moment, then,

"No thanks; I think I'll be going in soon."

He smiled and sat down again. Confirmation, he thought, she was in the same frame of mind as he was – too taut, too focused on the impending conversation in the next room to risk anxiety provoking a spill from a hot cup. But for all that, with the ice broken, they began to engage in the small-talk of strangers on a train – nothing of substance – words forgotten as they were spoken.

Two hours later, after a final grilling from the editor, luck went *Rick's* way.

In anyone's book, Juliet was an attractive woman but it wasn't just her looks that had drawn him to her but the way she had taken the news. She was calm, absorbing the decision, smoothing her skirt as she stood up, slipping her notes into a sleek black leather attaché. There was something in her demeanour that said this is no defeat, merely an irritating setback. If she was disappointed at losing to him, she didn't let it show.

On impulse, he asked, "Are you busy tonight?"

She turned to him, looking up from the attaché as she zipped a side panel. For a moment, the full force of those blue eyes settled on him. He knew what she was thinking – is this guy a straight-up type or is he a weirdo? Perfectly reasonable, he supposed – they'd set eyes on each other for the first time only a few hours before. There was a pause as she studied him, then –

"What did you have in mind?"

"Dinner on the Bay?"

She hesitated again, looked down and withdrew something from her attaché. "Pick me up at eight," she said, handing him a card and flashing a bewitching smile over her shoulder as she went to the door. He watched her go, savouring the warmth of that smile.

Rick thought of himself as a confident guy. He kept himself in shape and had been told once he had rugged looks and a winner's smile but Juliet was something else. She struck him as more than just a winner; there was a quality there he couldn't put his finger on. She may have lost *this* time but it seemed all part of a plan. Alone in the room, snapping shut his brief case, he was left wondering how he'd won out against her.

Arriving at her building just before eight, Rick peered

through the ornate glass door into the lobby. Before he could press the intercom to her apartment, she was there, stepping from the elevator just inside, shimmering in a blue satin cocktail dress. Her hair was loose now, falling to her shoulders. She saw him immediately, smiling at him through the glass. God, she was more beautiful than he remembered from a few hours ago.

Dinner was at a window table overlooking the water. He particularly remembered the lights from the boats out in the bay, their reflections broken by the restless waves. He liked to remember how she said she was struck by his dark brown eyes and quirky humour. He liked to remember the way her hair flicked from side to side when she walked and the dimple that appeared in her cheek when she laughed.

The second date had been two days later and left him with the expectation that, given a little time, this could go somewhere. They were calling each other frequently and life suddenly held a double promise – new job, new love. Then came his adventure on the Interstate and the long period of recovery. When he'd come round enough to think, the realisation that in the same way as one swallow doesn't make a summer, two dates and a promise of a third, was a long way short of making Juliet a stayer. The accident was on a Friday – the job at the *Times* due to start the following Monday. That fact, along with so many others, was a blur – a distant memory as he stumbled along the road to recovery through a fog of tumbling images and speeding nightmares which haunted him in sleeping and waking moments alike.

His parents and his sister, Sally, had been the constant throughout this uncertain time when doubts surrounding his ability to regain full mental capacity were never far from their minds. Looking back on the period, he marvelled how they had silently tolerated his frustration and mood-swings, how they had given comfort and encouragement until the day he'd finally felt able to start writing again. His father, in particular, had surprised him, taking time away from his manufacturing plant just to be with him. It was as if the business with its two hundred staff didn't exist.

Acutely aware of the sacrifices his family had made and how deeply they had been affected by the possibility they might lose him during that first comatose week after the crash, Rick silently vowed not to put them through anything like that again.

When he'd finally emerged into the light again, with a pain in his head bigger than the one he had when he woke up in the arms of coach Farley after being hit by a baseball in the Third Grade, the world had moved on. The nightmares were gone but he'd missed his chance at *The Times*. His place snapped up by Juliet who was now a features writer for the financial section. He liked to think he felt no animosity, hell, he'd have done the same. Nevertheless, the occasional photo of her in the *Times* society column, stepping into or out of the Ferrari of the young property magnate she was now dating, needled him but he had to swallow the pill and move on himself.

His attention was diverted elsewhere by the search for work but his efforts to secure a permanent position at any of the other newspapers in town had been fruitless. They'd taken occasional freelance pieces from him though, small mercies, he thought. Before he knew it, three and a half years had passed since he and the oak tree had met that night on the Interstate. Sally, whom he'd played hours of Frisbee with as part of his recovery regime, was now at law school in New York with a promising career ahead of her. The fact was, he was still at home at twenty-eight years old with no firm direction plotted and no job.

Rick considered himself healthy now despite the occasional dull ache in his shoulder when it rained. His exercise programme demanded by the physiotherapy department developed his body shape with a six-pack to be proud of. The confidence knocked out of him in the accident, was back along with that so called winner's smile – albeit he wasn't particularly winning at the moment. Possessing confidence is one thing, he reflected one morning in front of the shaving mirror, but without a new angle, he'd be stuck in a rut for a lifetime.

Television journalism had begun to catch his interest, a natural progression somehow – he wondered why he hadn't thought of it before. His father encouraged him to pursue it further. He looked for a university that would take him as a mature student and soon found the ideal fit – in London. His parents were hoping for something closer to home but he needed to get away for a while – lay a few ghosts. He enrolled for the September semester for a one-year MA course in television journalism at Goldsmiths, University of London. It was now March.

His thoughts were interrupted as Max whined again, this time, right outside the door. Rick ignored the cat's pleas and took a paper knife from the bedside drawer and slid it under the flap of his mother's letter, flattening four sheets of thin blue paper against his thigh and beginning to read.

Hardly thirty seconds passed before Max was determinedly making himself heard again, scratching at the apartment door and generally demanding attention. Rick could almost see the speech bubble above Max's head – "You know I'm out here and you know I know you're in there, so why in hell don't you let me in?" He looked up in frustration, stepped out of bed, pulling the blanket around his shoulders as he went to the door. It was barely open when Max pushed his way in and shot through to the kitchen giving an unspoken "About time!" as he scooted past. By the time Rick caught up, Max was standing next to the cupboard where several tins of cat food were kept for those times the Professor was out of town, quite often these days.

It was on his second day in London in the three storey apartment block, when Professor Milo Ferretti introduced himself in the corridor. Rick was grateful for a friendly face and a warm greeting. The Professor, it turned out, lived in the flat above.

"Why don't you come up later for a cup of tea; I can tell you about the place – where the shops are and all that. Four o' clock do you?" the smartly dressed academic invited.

At four, Rick found himself sharing a sofa in the Professor's flat with Max, a black Tom with a white patch over his left eye. Max had made his presence felt the moment Rick had entered the flat, settling on the arm of the sofa as Rick seated himself – letting him know who lived here and who the visitor was.

"Please call me Milo," the Professor said, as he brought a pot of tea, shooing Max off the sofa and resting the tray on a low table.

Milo looked impressive for his age. He was in his seventies at a guess, but with the easy manner of a much younger man. Bright blue eyes, a slight Italian accent and his smart appearance gave him a certain style. His deeply polished black lace-ups gleamed in the light of the table lamps and marked him out as one who came from an era when the shine on the shoe reflected the character of the wearer.

The layout of the flat was an exact duplicate of Rick's – small hallway leading to an open plan kitchen-diner cum living room. The only division was a small breakfast bar which defined the kitchen area. It was comfortably furnished with a few pieces of replica Georgian furniture, dining table with chairs, carving table and well stocked drinks cabinet. The only pieces that didn't seem to fit were a 1920s roll-top desk and a mission style grandfather clock of the same period. The sofa and two armchairs faced neatly filled bookshelves that lined both walls of the living area and a door at the back of the room, which, Rick presumed, would lead to the only bedroom with its en-suite bathroom.

Everything was in its place. From the beginning, Rick had Milo pegged as a very ordered individual, organised to the last detail. From the shining shoes to the way the silk handkerchief jutting from his jacket's top pocket matched his tie. It was clear this was no mad professor.

From that evening on, their meetings were frequent and pretty soon they'd established a routine of sorts. On Mondays, if Milo wasn't travelling, he would come down to Rick's and they would spend the evening playing chess over a Chinese take-out and on Wednesdays, Rick would dine at the Professor's flat and seek his advice on his course or whatever assignment he'd been set for that week. Although Milo had been a maths lecturer, Rick found his advice on revision technique and aspects of university life in London, insightful.

Over the weeks, Rick pieced together a little of Milo's life and background. He'd grown up in Reggio Emilia in Northern Italy and moved to London in the 1960s. He'd been a widower for twenty years and had no children. His only living relative was his niece who was a graphics designer with an ad agency in the West End. Rick caught a glimpse of her once, a silhouette taking the stairs up to Milo's – swaying hips which gave him a buzz he hadn't felt since Juliet. He hadn't seen her face though, only her long black hair that tumbled to her shoulders. It floated from side to side as she walked, laying a trail of whisked perfume on the air.

Milo had retired five years previously from his Head of Mathematics post at King's College in the Strand to "concentrate on a project of my own."

"What kind of project?" Rick had asked.

"Oh, just an idea – an ideal really."

Rick's expression of "please explain" drew no answer. The subject was obviously off limits. He hadn't pursued it further.

Occasionally, Milo would spend one or two nights away and would prevail upon Rick to see that Max was fed. The cat-sitting had started one morning, some two months after they'd met. The Professor had turned up at Rick's door a little flustered saying he had to leave for a few days and could Rick look after Max. He'd given Rick a key to his flat, telling him tins of cat food were under the sink and with that, had left.

The arrangement worked well. Whenever Milo returned from one of his trips, they would dine together swallowing a newly acquired bottle of wine between them. The Professor always let Rick know of an impending trip or, if Rick was out when Milo left, there would be a note slid under his door telling him how many days he should be feeding Max. So why was Max demanding attention today? There had been no note and, as far as Rick knew, Milo was upstairs.

While Max fussed over his food, Rick went back to bed and finished reading his letter. When he was done, he folded the sheets, sifted the rest of the mail and then lay for a while, working up enough energy to shower. He wasn't in the mood for any course-work and planned an afternoon in the West End with some of the other first-years who didn't seem to notice he was several years older than they were. A morning reading the newspaper and generally lounging around seemed the right strategy until it was time to leave.

2

"You say the Professor was dead when you went in the bathroom," it was more of a question than a statement.

"Yes," Rick replied.

"And what time was that?" Detective Inspector Newman asked.

"About eleven."

Newman was in his early forties with dark neatly cut wavy hair and, these days, looking trim and healthy since the warning from his G.P. of later heart problems if he didn't take care of himself.

James Newman had made D.I. only a few years earlier at thirty-nine but it seemed a world away now – obscured by the industry of murder and the paperwork that went with it. He glanced around the room as he jotted on the pad at his knee.

"And you touched nothing?"

"As I told you, I felt for a pulse and then called you guys."

"Did you see or hear anything unusual yesterday or maybe Thursday – any strangers hanging around?"

"No, and Friday I came home to change, went to the movies with friends and then to a club. I didn't get back until two."

Newman shot him a quizzical glance.

"It was Friday. We always go out on a Friday."

"Can you think of any reason why the Professor might have taken his own life?"

"I've only known him since September. I met him two days after I moved in.He invited me for tea, a sort of 'welcome to the building' kinda thing."

Newman stayed silent.

"In answer to your question, no, I don't know why he would kill himself and, the last time I saw him, he didn't seem in the mood for suicide."

"And when was that?"

"Wednesday evening – we had pizza at his."

"Would you say he seemed normal…..no appearance of stress….nothing unusual in his behaviour?"

"No, nothing. Now do you want to hear how we met or not?"

There was a pause as Rick waited for Newman to come back but Newman said nothing, merely gestured for him to continue.

"Well, anyway, I went up for tea in the afternoon and we became friends. We had a routine of sorts. Mondays, if Milo's around, he comes down to my place and we spend the evening playing chess. The only thing that interrupts us is the guy delivering the take-out. On Wednesdays, I eat at the Professor's and get his advice on my course work."

"I was under the impression the Professor's field was maths," Newman's tone was surprised, "your course is in journalism isn't it – how does that work?"

"Just because Milo is a maths guru, it doesn't stop him giving advice on revision technique and aspects of university life in London. I find it helpful – he has, sorry *had* great insight. I'll miss our talks."

"And you have no idea what he was working on?" Newman pressed.

"I told you," Rick replied, with a little irritation in his voice, "we met a couple of nights a week but what he did with the rest of his time, I couldn't tell; he kept off the subject. He went out a lot, that's all I know, where he went, I have no idea. He was working on something, that's for sure. I always figured it was something to do with maths because, as you rightly say, he was a maths lecturer once. He told me he retired to work on a project of his own; it could have been anything though."

"And you couldn't hazard a guess?"

"No, like I said," Rick replied, now more than irritated, "he wouldn't talk about it."

The detective looked at him as if he was deliberately leaving something out.

"He didn't tell me anything," Rick repeated.

"One more thing, did the Professor have any relatives you know about – next of kin?"

"He has a niece, Sophia. She works in the West End somewhere – at an ad agency, I think. I have no idea which one."

"Any last name?"

"I'm not certain but without teaching you to suck eggs, you could try Ferretti – the Professor's name. It might be the same if she hasn't married."

D.I. Newman closed his notebook with a weary look and made to leave.

Rick got up to open the door for the D.I. "Is that what it's going down as – suicide?"

"I can't say for sure, there're a few more things we have to check and there'll be the toxicology report – there was some bruising on his arms and neck and also around his mouth – we'll need to know what caused that but, right now, it certainly looks that way."

"But what about the apartment, the place was turned over. Don't you think it's a bit odd? Doesn't seem like the actions of someone about to commit suicide to me."

"When people kill themselves they're usually not thinking straight, they could do anything. I've seen cases where people have done their weekly shopping, packed it in the fridge then locked themselves in the garage with the car engine running. Only yesterday evening, my sergeant was late for his shift because someone threw himself on the track on the Circle line. That in itself isn't unusual but this guy came all the way from the Continent one day, to throw himself in front of a Tube train the next. So who can tell what's in a mind driven to suicide. In the Professor's case, there was no sign of forced entry and there's nothing to say anything was taken. Going on your statement, everything you remember being in the flat was still there, even if it was scattered around the floor. At this stage of the investigation, there's nothing in that flat to make us think it was anything more than a suicide."

As he closed the door behind the detective and returned to the sofa, Rick's instinct as a journalist told him there was something not right about Milo's death. It was the same instinct which had earlier forced him to overcome his nausea and go back into the bathroom. He'd snapped several shots of the scene with the camera in his phone before leaving and waiting for the Police downstairs in his flat. He'd taken more in the bedroom and others of the chaos in the lounge. The Police had taken thirty minutes to get there – plenty of time to download the shots onto an SD card and delete them from his phone. For safety's sake, he'd tossed the card into his shaving bag; it was lost amongst chap-sticks, tubes and shave cream.

Now alone, he flicked through the images on his laptop. He winced at the sight of Milo's naked blood spattered form, his white skin in sharp contrast to the dark red that pooled in the bottom of the bath. There was something not right, something about the Vodka bottle and a chance remark Milo had made that first time Rick had gone up for tea; for the life of him, he couldn't remember – definitely something about Vodka and not liking the stuff. At the time, Rick had been only half listening; he had been absorbed by the myriad of titles in the bookcase. However, if Milo didn't like Vodka, why would he make it his last drink. It didn't make sense.

The next picture flicked up. It was a long shot of the whole room. He zoomed in and began to track across the image, not knowing what he was looking for. The suicide of this man he'd had dinner with only a few nights ago and known for the last seven months, seemed all wrong for the cheerful character he remembered. He continued tracking, framed the section of bloody floor where Milo's mobile lay and zoomed in a little. Dark red filled the screen with the phone at its centre. Rick studied the image for a moment. One thing was for sure, he would be hearing from D.I. Newman again; the phone would have details of every call and Rick would show up as a frequent caller.

After twenty minutes with the laptop, he shut it down; it was making him depressed. It was three in the afternoon and he needed some air. The Police were still upstairs and they had his number if they needed him again. He zipped a leather jacket over a sweater and went out, heading up west.

3

Samuel Buckley rocked back in his chair, sipping coffee in his office on the tenth floor, a mile across town. The window behind his sleek oak desk spanned the width of the room from floor to ceiling and was, as were all the windows of the building, glazed with one-way glass. The block appeared as a tall mirror jutting into London's skyline. At this time every morning, Buckley liked to look out over the rooftops towards the west and watch distant planes lift into the sky from Heathrow. He would be fifty years old in four weeks and his birthday would coincide with the biggest deal of his life and maybe signal his retirement.

Samuel Buckley was the C.E.O. of Buckley Blane Marketing or BBM, the private company which would soon be swallowed by the U.S. giant Reimer Communications based in Seattle, just down the road from Microsoft. The past six months of negotiations had been tough but terms had finally been agreed and barring hiccups, the deal would complete the day before Buckley's birthday.

The intercom on his desk bleated.

"The head of I.T. is here, sir."

"Send him in."

As the door opened, Buckley came out from behind his desk and crossed to the sofas where he held his meetings. He gestured to his head of I.T, Natu Shah, to sit in the seat opposite.

"How's our project – is it done?" Buckley asked.

"Yes, all operational."

"Thank you, Natu. Please keep to the protocols you were given; this is between you and me only as usual."

"Of course, is there anything else, sir?"

"No, that's it."

Shah left his seat and went out. Barely five minutes passed before the intercom buzzed again.

"Mr. Blane's here to see you, sir."

"Send him right in please, Frankie."

There was a knock at the door and Sheldon Blane entered clutching a blue file.

"Sheldon," Buckley said, "everything okay?"

"Yes, I brought you a schedule, details of what will happen on what day – the handover and so-on."

"And what about you, are you okay? You've been a bit tetchy lately."

"I'm fine – just a few ripples needed smoothing before the big one. I've been making sure nothing screws it up that's all. Reimer's accountants have kept me at it. They've picked over everything but we're there now."

"Glad to hear it. I can't tell you how important it is that there are *no* surprises. We mustn't fall at the last hurdle."

"We won't," Blane said emphatically, "I'll see you at lunch." He placed the file on Buckley's desk and made to leave.

"So, there are no ripples remaining for me to lose sleep

over."

"None."

In the corridor outside, Blane opened his mobile lest he'd missed its vibration; there were no messages. He snapped it shut and made his way to his office. There *had* been a ripple but the last thing he wanted was Buckley meddling and moralising and urging tactics which would only delay the obvious and inevitable course of action, obvious that is, to Blane. A little bump had needed attention, that's all it was and it was being dealt with in the only way Blane knew how, silently and with what he liked to call, prejudice.

Though not as plush as Buckley's, Blane's office had a worthwhile view over the river with the same floor to ceiling windows and deep carpet. He was never worried about the view though; his focus had always been up. This office had to be functional, that's all; it was fine for his needs. He didn't want anyone else feeling comfortable when they visited him. He was the fire-fighter, the fixer of campaigns which were running into trouble or those little legal problems that could upset the running of the machine – and fix them he did before they reached Buckley's ears. He had no time for chit-chat and his P.A., Hennie, made sure he didn't have to endure any. The only concession he made to comfort was the meeting area in the centre of the room comprising a trio of black leather sofas set around a low table. It was here that any matters taking more than a few minutes of his time were negotiated or thrashed out. Visitors with day-to-day issues would perch on one or other of the two visitors' chairs which could be described as functional at best.

Sheldon Blane had known Buckley for four years. His rise

through the company had been meteoric and there was no doubt in *his* mind he deserved all that his status brought with it. He'd earned his position and earned his company shares and his partnership which brought with it the entitlement to have his name printed next to Buckley's on the company's letterhead. He'd grabbed every opportunity life had given him and taken a few it hadn't.

Suited at Savile Row, Blane was always immaculate in his appearance; exuding the attraction that comes with money and power over others. No altruist though, no smiling benefactor, more a white steel blade masked by expensive tailoring. There was one person in Sheldon's life and that person stared back at him every morning from the mirror; there was no room for anyone else. He was direct in his approach – blind to the people he'd pushed aside on his scything rise to the top, a trait he'd learnt fighting his way out of a rough upbringing in the East End of London and into university. Ten years ago he'd been working in a small ad agency, chasing small clients and small money but making a name for himself even then. Now, two jobs later – three in actual terms but he didn't count his first; it was short-lived and ended badly, though not for him –   and in his thirty-fifth year, he was about to become exceedingly wealthy.

His phone vibrated for a moment, jiggling in two short bursts on the polished desktop. A satisfied smile crept across his features as he read the short text message. No, he thought, as he read the words of confirmation, there would be no falling down now.

He called Hennie on the intercom.

"You can call it a day, Hennie, I'm just leaving."

There was no verbal response, only a click which said she understood. She never changes, he thought, a click sufficed, she felt no reason in wasting breath.

Henrietta (Hennie) Lawson had been with Blane from his first week in the firm. She had quickly gained a reputation as Blane's no-nonsense Rottweiler and had her ear to the ground for anything she felt he should know.

Only eight mourners attended Milo's funeral at the crematorium just a mile away and that number included Rick. A somewhat lonely end, he thought. An inquest, ten days after Milo's death, had been adjourned but the unofficial consensus among the Police was that the Professor had killed himself. Okay, the autopsy showed this was the most likely explanation but Rick was uneasy, he couldn't square the circumstances to fit; it seemed so unlike the man – moreover, there was no suicide note. He was shaken from his thoughts as the minister bade the tiny congregation sit; their shuffling echoed around the cavernous auditorium as they settled into creaking pews. The prepared précis of Milo's life began but Rick's thoughts were elsewhere. He drifted back to the day he'd made his gruesome find and the contradictory details – not least of these being the trashing of the flat. Then there was the toxicology report. It showed Milo had only ingested a small amount of Vodka, certainly not enough to give him the courage to go through with suicide or to sink into a stupor while his life ebbed away. There was, however, a significant presence of Valium. Vodka, there was *that* thought again. What was it about Vodka? Rick cursed himself for not paying attention to Milo's words that first night.

Immediately after the Professor's death, Max had realised there was a change in circumstances and made himself at home at Rick's. This was okay for the time being as Rick presumed Milo's niece, Sophia, would decide Max's future when she got around to it. He didn't want to bother her right now but, much as he liked Max, his plans for his time in London hadn't exactly included pets – well not of the four legged variety anyway. The Police knew he had Max and they'd assured him they would let her know. He'd seen Sophia one or two times coming and going from the building in the last week but never to talk to, only exchanging the occasional polite nod in the corridor as they passed each other. They'd never been formally introduced so it was unlikely she knew who he was.

With the exception of Sophia, the mourners were male and most were of the same sort of age as Milo. There was a man in his fifties who had walked in with Sophia, helping her to a pew. He looked different from the others – smarter in a pinstripe suit like some sort of professional, a lawyer maybe. He sat next to her; their body language suggesting they were acquaintances only. As Rick watched the coffin disappear through the curtains he wondered if any evidence pointing to an alternative cause of death was also going up in smoke.

Later, at a small gathering Sophia had organised in the Professor's flat, Rick watched her make small-talk and thank each one of the mourners for their presence. All were former colleagues of Milo's from King's with the exception of the man Rick had seen accompany Sophia at the crematorium – Milo's solicitor, he confirmed later by a quick scan of the book of condolence at the door.

The academics were caricatures of the professorial class, tweed jackets with elbow patches and bushy eyebrows. One peered out from a beard which almost totally obscured his face. Save the beard, he was a good deal smarter than the others, sporting a well cut suit and silk tie. He stood slightly apart from the group, only joining the conversation when compelled by a question seeking confirmation thrown his way. It was difficult to tell with the beard but, by the way he carried himself, he could have been a good deal younger than the others in the group. Rick's momentary curiosity was pushed aside as Sophia caught his eye.

The apartment was no longer the vision of hell he'd stumbled into on his last visit. It was back to its ordered appearance with everything in its place as if nothing out of the ordinary had ever happened here. Sophia had been busy. Gazing across the room at her, he studied her for the first time. Her black hair was tied back highlighting her dark eyes. Even in her sadness, Sophia was a beautiful woman. She caught him looking, smiled back at him and broke away from Milo's old colleagues who'd gathered round her in a huddle, threatening to corner her if she remained.

"I'm sorry I haven't been to see you before," she said, apologetically. "You're Rick Devan aren't you?"

"Yes," Rick nodded.

"My uncle mentioned you. How's Max?"

"Max is fine. He seems to have moved in without missing a beat."

"I'm sorry about that – I'll be taking him as soon as I finish up all the legal stuff."

"Don't apologise, Max and I are getting along fine. Take your time," he said, taking back all his thoughts of off-loading the cat.

She looked down for a moment and then said, "It was you who found him wasn't it?"

"Yes. It seems unbelievable; I half expect him to come in at any moment offering tea and biscuits."

Her dark eyes were welling. "I don't understand it; I saw him three days before and he seemed fine – upbeat even."

"Me too – I told the Police but they were pretty sure it was suicide right from the start. I'm not convinced though, not in the least. Milo just doesn't fit the profile of what I'd imagine a disturbed person to be. He was the opposite; laid back and taking life easy."

She hesitated then said, "If he didn't kill himself, what other possible explanation could there be for the way you found him?"

Rick thought about her question before answering; he didn't want to make things worse – mindful of her fragile state.

"Maybe we could meet a bit later – after the others have gone. I have a few questions I need answering before I can advance any theories. Call me and I'll come back up." He jotted his mobile number on a paper napkin.

"I'll do that," she said. "You're right, it'll be better later; I have one or two things to clear up with Uncle Milo's solicitor."

Giles Edwards checked his tie in the mirror; it was two fifteen – his interview with the senior partner at Hedges, Gretel & Smart was in an hour. He had time. South

Kensington Tube was seven minutes' walk from his front door. Allowing half an hour for the journey, he would still have twenty minutes or so to run through his spiel in Starbucks beforehand. He slipped on the jacket to his suit and smoothed the shoulders before donning his overcoat.

It had been a month since his ignominious departure from Jodrell Hope and at forty-five, he knew he was lucky to be offered an interview with another firm. Head-hunters these days mostly sought bright young stars in their twenties and, specialising as *he* did, in intellectual property, positions were scarce. The audience with Simon Hedges of H G & S must go well; he needed to ace it.

The walk to the station was under a heavy sky. A breeze snaked the occasional chilly breath under his coat despite the upturned collar. A hundred yards from the entrance, his mobile rang, forcing him into the relative quiet of a flower shop to shelter from the din of passing traffic. An assistant was busy with a customer at the other end of the store and didn't notice him at the entrance. The number of the incoming call was unknown to him.

"Giles Edwards."

"Mr. Edwards, this is Detective Inspector Newman from the Metropolitan Police. I wonder if you might have some time to talk to us in the next couple of days."

Giles was bemused. "You want to talk to me – what about?"

There was a pause. "Did you know Professor Milo Ferretti?" Newman asked.

Giles almost dropped his phone at the sound of the Professor's name. He struggled to keep his voice even.

"Well, we've never actually met but I know of him."

"Oh?" Newman sounded surprised. "It's just we found your number in his mobile."

Still off balance, Giles paused to gain control of his heartbeat, now accelerating at the expectation of trouble.

"Have you asked the Professor how it is he knows me?" he enquired, knowing full well that the Professor had no way of knowing his name.

"I'm afraid that's not possible; the Professor was found dead last week."

A small bead of sweat broke on Giles's forehead, his pulse now at light speed.

"Dead...how?"

"It's a bit early to say for sure but it appears he killed himself."

Giles, finding it difficult to breathe, was losing the battle to stay calm. His heart was pumping with a force that dizzied his head.

"I don't know what to say – I called him a couple times – that's all."

There was a pause on the line then the inspector said, "Why don't we meet tomorrow. We can talk about it then. Say about two at your flat. Your phone account shows you at number twenty-two Boswell Mansions; is that right? "

"Yes," Giles answered, fighting to keep his cool. "I'll be there but I'm not sure I can help you."

"Well, we won't know that until we've chatted, will we? I'll see you tomorrow."

The line cut. Giles was shaking as he closed the phone. The assistant had finished with her customer and had seen him; she was walking his way and mouthing something about helping him. He held up his hand to halt her.

"I'll be back later," he called to her, and grabbed the handle of the plate-glass door. As he stepped out into the street, the cold air slapped his brow bringing him to his senses. He hurried to the Tube, an anxious swirl in his stomach.

Sheldon Blane snapped the catches shut on his brief case. It was five thirty; he was calling it a day when the phone on his desk shrilled.

"There's a Mr. Smith to speak to you," Hennie's voice was sceptical as he picked up. "He won't say what about – he's most insistent, says he has to speak to you."

Blane hesitated then said tiredly, "Okay, put him through." There was a click.

"Mr. Blane, is that you?" The voice was excited.

"Yes, it's me. What can I do for you Mr….Smith?"

"It's the Professor, Mr. Blane; he's dead."

"Oh, I'm sorry to hear that. You're telling me this because…?"

"Because I sent him to see you and now he's dead." Blane was becoming irritated but held his voice steady.

"Surely you can't be suggesting I had anything to do with his death?"

"I don't know what I'm suggesting," the voice was cracking now, almost sobbing. "All I know is that he was on the verge of a fortune and they say he killed himself. Something's not right. The Police.. they.."

"What about the Police?" Blane interrupted.

"They want to see me…they're coming to my flat tomorrow."

There was a pause in the conversation, then Blane said,

"Mr. Edwards – Giles, isn't it?" He paused as he let shock envelop the caller with the knowledge his true identity was known. Keeping his tone level, Blane said, "Giles, you made us aware of the Professor and his work for which you were paid a fee. A very handsome fee, I recall. We made contact with him but unfortunately, there wasn't anything of value to us in what he was offering. I know you thought differently but when we looked at the detail, we felt it would have little impact on our business. We had one meeting and that was the extent of our involvement with him. We don't want the fee back so I think that's the end of the matter. People kill themselves for all kinds of reasons; who knows what was troubling him."

"Maybe you're right." The voice seemed reluctant but calmer.

"Yes, of course I'm right; there's no way on earth you should feel responsible and we certainly have had no contact since our meeting with him."

"Does anyone know it was me who sent him to you?"

"Not unless it came from you," Blane said evenly.

"Okay then, maybe it's just coincidence."

"Exactly. Speak to the Police and then forget about it."

"I'll do that. Sorry to have bothered you," Giles said, sheepishly.

Rick sat in one of Milo's armchairs looking around him as Sophia came from the kitchen carrying a tray in the same way as Milo had done on the first day he'd met him just a few months before. In the 'getting to know you' small-talk before she'd gone to boil the kettle, he'd told her something about himself, his crash – his reasons for being in London – how he'd met Milo and Max, of course. He'd been careful to tiptoe around the subject of Milo's death hoping she would bring it up first.

"What's going to happen to the flat?" he asked, as she handed him a cup of tea.

"I haven't decided yet; Uncle Milo left it to me and there's no rent – he owned it."

"Do you think you'll sell it?"

"Oh, I don't know, it's all a bit soon. I thought about moving here myself. I'm renting at the moment – sharing with a friend in Fulham. I'm not sure though; it might be difficult knowing he died here."

Rick looked into her eyes; they looked tired but it was to be expected – she'd had a long day – the funeral, the wake and then the clear-up afterwards. The flat was neat again. She'd been busy. The dishwasher was swishing its rhythm and the kitchen was clear – no sign of dishes or the plates of sandwiches he'd picked at earlier.

"Did you finish up with the solicitor?" he asked.

"I have to go over the will at his office; I have a few questions and then there's his fee of course – I suppose there will be fees."

"Maybe he knew something about your uncle's work – anything. People have reasons for everything. If Milo killed himself, he must have had a reason. If he didn't, his work must have figured somewhere. Well, that's my theory anyway."

"He never talked about his work. Whenever I asked him he would say it's far too boring to discuss with such a beautiful woman." She smiled sheepishly.

"He was the same with me; I got the message early on –

he didn't want to talk about whatever he was up to." He sipped his tea, then, "You were Milo's only relative?"

"That's right. My father died when I was fifteen and my mother shortly after my twenty-fifth birthday. That was four years ago and I don't think Uncle Milo was over it – I know it'll take me a while yet, if ever. My mother never remarried, she couldn't think of it."

"What about Milo, did he have any lady friends? He was still a smart looking guy. He had that twinkle – you know." Sophia smiled at the notion.

"Not that I know of – if he had a girlfriend, he kept it very quiet."

"Well, it was just a thought."

"Uncle Milo was the closest thing to a father figure for me. We'd see him every Sunday for lunch and very occasionally, during the week for supper. I tried to see him as much as I could after Mummy died but you know how work takes over. We'd manage lunch or dinner maybe once every two weeks. Now I regret the times I was just at home watching TV or out shopping with friends; I could have spent those times with him."

"I don't think you need to beat yourself up about it. Life has a way of throwing up the unexpected; I know from experience," Rick said, reassuringly and pointing to the scar at his temple.

He took a sip of tea, hesitating for a moment before his question.

"So, what's your theory about what happened?" he asked.

"I have no idea. It looks like suicide but I just don't believe it of him. On the other hand, who would want to kill him?"

"I think we'll only find that out if we know what was going on in his life. If he was murdered, the murderer did a pretty good job of fooling the Police. It'll take a bit of digging to change their minds."

"Do you have something in mind?" she asked.

"Well, I only knew Milo for a few months but I *think* we were firm friends; I kinda owe it to him to ask a few questions. It's up to you though – I'm not a relative; I don't want to stir anything up if you'd rather let it go."

"Something's not right about the way he died," she said, looking into Rick's eyes, "I have the feeling that the Police have made their minds up; if I don't make an effort, no-one will. Yes, I'd like you to help – if you've got the time."

"I've got the time," he said. "What about Milo's solicitor, he must know something, even if he doesn't realise it. That's where we need to start. When are you seeing him?"

"Tomorrow afternoon – at three; can you tag along?"

"Of course, any way I can help," he replied.

"I'll be glad of the company; it's going to be difficult reading Uncle Milo's words in the will," she replied sadly. "Meet me here at two thirty and we can take a cab together."

"Okay, I'll check what lectures I'll miss; someone can take notes for me." He looked at his watch. It was nine already and he could see she was waning. He gulped the rest of his tea and stood up.

"Two thirty tomorrow," he said.

She walked him to the door. "Thanks for coming," she said and gave him a wan smile as she shut the door.

In the corridor, he wondered why she would ask him to go with her to Milo's solicitor; he'd met her that day for the first time. It seemed odd that she hadn't asked one of her friends to accompany her, someone she'd known for more than a few hours. He wasn't complaining though.

As sleep took him that night, his thoughts were of his friend, Milo and happier times.

The offices of Hollis, Jackman & Steer were in the West End, tucked between two private residences in Welbeck Street at the New Cavendish Street end. The pavement was mirror wet from the drizzle as Rick and Sophia stepped from the cab. They hurried for the shelter of a two-tone brick doorway. The words Hollis, Jackman & Steer were embossed across a brass plate in black letters. It was bolted to the brickwork to the side of a heavy door painted in black high-gloss. Rick pressed the button on the entry-phone and simultaneously looked up at the camera fixed to the archway's underside. It was evident that the semblance of security was only for show as the lock buzzed and clicked open almost immediately without challenge.

They sat on a small sofa in a passageway serving as a waiting area which, at one time, had been the front hall of an Edwardian private residence.

"He'll see you now," a female voice called.

Rick looked up to see a pretty girl in her early twenties beckoning them to follow. She led them to a door a few feet away, knocked, then entered without waiting for a response. The office was comfortably sized and wood panelled. The man Rick had seen at the funeral was seated behind a walnut veneer desk, his back to a rain spattered bay window which looked out to the street. He rose, stepping around the desk, his arm outstretched.

"Sophia; please sit." He gestured to a leather chesterfield and turned to Rick;

"I'm Freddie Hollis," he said, shaking Rick's hand warmly.

"Rick – Rick Devan," Rick replied to the question on Hollis's face.

"Please, have a seat."

Rick seated himself next to Sophia on the chesterfield. Freddie Hollis sat in a matching armchair opposite. He was dressed almost as formally as he had been at the funeral in charcoal grey pinstripe; only the tie was different.

Sophia spoke first.

"As I told you, Rick here found my uncle on the day….," she hesitated for a moment, "and I've asked him to come with me today as he's the only person, apart from you that is, who seems to have had regular contact with him; I have no idea about my uncle's work or anything in his life which could have driven him to suicide. I'm hoping you can throw some light on things. So, as you can imagine, I have some questions."

"I understand," said Hollis. "You're quite happy for me to speak freely on *all* matters with Mr. Devan present?"

"Yes," she replied. She turned to Rick. "Please butt in if you have something to say."

Rick nodded.

"Before we start, can I offer you tea or coffee?" Hollis asked. When they declined, he settled himself back into the armchair. He laced his hands on his lap and began.

"I met Milo twenty years ago. I hadn't made partner in those days and I was in the process of building up my client list. Milo rang the switchboard out of the blue one day asking for a solicitor to make a will for him. I was free and he turned up that afternoon. His wife had died a month before and he was still suffering. It made no difference though; he was determined to sort his will there and then. It took about three days before he had the actual document – somewhat of a record for us at the time I have to say, but, when he had it in his hand, it was as though a great weight had been lifted from him. I didn't understand his reaction at the time – there was nothing unusual about the will. It left everything to you, Sophia, as all the subsequent wills have done. Every time he updated, there were a few minimal changes. The sums involved grew, of course, but there were no other changes I would call significant."

"What about his work – is there anything you can tell me on that score?" Sophia asked.

"Not much really. About five years ago he came to see me. I thought it would be for another update of his will but, as it turned out, I was wrong. He'd come to ask me to recommend a lawyer or a firm who specialised in intellectual property. He didn't elaborate, only that he'd given notice to King's and he would be working on his own project from then on and he needed a patent."

"And did you recommend someone?" Sophia enquired.

"Yes, Jodrell Hope. I know he dealt with them because I had a letter from Gerald Hope thanking me for the referral."

"When was the last time you saw Uncle Milo?"

"About six months ago – he came to update the will – again."

"And how was he?"

"He was fine but there *was* something he said which was unusual. He was always very careful only to refer to his project as 'my work' but in an unguarded moment he referred to it as 'my scale'. I could see it was an accidental slip and when I asked him what he meant, he didn't answer – he changed the subject back to the will. His reaction made me remember it."

"My scale," Sophia repeated the words. "What does it mean?"

"I think you should ask the patent lawyer," Rick said. "All roads seem to go that way."

"As I mentioned to you at the funeral," Hollis continued, "Milo called me the Wednesday before he died; he made an appointment to see me on the Friday of the following week. He was very excited – elated even, said he would have something to tell me by then. As usual, he didn't elaborate – said he would tell me everything when he saw me. He didn't make it of course."

"By all accounts, something good was happening for Milo," Rick said. "So why would he kill himself; none of it makes sense to me."

"Based on my last conversation with him, I have to agree with you," said Hollis. "He was very positive on the phone."

Sophia spoke. "I think we have to see the patent lawyer as soon as possible. Who did you say he saw – Gerald..?"

"Hope," Hollis filled the blank.

"Yes, Gerald Hope – it's the only way we're going to get any further. Can you arrange it?"

"I can call him but he might not talk to you."

"Oh?"

"He may be a bit sniffy and take the view he can't speak to you until probate is granted but let's see what he says. I may be able to convince him; he ought to take my word you have the rights to whatever it was Milo was working on – which is precisely what the will confirms. Hope could dig his heels in though which will mean you'll have to wait."

"How long?" Sophia asked.

"A month – two maybe. Even though I can tell you what's in the will today, we can't enact its demands until probate is granted.

Hollis pressed the intercom on his desk. A female voice answered.

"Jane, could you get Gerald Hope from Jodrells on the phone for me?"

There was a crackled, "Yes, Mr. Hollis," from the speaker followed by a loud click as the line was cut.

Sophia broke the momentary silence.

"What is in the will?" she asked.

"It's to the point," Hollis replied as he reached for a pair of documents on his desk. "This is a copy," he said, passing her a sheaf of three pages stapled at the top left corner. Hollis glanced at the preamble on the cover of his copy and then turned the page.

"The inheritance breaks up into three parts. There's the flat, of course, then cash and shares to the value of seven hundred and fifty thousand pounds and…"

"How much?" Sophia interrupted, clearly startled by the sum.

"Seven hundred and fifty thousand pounds," Hollis repeated.

She looked at Rick. "I had no idea," she said, disbelievingly.

"I can assure you the figure is correct." Hollis was running his finger down the page. "The last clause refers to his work. It gives you full title but doesn't actually say what his work is. I would like to think he was coming to see me to finally reveal all."

"I doubt we'll ever know for sure," Rick said, with a sad finality.

"I think you may be right," Hollis agreed.

The intercom clicked and the female voice broke in.

"Gerald Hope is with a client; I've left a message for him to call you." There was another click as the line cut.

Hollis scribbled something on a pad then tore the sheet from its binder and handed it to Sophia.

"Here's the address for Jodrells; I'll call you when I've heard from him. I'll have them pencil an appointment for you but you'll have to confirm it."

Sophia took the paper from him and stood up to leave.

"Thank you for your time, Mr. Hollis. I'll come and see you again when the will can be dealt with," she said, "in the meantime, I'll wait for your call."

Today had been a better day. Sophia kicked off her shoes and curled against the arm of the sofa back at her own flat, a glass of wine in one hand and the TV remote in the other, flicking channels with the sound low. The ride home had taken twenty minutes in a taxi. She sipped. Yes, today had been a better day – she felt she was doing something, taking a step forward at last, away from the day of the message on her machine requesting her to call D.I. Newman. The day the final connection to childhood memories and family had been broken, Uncle Milo had been her touchstone. The memories were still there but the colour had gone from them leaving them in flickering monochrome.

Claudia's postcard caught her eye on the side table – the Chrysler Building. She lingered on the image for a moment, picturing Claudia and Josh pounding the streets of New York. Claudia had chosen a fine time to be away but then again three months touring the Americas with your boyfriend would beat winter in London hands down. The flat was a quiet place without Claudia and some of her really annoying habits – like kicking off her shoes as she came in from work for all to trip on. Still, Sophia missed her. She sipped the wine again and smiled as she looked down at her own shoes, strewn across the carpet, Claudia style.

Her mobile beeped with an incoming text; the third from the same sender in the last hour – Jake. She ignored it. Claudia and the rest of her female friends had warned her about office romances but Sophia had felt Jake didn't count – he was one of the firm's partners; she didn't really regard him as a co-worker. Those divisions didn't seem to matter now; two years on and the relationship was going nowhere, only the promise of the next week away in some fashionable hot spot. That was all well and good for a while but it was wearing thin. Jake wasn't the type of person she could lean on at a time of crisis, he was too much of a good time boy and when Uncle Milo died, that fact was brought into sharp focus. She needed to move on whatever the fall-out. In some ways it was a relief that Claudia wasn't around to give her the 'I told you so' looks.

The phone gave a beeped reminder. She switched it off. Jake would be tomorrow's problem.

4

Giles Edwards's flat was on the second floor. A sodium street lamp shot crazy yellow streaks on rain spattered windows. He stood in his shirtsleeves sipping brandy – peering through the glass at the umbrellas that seemed to float by themselves along the glistening street below. He turned back to face the room. It was homely enough, Giles thought, cosy in its own way with deep pile carpet and his share of the furniture from his house, sold to satisfy the divorce settlement. He was sure the forced sale was to relieve some spiteful desire of his ex but, in his usual philosophical way, he brushed the thought aside; he was here now and had to make the best of it.

The interview with Simon Hedges had gone well – very well; the position was his. Barring any hiccups, his employment would start at the intellectual property firm, Hedges, Gretel & Smart at the end of the month; finally something is going right, he thought, swirling the brandy in the balloon. "I could have done without the call from the Police though," he muttered. It had left him rattled – shooting the occasional squirt of adrenaline and flipping his stomach when he thought about it. The call had put a cloud on an almost perfect day.

He thought about the Professor and tried to imagine what

could have driven him to suicide? Did I have a role in it somehow? he asked himself. Surely not, he'd spoken to the Professor only twice and the man seemed quite amenable. He had merely made the Professor aware of an opportunity – arranged an introduction, that's all. The Professor seemed curious to meet the company who, at worst, he might have regarded as the opposition but nevertheless, the people there would give him their views if nothing else. Giles sipped the brandy again. He hadn't cared what the motives were; his only interest had been in the brown envelope he would collect from the reception desk at Buckley Blane's glass tower.

Professor Ferretti had been more than curious to know who *he* was, Giles reflected, and, moreover, how Giles had come to know of his work. It was of particular interest to Ferretti as, besides himself, his patent lawyers were the only others who knew of the novelty his formula possessed. It had been quite difficult to steer the Professor away from this line of questioning, Giles recalled, but, when the old boy had realised he would get no further, he cut to the where and when. Buckley Blane would make contact with those details, so Giles's job was done.

He had been careless though; he should have called from a pay-phone – a phone whose number was meaningless. Using his mobile had left a trail to him. He cursed himself for his stupidity. In his defence, he hadn't expected the Professor to top himself and cause an incident which would attract Police attention. He was calmer now though – unsure if it was the brandy or the chat with Blane that had allayed his fears. All the same, right now was not a good time for any shadows to be cast over him. If Jodrell Hope, his previous employers, were to hear his name linked to the Professor's it might light a bulb in someone's head. It could trigger some elementary calculations which would arrive at the conclusion that he, Giles Edwards, disgruntled employee, the same Giles Edwards who had been turned down for a partnership and who had resigned acrimoniously a few weeks ago, may have copied privileged information and used it for his own gain. No, not a good time at all but so far, he seemed to have got away with things as far as the old firm were concerned. He concluded the Professor had heeded his advice, for the moment anyway, and not told his patent lawyers of the anonymous calls pointing to some opportunities he might not otherwise have thought of. If the Professor *had* called them, they would have been actively looking for the leak and Giles's reference would have been mud. He'd been offered a job today so his references still checked out; Jodrell Hope knew nothing. Giles smiled for a moment then grimaced when he remembered the Police were coming to interview him the following day; he took another gulp.

What on earth have I got to worry about, he reasoned; I've committed no traceable crime. Admittedly, there were the photocopied files of three of Jodrells' clients, the ones he'd thought had immediate potential for a cash introduction to interested parties but the Police would not know this. He chided himself for the momentary loss of composure which caused him to phone Blane in a fit of blind panic. Blane knowing his real name had thrown him for a moment though but, that aside, he was okay; all that was required of him would be to keep his head – and yet…

As far as Jodrells were concerned, his conscience was clear; he'd had no qualms lifting the files from them – they owed him. He'd done his time there, six years and the promised partnership had gone to a snot-nosed junior with half his experience but whose uncle was the Attorney General. Giles couldn't stay, of course, not with such disrespect; his position within the company had been thoroughly undermined. C'est la vie had been his reaction after he'd got over the initial anger but, if he was leaving, the files would be a little something to tide him over.

Blane had paid well and Giles had always been confident someone would. Giles made it his business to know what was going on in the City and who was going up and who was on the way out but also, who was buying whom. He was well aware of BBM's speciality and speculated that the impact of the Professor's work, if published, would have a devastating effect on the talks with Reimer. He'd been following Reimer's on-off romance with BBM for some time and guessed the engagement would be broken off if BBM's core business was undermined. Giles had chosen his moment carefully and telephoned to speak with Samuel Buckley. He'd calculated negotiations with Reimer were at a critical point. When he'd navigated the road blocks thrown up by secretaries and a P.A., he had finally been put through to Buckley's office, not to Buckley himself though. Instead, a male, who Giles had taken for Buckley's P.A., answered and had listened to the bare bones of what Giles had to offer and then was very specific in his reply. This was not for Mr. Buckley; Giles must call Sheldon Blane. Not his intended target but, as it turned out, the right one. Blane was understandably suspicious. Well, who wouldn't be? Out of the blue, he receives a call from a 'Mr. Smith', the well known telephone whisperer, whistle blower and, in another guise, frequent afternoon hotel visitor in the company of Mrs. Smith, with news that there's a Professor who has the potential to blow the takeover out of the water. After five minutes of stilted chat during which time Giles passed on enough detail to whet the appetite, Blane was convinced. At six that evening, they had a 'Deep Throat' at the Starbucks in Wardour Street and the deal was done.

It had never entered Giles's head that he would engage in any further dealings with either of his 'clients'. Despite the call from the Police, he hoped events would maintain the status quo.

It was seven thirty. Giles went to the kitchen and scanned the contents of the fridge; he needed to shop. He'd been putting it off as he always did until everything was out, which was usually at an inconvenient time. Tonight's inconvenience was the rain. He knew he'd have to get on with it or go without dinner and breakfast. How life had changed since the divorce. There was a hole in the trouser pocket of his suit; it had been there for months – something that once upon a time, would have been fixed at the very mention of it, by the lovely Fay – well, back then, she was lovely. The description changed shortly after he discovered she had been spending her afternoons with an incarnation of Mr. Smith, known in this case as Mr. Jones, the private detective had told him.

Nothing now was as it was and nothing appeared on the table these days without *his* effort which was an obvious truth but a bloody nuisance.

He checked the cupboards, making a mental note of what

was needed, put on his coat and left. He took the back stairs to the rear exit of the building and the alley. Dimly lit, it cut through to the high street shaving five minutes off the walk. He passed no-one on his way and was in the Tesco Express fifteen minutes later – cruising the aisles on automatic, loading his trolley without a second thought in a way "*only men are capable of*," he could hear Fay bleat in his head.

At the checkout, he entered his PIN and looked up and caught a glance from a man paying two rows down. He looked vaguely familiar but Giles couldn't place him. He was tall – six feet or more, well built, wearing a long dark raincoat which almost reached the ground and black leather gloves which he kept on, despite the clumsiness as he handled his change. Where was it now? Giles knew that face from somewhere and judging by the way it had turned away quickly, the face knew him.

A seven year old girl in the queue behind him suddenly shrieked causing Giles to turn around. A boy of about ten, presumably her brother, had whacked her with a baguette he'd taken from his mother's trolley. When Giles turned back, the face had gone. He looked around him again in a vain attempt to catch a glimpse of the distinctive long coat – nothing, just trolleys and mêlée at the tills.

Giles left the store with two bulging plastic carriers in each hand. They were heavy and their handles were beginning to cut into his fingers. The rain had picked up again and he hastened his pace. Who was that guy in the store? The question diverted his attention as he entered the alley, unaware of a figure slipping in behind, twenty yards back.

He was cold and getting wetter by the second; what he'd give right now for a steaming cup of coffee. That word 'coffee' triggered a memory – the one and only meeting with Blane in Starbucks. The face, now he remembered. It was in Starbucks; the guy came in about three minutes behind Blane. Giles had noticed the man squeezing his six foot frame behind a table near the door. It was no coincidence – he must have been tailing Blane. Maybe the guy was Blane's minder – Giles didn't think so; he seemed too detached. Maybe he'd been following me, Giles thought in a moment of panic. What Giles *did* know was that money was involved and there were too *many* maybes. Suddenly, Giles could see the danger. He'd been a bloody fool; he'd made somebody nervous. Who, he could not say for sure but the realisation was gut-wrenching – he was a liability, a threat to deals in numbers difficult to visualise. He quickened his pace, aware of footfalls behind him. He cursed his stupidity in panting breath. A long shadow overtook him as he turned in terror into the blade that buried itself into his heart. Giles slipped to the wet tarmac, scattering the contents of the bags as he fell. He lay helpless while his pockets were expertly rifled, the contents strewn not taken. Rivulets of rainwater ran across his cheeks mixing with a crimson trickle from the corner of his mouth. In his last conscious moments, lying amongst a rainbow of burst packaging, he watched his assailant casually trot back up the alley towards the light, raincoat flapping out behind him.

Juliet Laskey was in her room on the twentieth floor of the Park Lane Hilton. She'd been in London for five days putting together two stories. One covered the expansion of a sea food chain whose beginnings hailed from Seattle in the 1970s, the other, the Reimer takeover of BBM. The sea food piece was pretty much wrapped up and the background to the Reimer takeover of BBM was in place. She'd written up her interviews with Reimer's CEO and his deputy before leaving Seattle but she was yet to interview Samuel Buckley, the chairman of BBM or Sheldon Blane, the other shareholder.

Juliet's boss, Dick Frampton, had taken some persuading to send her to London to cover the British end of the story; the *Times* had a stringer in London, Jack Tennant, who was perfectly capable. However, Juliet had managed to sway Dick to her point of view that Reimer needed to be covered more specifically by the Business and Financial section rather than by Jack who, she pointed out, although extremely competent, usually filed more general stories. It had been a tough sell but showing him the work she had already done, broke his resistance.

"You're on a budget, remember; I'll be checking the receipts myself," he'd warned. "Oh, and one other thing, work with Jack while you're over there – it's his turf after all and he's good – he'll be sharing the byline with you."

She sat at the window focusing on her laptop – open on a small breakfast table designed for two. She turned and looked out over Hyde Park, admiring the view. It was a frosty morning lit by brilliant sunshine. Juliet sipped her coffee looking down on the joggers following their routes and pedestrians wrapped against the cold, breaths in white puffs as they chatted. Back at the computer, her thoughts were directed to planning the interview with Buckley.

From everything she'd read about him, he seemed a pretty straight forward kind of guy, a plodder who would always get there in the end. He'd built a moderately successful company during the 1990s but business really took off in the years after Sheldon Blane had come on the scene. Although the interview was an essential part of the piece, she had a feeling she'd be just going through the motions with Buckley who, not to put too fine a point on it, seemed dull; the session she really wanted was with Blane. *He* was not at all straightforward, anything but and difficult to flesh out. It was proving almost impossible to get any kind of long-term history for him – a state of affairs which was always suspicious in her book. It seemed he worked for two agencies before meeting Buckley but Jack Tennant had discovered a third. There had been some kind of cloud over an incident involving Blane but getting any detail was again, proving difficult; the agency was no more and the personnel had scattered.

Her mobile rang.

"It's Jack; I've got a name. I'll be at your room in ten minutes."

In fact, it was twenty before there was a rap on her door.

"Jack, come in."

They sat opposite each other at the breakfast table.

Jack Tennant was in his forties and had transferred to London with his wife and two children for a quieter life than the one he'd had during the previous years as a correspondent in war-torn Eastern Europe. He still had a piece of shrapnel in his leg from an incident that killed his photographer and left him with a slight limp which he managed to disguise in all but damp weathers. The event had been the catalyst for an ultimatum from his wife to which he had willingly succumbed, although he sometimes missed the rush. He was content though; the weeks in hospital had made him acutely aware of where his responsibilities lay. He was slim with brown hair and plainly took care of himself. The lines through Jack's features reflected a back-catalogue of nerve-racking experiences like a map of mountain tracks but for all that, he retained a mischievous twinkle in his eyes.

"Help yourself to coffee," Juliet said, handing him a clean cup. "You said you had a name?"

"Melvyn Carter."

"Go on."

"Ten years ago, Carter had a small advertising agency, Carter Gibbon Snell. The two junior partners were, Harry Gibbon and Marilyn Snell. They'd been running about five years and were beginning to make a name for themselves. I got this from the archives of Campaign."

Juliet gave him a quizzical look.

"It's an ad industry mag."

She nodded her understanding and gestured for him to continue.

"Issues of Campaign in mid 1999 were following the agency's expansion and predicting big things. They were right; Carter landed three major accounts almost immediately. It was about that time they employed Sheldon Blane. Eleven months later, Marilyn Snell was dead – suicide – and the agency consigned to history."

"What happened to Carter and Gibbon?"

"Gibbon seems to have vanished; there were rumours he'd

gone to Spain but I've had no luck tracing him."

"And Carter?"

"I've had better luck there. He dropped off the face of the earth for a couple of years but now lectures in Media Studies and Communications at Goldsmiths College here in London. The bad news is he won't talk to me or 'anyone from the Press' – a direct quote."

"Any idea what happened?"

"Not specifically, but there were a lot of rumours going around at the time."

"What kind of rumours?"

"You know – the sort of stuff that happens when success beckons, professional differences I gather from a copywriter I found in a Soho bar. The bickering started almost from the moment Blane joined. There was also a rumour about him and Marilyn Snell – nothing concrete though."

"How did you get hold of Carter?"

"I didn't actually get to talk to him."

"You said you had a direct quote."

"Well it was a direct quote, but it came via the department secretary."

"Oh… seems he means it," she remarked.

"I'd say so. Where do we go from here? I think we're stuck unless you can find someone to persuade Carter to talk to us – either that or we need someone who was on the inside back in the day." Jack was talking but he could see Juliet was somewhere else. "Juliet, I was saying…"

"Yes, sorry; I heard you," she said, holding a sudden thought somewhere safe before replying. "Have another go at finding Harry Gibbon or any others who worked there."

"Okay. What about Carter?"

Juliet was silent in thought; she'd remembered something one of the photographers had said before she left Seattle.

"I just had an idea; it's a long-shot but worth a try," she said finally.

Jack got up and made for the door.

"I'll call when I have something."

When she was alone again, she opened her staff contact list, scanning for a name – Seb Morgan. The bedside clock showed eleven thirty. That would make it three thirty a.m. in Seattle. She didn't know Seb that well but he worked for a newspaper and shouldn't be surprised to get a phone call at anytime. She was dialling and debating the rights and wrongs of waking Seb when the line began to ring at the other end and the decision was made for her.

After the fifth ring a voice, groggy and with a 'who the hell is calling me at this time' intonation, came on the line.

"This is Seb Morgan."

"Hi, Seb, it's Juliet." There was a pause. "Juliet Laskey." Another pause. She was about to repeat her name when Seb came to life.

"Juliet, do you know what time it is?"

"Seb, I didn't call you to get the time."

"Very funny; anyway, what do you need?"

"Just before I left, you told me that friend of yours, Rick, was at college in London."

"If I remember, he was also a *friend,*" he emphasised the word, "of yours, at one time."

The conversation missed a beat.

"Seb, can I get back to the reason I'm calling you."

"Yes, yes, what do you want to know?"

"Did you say he was at Goldsmiths College?"

"Yeah, he's doing TV journalism."

"What about a number, does he have a cell?"

"I don't know what he does for a phone in London but I can give you an email address."

She took down the address.

"Seb, thanks, now go back to sleep."

"Yeah, right."

She cut the line.

5

It had been two days since the meeting with Freddie Hollis. Rick was busy with a three thousand word piece to hand in by the end of Friday and that was tomorrow. He blessed his laptop every time he hit the keys, thinking of how it must have been for hacks before computers – pages of score-outs and a text which had to be hammered out on a typewriter to be legible. These days you could cut to the final with one glance at your notes and no need to assault your senses with wafts of correction fluid.

He was spending the afternoon back at his flat; seven hundred words to get down and he was done. Two hours ought to do it; he had more than enough planned. Lunch had been a take-away pizza picked up on the way back from college. Half-chewed crusts lay where they'd been tossed in the open box – shoved to the back of the table behind his laptop. Max was asleep on the arm of the sofa.

Rick was re-reading a passage, swigging from a Coke bottle when his mobile vibrated, resonating on the surface of the table.

"Hey, Sophia," he answered. "Yes, okay – at two thirty; I'll be waiting at the station entrance." He snapped the phone shut. They were seeing the patent lawyer at three.

Sophia had been on his mind since the day of the meeting

with Hollis. He still didn't know much about her, only the sketchy details she'd given him of her mother's death and how Milo had figured in her life. She was an attractive woman and, he presumed, there must be a man in her life. It was puzzling though. If there *was* a man in her life, where was he now, at her time of need? Now was not the right time to ask her, don't want her getting the wrong idea, he thought but, then again, he hoped she was single. Hitting on her though, with everything that was going on, might not go down well. Let's just go with the flow, he mused, as he pulled on his leather jacket.

Argyll Street exit of Oxford Circus Tube – she'd be there at two thirty. He was five minutes early but, climbing the steps to the street into the sunlight of a chilly afternoon, he could see she was already there, stamping the pavement to keep the cold at bay. Her hair spilled from beneath a knitted beret to her shoulders. A scarf twirled once around her neck and hung over her coat to her waist.

"Sorry if I've kept you waiting," he said, as she turned to face him.

"Don't worry about it; I was early," she said, smiling. "I hope you don't mind."

"Mind? Mind what?"

"Coming here at a moment's notice," she replied.

"Of course not; I've been looking for an excuse to…" he wanted to say 'looking for an excuse to see you' but remembered what he decided earlier and continued, "to get away from the books."

"It's okay then? I'm not dragging you out of lectures?"

"Not at all, I was stuck at home writing a piece to hand in. I'm nearly done with it, so I was glad you called. As I said, any excuse." He was smiling back at her.

"Okay then, let's go."

Jodrell Hope had the first and second floors of a Regency style building in Wigmore Street. It was a ten minute walk accompanied by the din of heavy traffic and clicking stilettos on busy pavements. They arrived very early but didn't mind waiting, thankful to be out of the cold. The interior of the building was modern – sleek furniture and high-tech electronics. They were shown to a windowless waiting area illuminated by concealed lighting which reflected off a white ceiling. Evenly spaced brushed steel panels concealing fluorescents were set away from light grey walls. It wasn't the picture Rick had in his mind of how a lawyer's office would be decorated; it was more like the flight deck of the Enterprise. A secretary sat stabbing a keyboard at a desk outside a door labelled Gerald Hope. She rose to greet them and offered them tea as they seated themselves on a black leather sofa then disappeared to a small kitchen behind her desk. She reappeared a few minutes later carrying a tray holding two cups and a teapot.

As they waited, sipping tea and chatting aimlessly, there was the growing sound of muffled voices coming from inside Gerald Hope's office. The pair looked at the door in expectation at first, then surprise as it opened. D.I. Newman stepped out accompanied by a second man of similar bearing –another policeman, Rick thought. A third, whom he took for Gerald Hope, followed them. Newman didn't see Rick and Sophia at first; he was busy with Gerald Hope.

"You'll tell me if you think of anything else," he was saying over his shoulder.

"Of course, I'm still finding it hard to believe. I suppose it can happen to any one of us," said Hope, as the group came to a halt in the waiting area. "Wrong place at the wrong time."

"Er.. yes," Newman agreed. As he turned to leave, he noticed Rick and Sophia.

"Miss Ferretti," he said, surprise on his face, "and Mr. Devan. Now this is a coincidence."

They got up from the sofa.

"Inspector, are you here on official business?" Sophia asked.

"I was about to ask you the very same question."

"Nothing mysterious I'm afraid; I'm just tying up some loose ends in my uncle's estate. Mr. Hope was his patent attorney."

"Oh, I see. Well, I won't hold you up." He gave a forced smile and made to leave, then hesitated. He turned back to Sophia.

"Just one more thing, Miss Ferretti; have you ever heard the name Giles Edwards?"

"No, Inspector, should I have?"

"No, no. Forget I asked; it was just a thought – that's all."

He gave another humourless smile and made his way out. Gerald Hope stood at the entrance to his office. Rick studied him. He was tall with fair hair, blue eyes and in his fifties sporting the lawyers' pinstripe uniform and a welcoming smile.

"Please, come in," he called to them.

In contrast to the artificial light in the waiting area, Gerald Hope's office was bathed in sunlight from a bank of sash windows along the street side. The ceiling was high and the walls were painted in white matt giving an airy feel to the space. A plush light grey carpet covered the floor from wall to wall, deadening every sound. An aroma of furniture polish and old leather came from walnut veneer units crammed with bound legal volumes. Rick and Sophia seated themselves on visitors' chairs at the front of Hope's desk. He sat across from them with his back to the windows.

"Thank you for agreeing to see us," Sophia said.

"I'm happy to," he replied. "Freddie filled me in on the details and as you are Milo's only beneficiary, it was important that we met as soon as possible. Had Freddie not contacted me, I would have been contacting him sooner or later. Your uncle's work had reached a critical stage." He turned to Rick.

"Devan, Rick Devan." Rick answered the unspoken question.

"And you're happy for me to talk in front of Mr. Devan?" he looked at Sophia.

"Yes," she replied, shooting a quick glance and a smile at Rick.

"Very well," Hope said, and opened a wallet file on his desk.

"Before we begin," Sophia said, "the Police, Inspector Newman – was he here about my uncle?"

"No, not at all – a tragedy concerning one of our former lawyers."

"Giles Edwards?" she asked.

"Yes, he was murdered two nights ago. The Police found one of his old business cards in his wallet."

"Do they have any idea why?" Rick asked.

"It seems it was a mugging. The Police think the robbers were disturbed before they could take anything. His wallet was by his side with two fifty pound notes still inside."

"Maybe money wasn't the motive; maybe they were after something else," Rick speculated. "Maybe it was his phone. Cell theft is big in the States; it must be the same here."

"Well," Hope said, "if that's what they were after, they were out of luck. The Police found his phone stuck in the lining of his trousers half-way down his leg; it had fallen through a hole in his pocket."

"How did…." Sophia began.

"A stab wound to the heart."

She winced at the reply.

Gerald Hope pulled a sheaf of papers from the file in front of him.

"Shall we get on," he said, turning to the first page.

Sophia looked at Rick and then back to Hope.

"Just one more question," she said, "and then I promise I'll leave the subject."

"Go ahead," said Hope.

"The Inspector asked me if I'd heard of Giles Edwards. Seems a bit odd unless he thought Giles Edwards was connected with my uncle in some way. *Was* Giles Edwards dealing with my uncle when he practised here?"

Hope was shaking his head.

"As far as I know, Giles never had occasion to meet your uncle. All Milo's dealings were with me. There would've been no reason for Giles to have come into contact with him."

"I found the Inspector's question curious, that's all but maybe he was just being a policeman – you know –

suspecting everyone." She smiled and let the subject go.

"Okay then," Hope began. "I think before we start on your uncle's case, it might be useful to outline exactly what it is we do here."

Rick and Sophia nodded for him to continue.

"Patents are all about novelty. If you want a patent, you have to demonstrate your idea has novelty. In other words you have to show that nobody else has patented the same idea. It's obvious but not as simple as it seems. We make a search of applicable registered patents and sometimes we find that someone else has patented a similar idea. However, if we can show that your idea differs from theirs, you can still apply for a patent provided you acknowledge the existing patent which is referred to as 'prior art'. I'm mentioning this because it has some relevance in your uncle's case. The Holy Grail, of course, is to register something where there is no prior art.

"Are you saying that my uncle filed something with 'Prior art'?

"I'll come to that in a moment. Anyway," Hope continued, "once we've established it's worth applying for a patent, we send off the papers. From that moment your idea is protected. You are able to enter negotiations with interested parties who might want to market the idea. It can take anything up to a year for the patent to be granted in this country, so it's advisable to talk to prospective customers while you're waiting. After that, depending on the commercial viability of the idea, we set about registration in other territories. The whole process takes money of course but Milo never seemed to be worried on that front. Are you following me so far?"

Rick and Sophia nodded.

Hope continued. "At this practice, we also become involved in getting the idea or product to market. We were a good way along the road with your uncle on that score."

Sophia could contain her curiosity no longer.

"I understand the background, but now, please tell us what Uncle Milo invented."

Gerald Hope smiled. "Milo devised a mathematical formula that has the potential to change the way we live. In simple terms, it calculates the true value of any product or scheme offered for sale."

"With that one sentence," Rick said, "I'm totally confused."

"Me too," agreed Sophia.

"Let me explain," Hope continued. "Every day, the consumer is bombarded by offers devised by marketing companies. They are designed to be confusing – whether it's a mortgage or a mobile phone contract; it's very difficult to work out if you're getting value for money. You may think you're getting a good deal but to actually analyse the pros and cons of a scheme and make a true assessment, takes an expert or a lot of time. Most people don't bother and are fooled by the headline of the offer. They might think they're buying a cheap package holiday only to find the hidden extras have cost them double. A very simple example would be a product offered for five pounds ninety-nine. The fact that this is one penny short of six pounds doesn't register; it's the figure *five* that sticks in the mind. As I said, that's a simple example with one device of 'trickery', Milo's word not mine. Anyway, imagine the complications when several devices of 'trickery' are employed, a mobile phone contract for instance. You may be offered a number of free texts and air time provided you sign a contract of a particular length. The average consumer has no way of knowing the true value to enable comparison with an alternative supplier."

"Okay," Rick said, "I'm with you so far."

"In very simple terms, Milo's formula cuts through all the confusion by setting a benchmark allowing similar products to be instantly rated against one another on a scale of one to ten – the higher the number on the scale, the better the value. There is no area where the scale could not be applied."

"The marketing companies won't be happy when this breaks," Rick observed.

"Nor the websites that offer price comparison, there'll be no need for them," Sophia added."

"Exactly," said Hope. "Some companies have built their fortunes on the practice of devising confusing campaigns. They have whole departments concentrating on the creation of these schemes for their clients."

"Their clients – would they be the mortgage lenders and phone companies?" Sophia asked.

"Not only mortgage lenders and phone companies. Airlines, supermarkets, banks, insurance companies, chain stores, gas and electricity suppliers – all the big players will be affected."

"Where was Uncle Milo in the patent process?"

"It was granted two months before he died; there'd been a hiccup but it was overcome."

"What kind of hiccup?"

"It was a claim of 'Prior art' by one of Milo's students

from his time at King's."

"One of his students?"

"We were surprised the chap was even aware of the filing having been careful not to hint at how the formula might be applied. There was no basis for his claim though; he'd merely made some comment on one of Milo's documented lectures. We thought that and the examiner agreed."

"So, who was this student?" asked Rick.

"Walter Nestrom, Milo ran his degree course."

"Walter Nestrom?" Sophia cut in. "There was a Walter Nestrom at the funeral. I'm not sure, I was a bit dazed on the day but I think he was the guy with the beard. Does that sound like the same person to you?"

"I couldn't say; we never met. Correspondence came through his lawyer."

"It must have been him – too much of a coincidence to be otherwise. Seems odd he would come to Uncle Milo's funeral if they were arguing."

"I agree but he must have had his reasons. Anyway, as I was saying, Nestrom claimed that Milo had stolen the idea from an essay he had included in a module handed in to Milo; he refers to it as his 'Thesis'. He went on to propose that Milo could not have reached any conclusion without the initial calculations and theory put forward in the essay. Milo vehemently denied this and pointed out very competently, the flaws in Nestrom's argument. The Examiner agreed with Milo."

"Did Nestrom drop his objection?"

"He had no option. However, from what his lawyer told me off the record, Walter was not happy to put it mildly."

"How unhappy was he – unhappy enough to cause harm

to my uncle?"

"I don't think so. He has a very successful business providing statistical forecasts to industry; he employs fifty people in this country and almost a hundred in Germany and branches of his business in the Far East. Walter Nestrom was a millionaire by the time he was thirty. He's a bit too high profile to be getting his hands dirty these days."

"Oh, I see. I still find it odd though….him at the funeral and then back to what was Uncle Milo's home, creepy really."

"Forget about Walter Nestrom. Let's talk about Milo's work – his Scale. "

Sophia was silent. She seemed reluctant to move on from the strange events involving Walter Nestrom. Finally, she asked, "How would you market something like this, I mean, who would actually pay for it?"

Hope's answer was short. "The E.U."

"You'll have to explain."

"Milo had been having meetings in Brussels for months. He dealt with one of the commissioners for consumer affairs, Frans Helder. The proposal was to bring forward a European law which would require any product or scheme sold or marketed within the E.U. to carry the scale, the Milo Scale. It would be printed on a label giving the rating. There are plans to set up a ministry to implement the scheme."

Rick's expression begged further explanation.

"Yes, a whole ministry", Hope continued. "It will take preparation."

"I think you need to give us more of an understanding of

how Milo's Scale works," Rick said, "I know you briefly outlined what the end result would be but, if Sophia goes along with me on this, I think it's important for her to know how the Scale arrives at its conclusions." He looked at Sophia who nodded her agreement.

"Yes… let me think of the best way to explain." Hope paused for a moment. "Milo's Scale regards any product," he began, "as being made up of positives and negatives. The positives are what you get for your money and the negatives make up what you pay. Now this may seem obvious until you consider that what appear to be positives can, in some cases, actually have a negative effect." He paused again, giving Rick and Sophia a 'with me so far look.' They nodded in unison. "Good, now let's take a mobile phone contract as an example. Most contracts offer a free amount of data transfer, a number of free call minutes as well as a number of free texts. In return, you might pay a lump sum for the phone and sign up for a minimum period – eighteen to twenty-four months. Taking the positives one-by-one and applying the formula calculates a value for each. The same method is also applied to the negatives and gives a numeric value. By weighing the negatives against the positives and applying the second phase of Milo's formula, a final score on a scale of one to ten emerges. It will be a huge task but worth it to consumers for clarity and the E.U. in revenue."

Rick looked sceptical.

"How would this work with…a can of beans..say? Where are the positives and negatives?"

It was evident Gerald had been expecting the question.

"Initially, the service sector will be targeted – banks,

mortgage companies, telecommunications and the like but food will be tackled in turn. Beans are a finite product and easier to calculate. The weight of the beans themselves – positive, this is what you are getting for your money. Is it a multi-pack? This can be both positive and negative; sometimes it's cheaper to buy the tins individually. The scale will wipe any deception away.

"So what happened?" Sophia interrupted excitedly.

"Nothing yet, Milo died two days before he was due to make a formal presentation to an assembly of commissioners. The first I knew something was wrong was when I got a call from Frans saying Milo hadn't turned up for the meeting."

"And now?" asked Rick.

"Everything's on hold. The commissioners had the meeting anyway with Frans filling in for Milo. They want to go ahead and are keen to release a statement to the press – a trailer for the proposed regulation. They are unable to do so, of course, without the permission of the owner of the rights." Hope looked at Sophia. "From what I understand from Freddie Hollis, it's you they need to speak to."

Sophia remained silent, suddenly realising the enormity of her uncle's work and, as every second passed, becoming more unsettled by D.I. Newman's question about Giles Edwards.

"I want to ask you something," she said finally,

"something you might find silly but I have to ask anyway."

"Ask away," Hope responded.

"Do you think I'm in danger? What I mean to say is…if there is so much money attached to keeping things the way they are, would there be people out there who would go to any lengths to stop an E.U. law coming into being?"

Hope hesitated. He could see Sophia was genuinely concerned and he was careful with his reply.

"Until Milo's will is published, it's only us, here in this room and Freddie, of course, who know that you are the owner of the rights. So, for the moment, it's not one of our worries but in any case, this is England – the type of thing you're worried about doesn't happen here."

"You understand why I ask. Uncle Milo is dead for no apparent reason and so is Giles Edwards who, although not working on Uncle Milo's project, was nevertheless, connected to Uncle Milo's patent attorney. I have no wish to be the next victim connected by *coincidence*." She made speech marks in the air.

"I can see why you're concerned but I really think you're worrying unnecessarily. There's no reason to believe anyone else knows about Milo's work apart from us."

"What about this Frans guy and the others in Brussels? How well do you know them?" Rick asked. "Can they be trusted?"

"Only Frans knew Milo's identity and I can vouch for him. I've known him for eight years and we've co-operated on several projects in that time. We are friends to the extent that we took our wives on a joint skiing trip last year and we're planning another. No, there are no worries there. The other commissioners had never actually met Milo and only knew of him by pseudonym. They were due to learn of his real name at the meeting he never made. So, at this time, they're none the wiser."

Rick glanced at Sophia; she seemed reassured.

"What do you suggest Sophia does now?" he asked Hope.

"Well," Hope replied, looking directly at Sophia, "assuming you want to go ahead, you'll have to confirm the continuance of Jodrell Hope on the project and then we pick up where Milo left off."

"And where was that?" she asked.

"After the planned presentation to the commissioners, Milo was due to make his royalty demands known. As you might imagine, the numbers are significant."

"Without seeming rude, what does your firm get out of the deal?" Sophia asked.

"Our fees are paid up to date; Milo was very particular to keep on top of them."

"I'm sensing there's something else," she stated politely.

"Yes, there is," returned Hope. "There's a contract giving a charity nominated by Jodrell Hope one quarter of one percent of the first year's royalties."

Sophia looked surprised but said nothing.

Hope continued. "Strictly speaking, we should wait for probate to be granted but I see no harm in starting the ball rolling again. You need to meet Frans Helder, that would be a start. If he can't manage to get to London, maybe you could take a trip on the Eurostar to Brussels. It's a two hour trip – you could be back by the evening."

"I'm not sure I'm ready to meet him without you if I have to go to Brussels; I'll need some coaching."

"I'm happy to accompany you," Hope said.

"Good, make the arrangements for next week sometime; I'll wait for your call." She opened her bag and after fumbling in its interior, drew out a business card. "Here," she said, handing him the card. "Ignore the work number, ring the mobile."

Hope took the card. "Thanks," he said, taking a momentary glance at the number before tucking the card into the inside pocket of his jacket.

Sophia stood up and gave Gerald Hope's hand the briefest of shakes.

"Thank you for your time, Mr. Hope."

"Not at all, I'll be in touch."

Rick was already standing. He shook Hope's hand and followed Sophia out.

As they stepped out into the chilly air and noise of the street, Rick checked the time at his wrist; it was just after four.

"Can I buy you a cup of coffee?" he asked.

"Why not," Sophia replied, looking up and down the street, "which way?"

"Back up to Regent Street, I saw a place on the way here."

"Okay, let's go." She surprised him by hanging onto his arm as they walked.

The small café was a short walk. Rick went to the counter and ordered as Sophia found a table at the window. The place was warm and busy with shoppers relaxing at the end of their day in town before the trip back to the suburbs. Sophia was staring through the window at passers-by when Rick returned with two mugs of coffee. She looked up at him and smiled as he put the mugs on the table. They hadn't noticed the well-built man wearing a long dark raincoat and black leather gloves slip into the café behind them. Now positioned at a table across the room, he casually observed them from behind a newspaper.

6

Sophia had left Rick at the Tube and taken advantage of the nearness of Marks & Spencer to shop for food. It was only as she entered her flat after a taxi ride in heavy traffic that she remembered she'd switched off her mobile for the meeting with Gerald Hope and had forgotten to switch it back on again. The winking light from her answer machine on the hallway table signalled the frustration of those who'd given up calling her mobile. She set down her bags and hit 'Play'.

"Five new messages," came the robotic squawk from the speaker. "Message one." The machine began its list.

There were two calls from Sadie. The first, asking her out to a movie and a drink later with the others; the second, complaining about the mobile still being off and call her "Before she asks a deserving man!"

The other messages were different. There were two hang-ups and a curious message from a head-hunter. It was curious because she had not contacted a head-hunter and more curious because her number was unlisted.

It was a man's voice that introduced itself as Sam Weller.

"I'm sorry I haven't got back to you sooner Miss Ferretti but I think we have something for you now. Please call me on…." The voice gave a mobile number and then hung up. She scribbled the number on the pad she kept by the phone then carried her shopping to the kitchen with an uneasy feeling gnawing at her stomach. Who was Sam Weller – certainly no-one *she* knew and how did he get her number? The questions were tumbling around in her head as she loaded the fridge. Then it came to her – Claudia. She'd been banging on about Jake and the only way Sophia could get shot of him was to change jobs.

"Someone like you is a head-hunter's dream," Claudia had raved – "You'd have no problem, more money and a better place for your head."

Yes, this was Claudia's work alright and she was conveniently away when the call came. But, for all her clumsy methods, maybe Claudia was right. It would be much easier to make her break from Jake if she didn't have to see him every day.

She poured a glass of Chablis from the bottle she'd started the night before and flopped onto the sofa. She took a sip then studied the number on the sheet she'd torn from the pad. Sam Weller – she knew the name but couldn't remember from where. She flipped open her phone and dialled.

"Sam Weller," the voice was crisp with a gravitas she found surprising almost threatening, a little different from the tone recorded on her machine – caught almost unawares.

"Mr. Weller, you left a message for me. I'm Sophia Ferretti."

"Oh, yes – Miss Ferretti – glad you could call back." The voice was now silky like melted chocolate. "I'm sorry it's taken a few weeks to contact you but you were explicit in your call and in your letter to us."

"I was?"

"Yes. We were not to bother you with anything that did not fit your strict criteria and only contact you if we felt we had the absolute match for your skills and salary requirements." Claudia had done well, Sophia mused.

"And have you found something?"

"We think so. I'd like to discuss the position with you in person as soon as possible before arranging an interview with the company."

"Would tomorrow do? I could take a long lunch," she offered. "I'm afraid I can't remember your address."

"It's in Holborn but we're decorating at the moment. Could I meet you at a place of your choosing?"

Sophia thought for a moment. She had no idea who this man was but was sure the road led back to Claudia. Nevertheless, she'd be careful. She'd meet him in a very public place – a hotel.

"Do you know the Grosvenor House on Park Lane?"

"Yes, I know it."

"I'll see you at 1.20 in the lobby; we can talk there."

"That'll be fine."

Sophia was about to hang up but then thought the better of it.

"Mr. Weller, forgive me, I've forgotten the name of your company."

"Weller and Associates."

"I'll see you tomorrow," she said, and hung up.

Taking another sip of the Chablis, she wandered over to her desk by the window and turned on her computer. A few minutes later, she was Googling Mr. Sam Weller and discovering where she'd heard the name before – in

Charles Dickens's first novel, The Pickwick Papers. She'd read it for a school assignment. She remembered now, Sam Weller was the comic character and valet to Pickwick but the Sam Weller she would meet tomorrow didn't sound much like a barrel of laughs; there was no humour in that voice but hey – it takes all sorts, she thought.

It was on the fifth page of hits that she came across Weller and Associates – Executive Placements but, when she hit the link, a 'site under construction' page came up. There was a phone number though. It was the same one she had just called. Seeing a reference to the company eased her mind a little though. She was reassured that the complete stranger she would meet wasn't going to drug her and sell her into slavery. She smiled at the thought and the memory it brought with it of her mother using those words to her as she set off for her first term at university, car crammed to the gunnels, all her belongings pressed against the windows.

Sophia had never been away from home on her own before. There had been school trips of course, but that didn't really count; she was with all the friends she had grown up with – a noisy collection of girls who her mother knew from sleepovers and, in the early years, face-painting parties of jelly and ice-cream. The longest time she'd been on a trip was ten days. This time it would be different.

Always supportive, her mother had given Sophia the encouragement she needed to win her place at university but it didn't stop the natural worries of a mother concerned about her little girl. There would be periods of no contact when her mother would wonder what she was doing and who she was with and what she was doing with the people she was with.

Sophia had tried to soothe her mother's anxiety but it was an exciting moment of anticipation. She had been taking a first real step into the world. As she had driven away, slipping into second gear, she'd taken a glance in the mirror expecting to see her mum waving but the pavement had been empty. She had understood why.

The man calling himself Sam Weller cut the line. So – she would meet him. He wondered if she would hear him out or leave the instant he revealed the real purpose of their rendezvous. He hoped she'd be reasonable but people are unpredictable, he thought; there was no telling what they might do.

Sophia, please do the right thing, he thought. This was one of the very few occasions in his life where he did not have complete control of the situation. He wasn't at all sure where events would take him, though he was sure of the eventual outcome – what it *must* be. With the removal of that fool Giles Edwards, he was in too deep to turn back now. One more unexplained mugging was neither here nor there.

"Sophia," he said her name in a whisper, "take the money."

Detective Sergeant Dave Gorman poked his head around the door of Newman's office. It was a relatively quiet sanctuary, sectioned off from the busy open-plan floor where eleven other detectives worked on their case loads. Despite the heavy carpeting and sound-deadening ceiling panels, the occasional raised voice or the ring of a telephone could still be heard through the glass panel window which looked out at the industry of police work.

Newman was at his desk; he looked up as the D.S. entered clutching a sheaf of paper.

"There's something on that Belgian bloke," the D.S. said, as he handed Newman the single sheet.

"Belgian bloke?"

"The one under the train."

"Oh, yes – sorry, I was miles away; tell me."

"I sent the details from his wallet through to Brussels. We got a hit."

"Just a minute, are you telling me you only just sent off the enquiry; it should've gone on the day we pulled him off the track. It's been a couple of weeks."

The D.S. looked sheepish.

"Er.. sorry sir, there was a bit of a cock-up, Burrows went sick on the day and he forgot. He got back yesterday. That's when we found out; it'd been sitting on his desk I sent it off straight away."

Newman gave an exasperated shake of his head.

"Go on."

"There's an Inspector Daniel Grenard who'd like to talk to you; seems they were looking for our jumper. Grenard would like you to call him – his number's on the page."

"Okay, thanks."

As Gorman left the room, Newman picked up the phone and dialled.

The line was answered almost immediately by a businesslike voice which uttered something in French, unintelligible to Newman, but he made out the word "Grenard".

Newman cut in. "Inspector Grenard?"

"Yes, this is Inspector Grenard." The English was perfect with only the slightest trace of an accent.

"This is Detective Inspector Newman from the Metropolitan Police in London."

"Oh yes, Inspector; thank you for calling back. You're holding Luc de Grood I believe."

"What's left of him – yes."

"He was killed by a train; is that right?"

"Yes, almost two weeks ago now, witnesses say he jumped. Can I ask why he is of interest?"

"Of course," Grenard replied, "murder – the murder of his wife. There is evidence leading to him. We have a witness who puts him in the building at the time of death and some other circumstances."

"I see. How…"

"She was in her bath with her wrists cut. He tried to make it look like suicide."

"Seems curious that he would come all the way to London to kill himself," Newman remarked.

"We are also puzzled. There must have been a reason but, we have no idea what it was. I was hoping you might know something we don't."

"Not yet, I'm afraid," replied Newman. "I'll let you know if something comes up."

"Thank you. One other thing, de Grood has a brother, he'll be contacting you to make arrangements to bring the body back to Brussels."

"Understood, I'll be in touch when we know more of de Grood's movements in London before he jumped."

"Thank you."

Sophia pushed through the revolving door, shedding her coat and slipping it over her arm as she stepped into the lobby. There were a few people queuing at the reception desk. Her heels clacked on the marble floor as she made her way around an extravagant arrangement of lilies bursting from a tall glass vase to a waiting area bounded by sofas. The sofas were laid out in a semi-circle facing a fireplace with a blazing fake log fire at the far end of the atrium. Walkways either side led away to other parts of the hotel. An elderly couple sat facing the fire, luggage standing next to them as they waited patiently for their room to be prepared. There was no sign of Sam Weller. She was about to sit when her mobile rang.

"Miss Ferretti?" It was Weller.

"Yes."

"I'm in the coffee shop behind the lobby."

"I'm on my way." She was walking with the phone to her ear. There was an opening on her left which led to the coffee shop. It was busy with diners taking lunch; the babble of their conversation spilled out into the entrance passageway. Waitresses cruised the tables, trays laden.

A man sitting on a bench seat at a table along the rear wall waved to her almost as soon as she stepped in. Sophia slipped her phone into her bag and made her way to him.

"Hello Miss Ferretti. Please – sit."

"Thank you." He was not at all as she had expected. He was late thirties, she guessed, well groomed and wearing an expensive suit. Business must be good in the executive placement line, she mused. There was a sleek attaché at his side. A red baseball cap rested on the seat next to it. It seemed out of place. It didn't go with the suit so probably wasn't his – left behind maybe by a previous customer in a hurry.

"Can I get you anything – tea – coffee maybe?" he offered, with a welcoming smile.

"No thanks, I have to get back. I'd prefer to get down to business."

She pulled up a seat opposite and set her bag down on the floor at her feet; her coat was slung on an adjacent chair.

"Very well," Weller said, and leaned back. "I have a confession to make," he began.

Sophia shot a quizzical glance at him.

"I haven't come here to introduce you to any company; I'm here for an altogether different reason."

"Oh?" she said, with calmness she didn't feel, aware her heart had stepped up a gear.

"I'm here to talk about your uncle."

Now her heart was thumping with an intensity that made it hard to breath. She made to get up.

"Please, hear me out; I'm here to help."

"Who are you?" She was angry now. "My uncle's dead – but I suppose you know that. Tell me, who you are and how you got my number."

"Who I am is not important; it's what I can do for you that is."

Sophia was standing now, turning to go.

"It's worth half a million pounds – it could be in your account this afternoon."

Sophia hesitated.

"Sit down – just for a moment," Weller continued, "it can't hurt to hear what I have to say."

She sat with reluctance.

"This better be good or I'm gone – now, what about my uncle?"

Weller put his hands together under his chin as if he was about to pray then he put them on the table in front of him, spreading his fingers.

"Your uncle," he began, looking straight into her eyes in a way that made her uncomfortable. "His work, I know that since his unfortunate death, the rights to his formula have passed to you and you intend to continue…."

"What do you know about his work?" Sophia cut across his words.

"I know it will take time before circumstances allow you to see any return, it may be years. Committees in Brussels are notorious for their procrastination."

"You seem remarkably well informed – I don't know how, but it can't be legal."

"Let me get to the point."

"I wish you would."

"I am interested in the rights to your uncle's work and I'm prepared to pay."

Sophia tried to keep her composure but she was angry and a little frightened – no, she was more than a little frightened. It was like a bad dream. There had been no threat but she had the feeling it would be implied at any moment. She tried to calm herself remembering Gerald Hope's words of reassurance.

"Go on."

Weller reached for his attaché and pulled out a blue folder.

"I have a contract here. It confirms that five hundred thousand pounds be paid to you in return for relinquishing all your rights to Professor Ferretti's formula and that you make them over to me. All you need to do is sign it in front of a witness – any one of these waitresses would do," he gestured about the room. "I could have the money wired to your account while we're sitting here."

She was about to speak but was interrupted by the ring of Weller's mobile. He was holding her gaze as he answered – speaking softly into the phone.

"Yes, I've got that," was the extent of the conversation before he cut the call. "Now, where were we? Ah – yes, you were about to consider my offer."

Sophia remained silent for a moment. She looked at the blue folder containing the contract and then flicked her eyes back to his.

"My uncle spent years developing his ideas into a workable formula. I don't believe he did it just for the money. I now know he believed he could help ordinary people even the score. If you know so much about me, why, in God's name, did you think I would sell him out? How did you even think I would come to this meeting? Were you just guessing I was in the market for a new job?"

Weller's face lost a little of its charm as his mouth tightened around the edges.

"Yes, I was guessing you would be like ninety percent of the population and be curious to see if the grass was greener somewhere different and I was right, you turned up."

"You didn't answer my question. Why would you assume that I would sell out my uncle's work?"

"Well, my dear – for one thing, you are not your uncle. You have different pressures – concerns, should I say?"

"Pressures? – what pressures?"

"For instance – twenty-two thousand pounds of yet unpaid

university fees in the form of a loan," he replied, breaking a smug smile. "It's been a while since you were at university so it's safe to assume your bank balance could do with some help."

"How..?"

"Never mind how I know. All I'm asking is you think about it."

Sophia was winded for a moment at the ease with which this stranger had obtained the details of her bank account. Devious as he was, however, he apparently had no knowledge of the cash bequest from Uncle Milo which languished in Freddie Hollis' client account collecting interest for her while she waited for probate. The pressure, she supposed, had vanished when Uncle Milo's will was read to her in Freddie's office but Weller couldn't know that.

"And if I refuse?"

"If you refuse…. It would be your loss and mine. You will still struggle on trying to pay your debts and I would have to find some other proposition to spend my money on."

"So…" she said, hesitantly, "you expect me to sign all my rights over to you without even a lawyer looking at the contract first? – I don't think so." She stood, picking up her coat and bag in one movement. She wanted to be out of there – something about Weller or whoever he was, gave her the creeps in a frightening way.

He held the contract up to her. "At least consider it. As I said, I'm offering to help you."

She turned back to him. "Okay, I'll think about it." She had no intention of doing any such thing but thought that if she took it from him, she could, at least, get away and out into the street. "I'll let you know."

"Don't leave it too long," he said, almost inaudibly in a tone that implied consequences as he watched her out of sight.

7

"Don't date the help," were the words bouncing around inside Jake's head. Spoken by his business partner, Adam, who had gone on to add a few more words of warning along the same lines but all leading to a conclusion which featured a summation containing the phrase 'crap on your own doorstep'. However, Jake had believed things would be different in his case and he'd gone ahead and started something with Sophia, the 'help' referred to by his 'oh so wise' and occasionally smug partner when giving his unsought advice. There was no doubt however, that his thing, relationship, affair – he hadn't quite decided which heading it went under – with Sophia, was hitting a decidedly tricky stage. She wasn't returning his calls and his texts went unanswered. Yes, something was going wrong alright and he'd better fix it before Adam's prophecies of an uncomfortable mess at the office became reality.

"She's not there," Dawn, one of the copy-writers who sat in the outer office, had told him as he made to knock on the studio door where Sophia sketched her designs. "She's gone out to lunch."

"Oh."

"I don't think she'll be back today; she took work home."

At thirty, Jake was unmarried and still having a good time. His easy-going demeanour and glamorous profession had ensured he was never short of female company willing to party. Nevertheless, he was aware it couldn't go on forever. Sophia was his first attempt, half hearted though it was, at a more permanent arrangement. She doesn't seem to be getting it; I'm not getting my message across – no product recognition, he pondered in advertising speak as his cab drew up to her apartment block. He paid the driver and used the key he suspected he might be returning at any moment – the one Sophia had given him a few months after their relationship began. Relationship – this is what he finally decided they had together but there was a nagging feeling at the back of his mind that maybe the accolade had been awarded too late.

I'll give it my best shot even so, he thought, as he bounded up the stairs to the first floor – too impatient to wait for the lift.

The stairs and corridor were laid with heavy carpet; his footfalls were absorbed by the deep pile. As he approached Sophia's door, he noticed it was ajar. He was about to knock but checked himself. There was a rustling sound coming from inside then a man's voice. He withdrew his hand. She's got a guy in there! No wonder she's not coming back to the office. He turned to go but stopped as he realised the voice was speaking into a phone. He strained to hear, tilting his head closer to the opening.

"I've got the latest statement from her bank in my hand." The voice was deep and accented – German maybe. It was slow in it's delivery but something with weight behind it. "She's twenty-two thousand in hock to the university loan company and almost nothing in her current account." The voice went quiet for a moment as if listening to a response from the other end of the line then said, "Okay, I'm out of here."

At that point, Jake, who had been leaning to crane his head, lost his balance and fell against the door. It offered no resistance and swung open. A tall muscular man looked up from the bureau where Jake knew Sophia kept her personal papers. He rushed at Jake, crashing into him with the force of a hurricane. The pair reeled sideways splintering a coffee table of wood and glass as they tumbled to the floor. An instant later, Jake felt a fist the size of a bowling ball collide with the side of his head. He felt warm blood on his cheek. This guy's going to kill me if I don't get up, he thought, rolling left to avoid another one of those bowling balls. He struggled to his feet but the giant was on him again. He managed to parry one blow but the next knocked the wind from him and he fell backwards towards the French windows. As he hit the floor, he caught sight of the glass Nautilus bowl he'd bought for Sophia from Steuben in New York on their first trip together to the Big Apple. It had fallen just within the reach of his outstretched arm. The edge of the bowl rose up at one side in the shape of a mollusc making an ideal handle. He grabbed it and with all the strength he had left, brought it up in a perfect arc against his assailant's head as he was coming in for the final strike. Jake watched the massive fist halt mid-flight, waver for a split second and then fall away as its owner landed squarely on top of him. It was like being crushed under the foot of an elephant and he thought he heard a crack from his ribcage. He wriggled free and stood up holding his head and feeling a sharp stab of pain in his chest. The world was spinning in a dizzy swirl and he collapsed gasping onto the only remaining upright chair. He closed his eyes but the spinning sensation kept right on. He needed some air. Opening his eyes again, he was relieved his vision was steadier now. There was a scene of upheaval around him. His assailant was still out cold, sprawled by the smashed coffee table in a sunburst of broken glass and taking shallow breaths with the occasional snort.

Jake stood up, swayed and then clung to the frame of the French windows. He wanted to get away before his new acquaintance woke up but he was nauseous and with every breath, the pain in his chest was like a jab with a sharp stick. He flung open the French windows and staggered out onto the small balcony, hoping the smack of cold air on his face would calm his wavy stomach and give him the strength to get the hell out of there. He took short breaths to avoid the pain in his ribs and stood leaning on the balustrade regaining his senses. The noise of the traffic below filled his ears and covered the sound of stirring shards of glass on the floor behind him. He didn't see the large hands that grabbed him and pitched him over. He was falling then, blackness.

Rick's mobile vibrated in his pocket; the 'Media Law and Ethical Issues' lecture was just wrapping up. It was Sophia. He snuck out of the lecture hall and into the corridor.

"I'm sorry to bother you in college but I need you to come over to my flat right away. Something's happened…and..," she was speaking in a rush.

He cut across her. "Stay cool – I'll be there. Give me the

address."

Sophia's apartment block looked a little out of place in a tree-lined avenue amongst expensive looking 1920s houses. It looked like something from the 1960s. What was definitely out of place though was the Police cordon of flapping plastic tape which sectioned off an area in front of the building like a restless snake. Behind the cordon Rick spotted D.I. Newman in animated conversation with two other men - more plain clothes Police, he presumed. They were pointing up and then to the car next to them. The windscreen had a spider-web crack and its roof was caved in.

"Detective Inspector," Rick called from behind the tape where he'd been restrained by a constable.
Newman looked up – took a beat to recognise him then waved him through.

"Seems like everywhere I turn these days, I bump into you and Miss Ferretti," Newman greeted him with resignation.

"What happened?"

"We're not quite sure what went on before we got here but when we did, we found a friend of Miss Ferretti's lying on the top of this car." He gestured to the distorted vehicle to his left. "At a glance, I'd say he fell from her balcony."
Rick opened his mouth to speak but Newman held one hand up indicating he wasn't finished.

"Miss Ferretti has made a statement but claims she wasn't here. She says she was at a meeting at the Grosvenor House Hotel. Do you know anything about that?"
Rick shook his head.

"It'll be easy enough to check of course." Newman went on. "Why don't you go up and have a talk with her – maybe she'll tell you more than she told us."

"The guy who fell, is he okay?"

"Too early to say, he's in a coma along with a few broken bones. We'll know in a few days."

Rick turned to leave.

"Just one thing Mr. Devan, why exactly are you here?"

"Sophia called me about thirty minutes ago. She didn't give any details, just asked me to come right away."

Newman gave a nod of understanding and waved him away.

Sophia's flat resembled Milo's on the day Rick had found his body staring back at him from the bath. Furniture and ornaments were strewn about and there was a smashed coffee table and a drying bloodstain on the carpet next to it. Sophia sat with a woman Police constable at the back of the room while two men, hooded in white coveralls, were putting something into a plastic bag. Sophia saw him and immediately went over to him and gave him the briefest of hugs.

"Thanks for coming, I didn't know who else to call."

"Don't worry about it; I'd finished for the day anyway." They went to the chairs where Sophia had been sitting with the Policewoman and sat down.

"I'll be with D.I. Newman if you need me," the woman constable said, as she left. Sophia nodded an acknowledgement and turned to face Rick.

He could see she was shaken and took both her hands in his.

"Now, tell me, what the hell went on here? Who's the guy

who fell?"

"Jake, it's Jake who fell. He's er.., someone I've been seeing," she replied, to the unasked question on Rick's face. "What he was doing here, I have no idea. We're in the process of breaking up. I can only presume he'd come to talk but I can't say for sure. All I know is that when I got back from Town, the Police were already here loading Jake into an ambulance."

"The place is a mess."

Sophia looked around at her scattered possessions. "The Police think there was a fight in here and whoever it was Jake was fighting with, pushed him over the balcony."

"Maybe Jake walked in on a burglar," Rick offered.

"Maybe, but nothing was taken – no, I think it had something to do with my meeting today."

Rick was puzzled. "Have you told Newman this?"

"Not yet but I plan to." She went on to recount the day's events and her meeting with Weller. "..and he got a call. Suddenly, he knew what was in my bank account and details I hadn't told anyone. I think whoever was on the end of the line was calling from here and was reading from my bank statement."

"Seems possible – it'll be easy enough to check, just press the redial. Did Newman make a guess at the owner of the blood on the carpet?"

"No, they took samples. Jake was bleeding so it's probably his."

Rick stood up. "I'd better get Newman; he'll be wanting to speak to this Weller character. The sooner you start talking, the better."

"Oh, I just remembered, he gave me this." Sophia held

out the two page contract Weller had pressed on her.

Rick took it from her and studied the text. "There's no name on it anywhere," he said, flicking the page over. "There are blanks where the names of the parties should be. He doesn't want you to know who he is until you agree."

"Yes, that seems about right. It was scary how he knew so much about me and Uncle Milo. When I think about it, he was a scary man; everything about him spelt trouble – I was glad to get away from him."

"I'm going down to bring Newman. I'll be back in a couple of minutes – will you be okay?"

"I'll be fine – these two will watch over me," she replied, gesturing to the two figures in white bent over a section of carpet.

He was almost at the door when she called after him.

"Can I ask another favour?"

"Go ahead."

"Can I stay at your place tonight? My flatmate's away and I'd rather not be here alone tonight."

8

For most people, rolling a car and spending sleep-time next to one of those machines that beeps every few seconds to let everyone know that the patient still had potential, would have been enough excitement to last a lifetime. However, Rick's life in the last few weeks had been turning into a movie plot – the kind he used to watch on re-runs of Dragnet. What a day today had been. It had started quietly enough with a brisk walk to college and coffee in the refectory with Reggie Lieu and his girlfriend, both students from Hong Kong on his course. There was only one lecture and they all went in together. Then came the call from Sophia and the tenor of the day changed. He had no idea what to expect on his way over to her place but was flattered that it was him she'd called. It still puzzled him though; it was as if she had no-one else to call – hard to believe but he wasn't complaining. She was an attractive woman and she was calling *him*; he needed no other explanation. Now that same attractive woman was sitting not ten feet away on his couch.

He got up and flicked on his laptop on his way to the kitchen.

"Coffee, tea or .."

"Tea," she called after him before he could finish.

He filled the kettle and went back to his computer to check his email while the water boiled. He scanned the list, deleting as he went but caught his breath as the highlighter rested on an address he hadn't expected to see in his inbox – ever... juliet.laskey@stimes.com. He was caught by surprise and his expression surely showed it. He glanced over at Sophia but she was studying her mobile; she hadn't noticed. He opened the mail, careful to put himself between the screen and Sophia; not that she would be able to read from ten feet away but you can't be too careful where women are concerned, he mused – they have the stealth of cats and the intuition to match.

'I'm in London for a week on a story. I heard you were here from Seb Morgan. I'd like to catch up. Email me, Juliet.'
What did she want; she sure as hell didn't want to catch up.

Sebastian Morgan – Seb, was a friend from high-school whom he'd kept loose touch with because they'd had the same ambition – journalism, albeit in different branches. Seb was a photographer and photo journalism had been his thing for as long as Rick could remember. They fantasised they would be a team with Rick writing the gritty stories and Seb taking the shot that would win him the Pulitzer for Spot News Photography. Seb was at the *Times* now. He'd got the job right around the time Rick was learning to get about again after the accident. They went for a coffee the day Seb had called at Rick's parents, taking a chance Rick might be there. It had been a full ten minutes of small-talk before Seb had told him.

"At least one half of the team is on the case," Rick had joked.

"Let's hope I don't have to wait too long for the other

half!" Seb had responded, giving a clear signal that he hoped he and Rick would ultimately fulfil the plans they'd made in their teens.

Who was Seb's other half these days? Rick wondered. Was he partnered with Juliet as the photographer of the team? Was that how they came to be talking about him? The questions kept coming and it was only the fury of the boiling water in the kettle which shook him loose of his thoughts.

Later, when Sophia was asleep on the couch – he'd offered to move out of his room but she'd insisted on the couch – he tapped out a reply. Nothing fancy or newsy, just businesslike – 'I can see you tomorrow. Send me a number to call you.' He closed the laptop and turned his thoughts back to Sophia. Max hadn't quite known what to make of it and spent a while darting from one room to another as the bed was being made up for her. He settled down though once he realised Sophia was staying. Rick didn't know why he was feeling a little guilty he hadn't told her about the email from Juliet but justified his silence on the subject reasoning that she had enough to keep her occupied without hearing about his ex. However, the truth was simpler, he didn't want any spoilers messing up the hopes he had for Sophia. Juliet would be gone in a few days; there was no sense in complicating things. Nevertheless, getting 'right down to the wire' truthful, he was more than a little curious as to why Juliet wanted to see him. The last he'd heard, she was engaged to her property tycoon with a marriage planned for next spring; not that he'd been following her career, just tittle-tattle from the *Times'* on-line pages.

Rick and Sophia had left the disarray of the flat at around six and had promised to meet D.I. Newman at his office the following day. Jake was in 'Intensive Care' and there would be an update in twenty-four hours. Dinner had been a take-out pizza, a meal that was becoming a habit with Rick; one he repeatedly resolved to kick every time he opened the box of the latest delivery and the aroma of topping mingled with warm cardboard hit his nostrils.

Over several glasses of wine from a bottle he'd been keeping for an evening when he might have company, Rick had listened to Sophia re-tell the story of her meeting with Sam Weller. The details of her time with Jake followed as the wine took effect. He'd always suspected there must be a boyfriend somewhere. No-one as eye-catching as she was would remain unattached for very long in any world he knew. Nevertheless, it still threw cold water on his aspirations with her even though she'd told him she was breaking up with Jake. Not wishing to be uncaring or callous in any way but, after today's events, there would be the whole sympathy thing while Jake recovered which could delay the final break or re-kindle their affair. In fairness to Sophia though, she hadn't shown any signs that Jake's airborne adventure which took off from her balcony, had changed anything. She was more concerned about her own safety and was now, more than ever, tempted to take the money offered by Sam Weller and run.

As Rick mulled it all over – everything from the time of meeting Milo to Jake falling and Sophia in his living room, the images began to jumble with unconnected memories from the distant past and sleep finally took him.

When he opened his email the next morning at eight, Juliet's reply was waiting with a mobile number. Sophia had beaten him to the shower; he could hear splashing sounds coming from the bathroom. Using the opportunity, he called Juliet.

"Hey Rick, thanks for calling. I wasn't sure you'd reply……Can you get over to see me?"

Straight to the point, no shilly-shallying with pleasantries; she'll go far, he thought. In the brief exchange that followed, they arranged to meet at her hotel that afternoon.

"We can catch up then," she said, and the call was over.

At eleven thirty that same morning, Rick, Sophia and D.I. Newman sat three abreast opposite a TV hooked up to a DVD player.

"We've edited the footage from several cameras in the hotel CCTV system," Newman said, turning to Sophia. "The time-line starts from the moment you enter and finishes when you leave. We've done the same thing with the recordings of the person we think you met."

"The person you think I met? So you're not sure I'm telling the truth." Sophia's temperature was rising.

"Calm down and watch," Newman replied, "You'll understand." He nodded to D.S. Gorman who was standing at the edge of the room holding a remote control. Gorman hit the play button. The TV screen flickered into life to give a not quite continuous series of images of people coming and going through the revolving entrance door of the Grosvenor House Hotel from the lobby side.

A rolling bar of numbers at the bottom of the screen

indicated the time on every frame as it flashed up. Sophia was caught by the camera entering the lobby at 13.19. A second camera, from a higher angle, picked her up crossing the lobby and a third, captured the moment she entered the coffee shop. The final view came from within the coffee shop. The shot was from the corner of the ceiling and showed her crossing to the table where she'd met Weller. Suddenly, she understood what Newman had meant. Only a third of the table was in shot. The bench seat, where Weller had installed himself, was not covered. The only time anything of Sam Weller entered the picture was at the end of their conversation when he had handed her the contract – and then only his forearm was visible.

"Are there any other cameras?"

"There's one directly above but behind," Newman grimaced, "we can see you clearly but all we can see of your friend, is the top of his head."

"There must be pictures of him arriving."

"Oh, there are," D.I. Newman maintained his grimace. "He didn't want to be seen though – take a look." He nodded to D.S. Gorman who hit another button on the remote. The screen went blank for a moment and then lit up with the shot of the revolving doors; the time code showed 13.12. Three blank frames flicked by, then a man wearing a suit entered. A red baseball cap with the peak pulled down fitted his head snuggly, completely obscuring his face from the camera. The sequence followed the same pattern as the previous one which had tracked Sophia until he went out of shot to sit down.

"That's it?" Sophia was incredulous. "That's all there is?"

"I'm afraid so. Whoever it was you met yesterday knew

exactly what he was doing. He knew where the cameras were and suspected somebody might be interested. Now, Miss Ferretti, over the last two-and-a-half weeks, I've bumped into you and our American friend here on four occasions and in circumstances which haven't been particularly pleasant. Your Uncle, found dead by Mr. Devan, then a lawyer connected to your patent attorney was found murdered in the street and another friend of yours thrown, we think, from your balcony. Don't you think it's time to tell me exactly what's going on?"

Sophia glanced at Rick.

"I don't know myself," she began.

"You can do better than that," Newman cut in. "For a start, you can tell me the real reason why you met with Weller. You said he made you an offer but you conveniently omitted to say what it was he was offering to buy. Now, you can tell me everything here or we can do this formally in an interview room downstairs."

It was true; Sophia had been economic in her description of events for the most part because she wasn't sure how much she *should* say. The world of patents and copyright was new to her and not having checked with Gerald Hope, she had no idea how much she could reveal without jeopardising any negotiations she might have in Brussels. She glanced at Rick again. He gave her a reassuring nod.

"You don't need permission from Mr. Devan. Let's hear it." Newman was becoming impatient.

"Okay, okay, but you understand I haven't spoken to my patent lawyer so I can't give all the details."

The D.I. frowned but gestured for her to continue.

"Uncle Milo," she began. "He was working on something

when he died, something which will change the way you buy," she paused for a moment then said, "anything."

D.S. Gorman, who, up until this point, hadn't being paying much attention, stopped fiddling with the DVD player and turned to listen.

"Without speaking to Gerald Hope, that's as much as I can say about his work."

Over the next five minutes, she went over the seventeen days since her uncle's death. Newman remained silent, nodding occasionally as she listed the key events – Freddie Hollis, how she'd learnt of her considerable inheritance amongst which were the rights to Uncle Milo's work and the meeting with Gerald Hope.

"I was a bit concerned to see you at Gerald Hope's office and a little alarmed when I heard that the man who was murdered used to work for him. Gerald told me it was nothing to worry about and certainly not related to anything Uncle Milo had been working on. The man who died…"

"Giles Edwards," Newman reminded her.

"Yes, Giles Edwards – he'd left the firm some time ago apparently. Gerald was convinced it was just Giles's bad luck he was in the wrong place. Well, I believed that until yesterday. First Weller offering money for my uncle's work and then what happened to Jake; I don't believe in coincidence – I think I'm right not to. Three weeks ago, all I had to worry about was the loan left over from my student days and when to go to Sainsbury's; now I feel like there's a target on my back and there's an open invitation for some very nasty people to take a shot at it."

"Where do you fit in this story, Mr. Devan?" Newman asked, turning to Rick.

"I don't really – other than what I told you at the time – I knew Milo. I found his body in his bath. You know this though."

"Yes, but you have a habit of turning up at venues where I'm investigating incidents which seem to lead back to the Professor – a bit odd don't you think?"

"Look Detective Inspector, I'm a friend of Sophia – not one of longstanding, about two and a half weeks actually but a friend nonetheless and trying to help out at a difficult time for her. Of course, I'm going to be around her – what can I tell you?"

"Okay," Newman held up his hand for Rick to stop. He got the feeling that if he didn't, the boy would keep going for ever. "That's all for now but I might be in touch with you again in the next few days. Hopefully Miss Ferretti's friend in the hospital will tell us something when he comes round. Just don't go far without letting me know. Here's my card, you can call me any time if you think of anything else you want to tell me." He handed Rick and Sophia a card each as they got up to leave.

"There is one thing, Inspector, I – we," she looked at Rick, "are going to Brussels for a couple of days next week; it's to do with Uncle Milo's work. You'll be able to get me on my mobile if you need to speak to me urgently."

Surprise must have registered on Rick's face because Newman asked,

"Is that right Mr. Devan?"

"Er – yes, absolutely."

"This a holiday as well as business?"

"As I said, it has something to do with Uncle Milo's work; I have to meet someone who works at the E.U. building."

"Okay, just let me know when you know which day."

They didn't speak in the lift but as they went out onto the street, Rick put his arm round Sophia's shoulder and smiled.

"So, you're taking me away to Brussels for a few days but you were going to surprise me."

"Sorry," she said, sheepishly, "I was going to ask you yesterday but the thing with Weller and then Jake, it clean went out of my head. Will you come? There's no way I want to go on my own and even if Gerald comes, I think I'd feel safer if you were there as well."

"I'm flattered, I'll be there. Who could refuse such an offer?"

"Thanks. Don't worry about any of the arrangements, Gerald will organise it all."

Nagging at the back of Rick's mind was a little voice telling him that he was supposed to be studying but, he thought he owed it to Milo to see things through and also, not let Sophia down. He was becoming fond of Sophia and it was no hardship spending time with her. He'd just have to find the time to make up any course work he'd missed. However, it was a relief to hear Gerald would be footing the bill. Even though Rick had readily agreed to go to Brussels, the cost of a ticket would have put a severe dent in his college budget. Mind you, if push had come to shove, he'd have forked out just to be with Sophia for a couple of days. He was a guy, after all and guys took chances where women were concerned and worried about the consequences later.

He turned to her, "I have to be somewhere this afternoon

but we could meet up later, if that's okay?"

"Can I stay at your place again? It'll be just for tonight, I promise."

"Are you sure you can survive the couch again?"

"No probs but I need to go back to my flat to pick up a few things and I want to ring the hospital to see how Jake is." There it was – the sympathy thing. "Yeah, of course, maybe he's come out of it."

Rick hailed a cab for her at the corner and when she was on her way, made for the Tube. He emerged at Hyde Park Corner. Park Lane was noisy with traffic as he walked the five minutes up to the Hilton. The din was replaced by low voices mingled with Musac the moment he entered the tranquil lobby through revolving glass doors. As instructed, he went around the lifts and up the double staircase at their rear to the mezzanine lounge.

9

Rick had a few reservations about this meeting; he thought he'd put Miss Laskey behind him but his uneasiness told him he hadn't. He was unsure if it was from guilt he hadn't told Sophia what he was up to today or if it was the anticipation of seeing Juliet for the first time in nigh on two years that was responsible for the troupe of butterflies doing back-flips in his stomach.

Juliet had left his life so suddenly; it almost made his head spin when he thought about it. There had only been two dates but, back then, he had convinced himself she might be the one. He was wrong, of course, he admitted reluctantly. She'd been to the hospital twice, he was told later, to satisfy herself, he suspected, that he would be okay. Once established, she'd moved on without a backward glance – or so it had played out in his head. Maybe the truth was something different but he'd been so high on every kind of drug in those early days, the line between reality and the weird dreams he was having at the time, was blurred.

He remembered how she'd been at the interview; how she'd taken defeat – or not as it turned out. Juliet Laskey was on a path and a team of wild horses would be unable to pull her off it and, thinking of his growing affection for

Sophia, he was beginning to feel right about how things had worked out.

That was before he rounded the corner into the open lounge. Juliet was sitting in an easy-chair next to a low table speaking into her phone, her hair back-lit from a standard lamp. She looked up and directly at him as he approached, locking her eyes with his just as she'd done on the day they had met. She was as beautiful as he remembered – more, maybe. She hung up the phone and got up to meet him, kissing his cheek before he could utter a word. Her perfume filled the air around him with an intoxicating effect. He thought he might stammer but finally got it together.

"Juliet, how are you – silly question really; I can tell just by looking at you. You look great."

"Thank you, Rick; you look pretty good yourself."

"Better than the last time you saw me."

There was an awkward pause. A frown clouded her features.

"About that….I'm sorry I didn't come again. I…"

"Forget it – I have." Well, he thought he had until thirty seconds ago.

She called a waiter over.

"What would you like to drink?"she asked, steering the conversation away from the past.

"Tea would be great; this is England and they drink a lot of it here."

She smiled and ordered.

"So, tell me, what's it like…. living here?"

"I'm having a good time. I forgot what it was like to be at college. It must be the same everywhere; only the accents change. And you – what's happening in your life?" He wasn't about to tell her he'd been following her career with interest; any more than he was going to tell her that he thought a friend in his building was murdered and, more significantly, he had designs on someone new in his life.

"I'm making steady progress…I think," she replied modestly. "I've a way to go yet though. You know how it is; you're only as good as your last big story and for me, that was a couple of months ago – I need a new one."

"Two months? You haven't turned anything in for two months."

"Oh, sure, there have been a few small pieces but nothing meaty."

The tea arrived and Rick sipped. Gaps were appearing in the conversation; he could see the pleasantries were draining away.

"Okay Juliet, let me make it easy for you. We both know you didn't come here to schmooze; judging by the rock on your finger, that role's gone already – what is it you need from me?"

She was silent, holding his eyes in hers again as if savouring the moment before it was lost in the real business of the day.

"Yes," she said finally, "there is something."

Rick knew as much but he'd hoped in some stupid way, she had genuinely wanted to catch up. He didn't let his disappointment show; he did a remarkable job in covering it – he thought.

"Go on."

"Well, I'm not sure how much you know of what I do."

"A little – you write for the Business section."

She showed surprise he'd been interested enough to find out. "Yes but not the straight forward stuff; I try to go deep into the background detail and the personalities."

"Okay.." he drew out the word. "I'm not sure how I could possibly help you though."

"I'm getting to that. I'm working on something at the moment here in London. A firm back home is taking over a worldwide marketing corporation; it has its head office in London. It has regionals in New York, Hong Kong and Tokyo; it's a massive deal. I need to get some information on one of the key players but the one person who can help me doesn't give interviews."

"I'm with you but still don't see my part in this."

Juliet paused, struggling for the right words to paint her in a light other than the one casting her as a manipulating journo who didn't care who she used, even old boyfriends, as long as she got what she needed. That was the case alright; it looked like what it was. There was no way other than to come out with it.

"You're at Goldsmiths, right?"

"Yes," Rick replied, with suspicion.

"The guy I need to talk to is a lecturer there; I was wondering if you knew him."

"And if I do?"

"Persuade him to talk to me."

Rick had no idea how many lecturers there were at Goldsmiths, fifty – a hundred, maybe. He had reasonable relationships with the ones on his course but the chances he knew even a fraction of the others in any more than a 'Hello how are you' sort of way as he passed them in the corridor, was minimal.

"Who is he?"

"Melvyn Carter – do you know him?"

"Yeah, I know *him*; he runs the media course."

"How well do you know him?"

"Well, it might be overstating a little to say I know him; he took three lectures when our regular guy was ill. I thought I got on with him okay – we chatted."

"So, do you think you could get him to talk to me?"

"I'm not sure; I only spoke to him on those occasions – I don't know what the name of his cat is or which day he goes to the laundromat. I guess it depends on the subject."

Juliet spent the next twenty minutes going through the facets of the take-over with a few facts about each of the senior executives thrown in. She left the intrigue surrounding Sheldon Blane until last, recounting Jack's discoveries and the questions they begged.

"Blane is a bit of a mystery man and supposedly, a ruthless one. All the people who have worked with him in the past, ones we've managed to track down so far, hold him in some kind of awe; I can't work out if it's out of respect or downright fear."

"And Carter, he has the goods on Blane, you reckon?"

"Yes, that's about it. He knows something – I just need him to talk about it."

Rick took another sip of tea to give him time to think about what she was asking of him. It would be difficult to refuse but then again, how could he approach Carter without drawing fire. He was a journalist himself – confessed by the very fact he was on a course to broaden his career. Juliet was studying him, not sure how he would respond, he guessed.

"Okay, I'll give it a go – but I'm not making any promises. He could tell me to take a walk the moment I open my mouth if your guy's experience is anything to go by."

"I understand. All I'm asking is for you to try. If we get nowhere, then I'll have to accept it…..but it's got to be worth a shot don't you think?"

"Yeah, it's got to be worth a shot."

She smiled at him, giving him the full force of those eyes again.

"You know what the next question is, I think."

"Sure, you want to know when. It'll have to be tomorrow; it's too late to go to college today."

"Okay, tomorrow then. No later, please, I don't know how much longer I can push my stay."

"I'll do my best." He drained his cup and got up not wishing to reach a point where his allotted time was up; he remembered how ordered she was.

"I thought you were free today," she said, with a look of surprise.

"No lectures but other stuff."

"Oh, I see."

She seemed genuinely disappointed as she handed him a business card.

"My cell's on this. You'll call me if you have anything?"

He nodded.

She stood and kissed his cheek. "Call me anyway."

He smiled and turned to leave.

"Rick…it was good to see you again."

"It was good to see you too, Juliet."

He turned back, kissed her cheek and made for the stairs.

Sophia lay awake on the sofa; it was midnight. Rick had turned in half an hour ago. Max, who apparently had got over his initial misgivings, was curled up on the carpet at the foot of Sophia's make-shift bed; his head nestled against his body in an alert sleep.

When she'd called the hospital, Jake was still unconscious but stable. There had been a slight improvement but it could be a while before he would be out of danger. Newman had posted one of his men outside the door –

"Just in case," he'd told her.

"In case of what?"

"In case he saw the face of whoever threw him off of your balcony. We don't want anyone coming back to finish the job, do we?"

This was all getting too much, thank god for Rick. She thought about him in the room next door. He was so different to Jake. She'd put up with Jake's dodges for so long, she'd forgotten what it was like to be in the company of a man who wasn't giving little hints that he was still in his free spirit days. Commitment, it was a word Jake avoided at all costs – he was as slippery as the weed covered rocks she used to paddle amongst with her crab catching net when she was five years old on holiday with her mum and dad in Cornwall. It was an analogy she often applied to Jake because it fitted so well. It was never possible to find a firm foothold on those rocks and Jake was the same; there was nowhere to hold on to. She was upset at what had happened to him, of course, and that he was lying in a hospital bed as a result of his desire to come and see her – but there was no going back. She'd have to tell him and soon, she thought.

She thought of Rick again and realised she had been thinking of him a great deal lately; he always seemed to be there somewhere. She turned onto her side in a fresh effort to sleep. Max heard the sofa creak and flicked one eye open and then closed it again when he was satisfied of the status quo, working his head further into the warm patch of carpet.

10

Annabel Price made her way back to her desk from the petite kitchen tucked out of sight of waiting visitors behind a wall at the back of the reception area. She gingerly set her coffee mug down on a coaster and sat surveying the pile of completed typing. She sipped her coffee. Only another three months of this and I'll be out of this place and in the sunshine, she reflected. Mustn't complain though, this job came just at the right time and was a stroke of luck. She'd only needed a six month contract and this little number had come into the agency while she was actually sitting there being interviewed by the boss of the place. The job was dull though and only served to convince her that when she eventually began her career, it wouldn't be in a patent lawyer's practice or any other kind of lawyer's office for that matter. She sipped her coffee again. Anyway, I've got a whole year in the South African sun before I have to concern myself with that. Right now, I need to keep my head down, smile and pander to the egos of the irritating men who work here and grab the pay.

The intercom buzzed.

"Annabel, can you come in please?"

"Yes, Mr. Hope."

Gerald Hope wasn't that irritating. He was pleasant enough

but he didn't seem to have a sense of humour, he was too focused on his work she supposed, though she *had* caught him looking at her breasts once or twice when she'd had one button too many undone on her blouse. So, there must be some life in there after all.

Hope put aside some papers as Annabel sat across from him with her pad, pencil poised.

"I want you to ring Sophia Ferretti and tell her I've penciled meetings on Wednesday of next week in Brussels. She'd better go Tuesday to be in time if the meetings start early. Check she can make it. She won't need me at this stage. Frans Helder will look after her. If she can make it, we'll fix her hotel and ticket on the Eurostar."

Annabel nodded as she scribbled.

Hope continued. "I've a feeling she might want to take a friend; tell her that's okay, we'll take care of everything. I'll be out at a meeting for the next hour. I'll speak to you when I get back."

As Annabel rose and turned towards the door, a smile began to light her features. Finally, she thought, something that's worth something.

It had been a week earlier. Annabel had been taking her lunch at her usual spot in the small diner a street away from the office and far enough away to ensure she wouldn't be forced to sit with any of her work colleagues. She always arrived before the rush. Twenty-six years old and with the savvy to work a sensuous glance, she never failed to secure her favoured table by the window from the young waiter she suspected as having the hots for her.

"Do you mind if I sit here?"

She looked up from the Coke she was sipping while she waited for her pasta.

"No, go ahead." She glanced unobtrusively at the handsome man as he took his overcoat to the rack in the corner. Mid-thirties, she thought, a suit from a different planet to those worn at her workplace and – money, she surmised.

Her pasta arrived.

"Is the pasta good here," he asked, as he sat down,
He caught her eyes in his.

"Er.. yes, it's always good," she replied awkwardly.
He turned and caught the waiter.

"I'll have the same."

Annabel didn't remember much of what they talked about at lunch. She must have told him how she was taking a year out to see a friend in South Africa who she'd met at Uni. What she did remember was dinner in the roof restaurant of the expensive hotel where they'd spent a night of urgent and sometimes rough sex drowned in Champagne. Even now, the thought of it sent a tingle to a place that made her shift position in her chair. The last six days had been like a dream – a dream she was astute enough to know would come to an end but one she'd squeeze until it was over. She glanced at the Rolex he'd given her after their third date.

Every day followed the same routine. He'd pick her up at around eight, dinner and Champagne and sex – not always in that order though. She was just about recovered enough every morning not to let the effects of the night before show at work but it was getting more difficult.

It was on their third date, as she sipped from her second glass of Champagne and a few moments after he'd slipped the Rolex on her wrist.   .

"I want you to do something for me." He was holding her hand as they sat opposite each other at a Pimlico bistro.

"If it's within my power – anything."

"I'll pay, of course. I know you need money for your trip; I can help."

"What do you want me to do?" She drained the glass.

"Nothing very much really," he replied soothingly, as he poured a refill. "I need a little information from your office."

"Information? I don't think I know anything important." He placed a wad of notes on the table.

"There's five hundred pounds, put it in your bag. There'll be another five hundred when you give me something I need to know."

She stared at the notes for a fleeting second of indecision and then buried them in her bag.

It had been a whirlwind of a week, she thought, as she returned to her desk and one I might choose to forget in later life, but here and now, I need the money and I don't owe the people here anything.

"Next Tuesday," she whispered into the phone, "I'll bring the itinerary tonight."

The man moving along the busy pavements of Soho was indistinguishable from any other pedestrian. He wore an overcoat with its collar up and a baseball cap, its peak pulled down, a Gap emblem stitched at its front. He crossed into Wardour Street, making for Starbucks. The fumes and noise of the traffic were replaced by warmth, a smell of brewing coffee and gurgling of espresso machines as he slipped in and made for a vacant seat. The shadow of a tall man fell across the table almost immediately. Gap-cap didn't look up, he didn't need to – it was Kierack, the fixer he'd found having crossed into East Germany on a week long trip advising a less than savoury debt recovery business. Kierack was an enforcer of kinds, schooled in all the ways of the underworld – one of theirs but dissatisfied. He'd been assigned to look after all the needs of the man opposite who would shortly become his new boss – as it turned out. A week later, Kierack was in a *new* town – London.

"Sit down," Gap-cap told him. "Now – you said you had something to tell me."

"Yes, something went wrong yesterday," Kierack replied, his accent tinting the words with a hint of defensive menace.

"Why didn't you tell me yesterday?"

"I couldn't, I had to be fixed up."

Gap lifted his eyes just enough to see the bandaged head of his companion.

"What happened?"

"Someone came in just as I was hanging up to you; he saw me."

Kierack's boss gave an exasperated sigh. "And…?"

"I dealt with him."

"Judging by your head, he seems to have dealt with you. Do you know who he was?"

"I've no idea and I didn't stay to find out."

"And you say he won't be causing any trouble?" his employer asked sceptically.

"He took a fall, too far to be getting up."

"Okay, I don't need the details. Nevertheless, you'd better take extra care."

"Don't worry, I got away clean." Kierack assured his boss who was eyeing him questioningly.

"Alright then, the girl – she's going to Brussels Tuesday. There's a meeting set for Wednesday. She mustn't make it there. Here, take this."

Kierack took the offered thick brown envelope as it was passed under the table. "If you haven't dealt with her before Monday, I want you to go to Brussels. Get yourself a room near the university – you're a stationery salesman selling to the university if anyone asks. Only pay cash and wait for my call. I'll have more details tonight."

"What if she has company?"

"Bad luck for them. Have you got that? Is it clear?"

"Crystal."

One short knock and the door opened interrupting Newman's perusal of a file containing the details of a male body pulled from the Thames that morning. He looked up; it was Gorman.

"Yes?"

"De Grood – the Belgian bloke in front of the train."

"What about him?"

"We've got the forensics back on his stuff." The D.S. handed a two page report to Newman. "Page two makes interesting reading."

Newman's eyes widened in surprise as he scanned the page before his features changed to carry a look of scepticism.

"Are they sure about this? Are they positive there's been no cross-contamination?"

"My thoughts exactly sir but they're adamant."

"Okay," he drew the word out in a 'You'd better be right about this' way. "Looks like we'll be taking a little trip."

Since the few occasions Dr. Carter had covered lectures during the flu outbreak which had put several of the teaching staff on sick leave, Rick had noticed him taking lunch at the refectory. He'd seen him before, of course, sitting alone scanning the pages of one journal or another but had no idea who he was until he'd appeared as a replacement lecturer to take one of his classes. The lecture was a divergence from the one his group had been expecting, Rick recalled, but Carter had tried to make a useful contribution at short notice covering ways of distinguishing real news from contrived P.R. That was a month ago.

By the time Rick made it to the refectory, it was one fifteen; the place was bustling and noisy. He glanced around the room; there was no sign of Dr. Carter but he didn't think he'd missed him. He went to the counter, loaded a tray with a Coke and a bacon baguette, then searched for a table over the head of the cashier as he paid. He set his tray down on one that gave a clear view of the entrance, sat and took a bite from the baguette.

Dr. Melvyn Carter entered at around one thirty. He was clean shaven, smartly dressed and in his late fifties. His neatly styled hair, jet black at one time, had a feathering of grey shot through it. He cut an impressive figure.

Rick watched as Carter filled a tray and found a place to sit two tables away when done with the cashier. He didn't seem to be in any hurry; he had no newspaper or trade magazine – he appeared more interested in his surroundings, sipping his soup starter from a mug.

Striking up a conversation with this man and holding it when its true purpose was revealed would be difficult at the best of times. Rick would be economic with the truth. He had no way of knowing if this was a good time or a bad one so he made the decision to jump in with a version and leave the rest for Juliet to fill in. He had no props to play with; his baguette was gone and there were only a few dregs left in the Coke bottle. No, he was going dressed as himself. He got up and walked over to where Carter was sitting.

"Dr. Carter, may I join you."

Carter looked up, studying Rick for a moment. "Go ahead," he replied finally. "Do I know you, your face seems familiar."

"You stood in for Professor Hoskins for a few classes. I'm in his group."

"Oh, yes, the TV journos, I remember now. Not sure I gave you your money's worth though," he chuckled.

"On the contrary, I found your lectures gave a different perspective."

"I'm glad you think so. Now, tell me, is this a social call or do you have something on your mind?"

Carter's directness took Rick by surprise. He'd intended to skirt a few topics before segueing into the real purpose of their *chance* meeting.

"Oh, is it that obvious?"

Carter nodded and took another swig of his soup, raising his head expectantly.

"Well..er.., I have a friend over from the States, she'd like to meet you," Rick continued. "She's a writer." He was bending the truth but it was the only way.

Carter eyed him warily. "And how do you know her?"

"She's from my home town, Seattle."

Carter seemed to flicker some sort of reaction at the mention of Seattle but then put on a puzzled expression.

"Why on earth would a writer want to meet me?"

"She's working on a history of advertising and needs some background; I suggested you."

"Mmm.., you *must* have been impressed by my lectures." Rick nodded in agreement.

"So, what's her name – your friend?" Dr. Carter had already produced pen and small post-it pad from the inside pocket of his jacket and was poised, ready to write. It was something about the lecturer's tone that flicked on a warning light in Rick's head. He needed to lie if the meeting was ever to take place.

"Juliet…Baxter," Rick replied, watching Carter carefully take down Juliet's cell number, sure the first thing the good doctor would do the next time he was in front of a computer screen, would be to tap the name into Google. If he'd have given Laskey as a last name, who knows what kind of stories and diatribes from aggrieved captains of industry who'd had their feathers ruffled by her, would have flashed up. He hoped Juliet Baxter, if there was such a person, had the profile of a Sunday school teacher or the like. Anyways, his job was to get Carter to agree to the meeting; Juliet would have to come clean when she was one-to-one. Carter tore the top sheet from the notepad and scribbled on the next sheet. He tore it off and handed it to Rick.

"Here's my mobile. I don't make a habit of this but your

bit of flattery about my lectures got you a few points. Tell her to call me at seven this evening."

"Thank you. I'll leave you in peace now."

Carter waved him away with a friendly gesture.

"Gentlemen and lady," Detective Inspector Newman addressed his assembled team, three male Detective Sergeants and one woman – a newcomer to the group, Jill Hargreaves, also a D.S. "I think we missed a trick somewhere along the line. In fact, I don't think it, I know it." He turned to the wall of photographs hastily pinned to a cork board by D.S. Gorman since the receipt of the forensic report on the effects of Luke de Grood, or 'Mr. Friday-night' as he was referred to by Gorman, a Friday night being the night when de Grood had chosen to leap into the path of a Circle Line train as it came into High Street Kensington station.

The photos all covered the death of Professor Milo Ferretti – images of his body lolling in his bath, his wrecked flat, even a shot of Max, his cat.

"Come on, you were all there, what did you see?" Newman's gaze fixed on Burrows, still in the doghouse for his tardiness in contacting the Belgian force, his excuse of illness not accepted.

"Well nothing out of the ordinary in the flat, the usual middle class crapjets d'art but spread over the floor. Conclusion – the guy beat up the place then topped himself."

"Well, assuming we believe our colleagues at forensics, we can probably discount *that* theory," Newman said, pointedly discarding Burrows' views and ignoring the bored, 'Where's all this leading' expressions on the faces of his team. "Mr. de Grood," he continued, "was considerate enough to leave his rucksack on the platform before he jumped. He was wearing a sweater and jeans when he was hit by the train. The attending officers had a messy time fishing his passport and wallet out of his back pockets."

"Sir, what's all this got to do with Milo Ferretti?" Burrows asked.

"If you let me finish, you'll find out," Newman replied, nodding in Gorman's direction and gesturing to the documents the detective was clutching. Each of the group was handed a copy of the forensic report.

"You'll see from the report that de Grood had a change of clothes in his bag – a jacket and trousers. You'll also see there was a considerable amount of blood on the items, the Professor's blood."

The air of indifference had lifted by now and was replaced by sudden interest as they skipped to the second page.

"I can see I've caught your attention but now comes the question, how did Milo Ferretti's blood come to be on Luc de Grood's clothing? Knowing what we now know about Mr. de Grood, albeit ten days late," Newman gave an askance squint at Burrows, "I think we know the answer to that one but it raises several others – *why*, being the principal one. Then there's the vandalism at the flat. Did de Grood do it? I don't think so now and I think I'm going to have to eat some humble pie on this. Sophia Ferretti's friend, Devan, has been on at me about the time of the Professor's death and the time on the Grandfather clock. He's been adamant that there was no suicide and the vandalism in the flat was not down to the Professor. If we were now to believe the time on the clock – twenty past twelve midnight in the early hours of Saturday, then we have to assume someone else was in the flat after the Professor's death. We discarded the idea in the first place on the say-so of that expert of yours…" He was looking at Gorman.

"Getz, Heini Getz," the D.S. filled the blank.

"Yes, well, Mr. Getz said we couldn't rely on the date. A fall to the floor like that could click the mechanism to the next day or even later, he'd said according to your notes." Newman's gaze rested on Gorman. "However, your notes also suggest Getz later said there was a fifty percent chance that the day and date might be accurate and the mechanism could have withstood the shock as the clock hit the floor." Newman's features clouded with the unasked question, 'Care to explain why only Getz's first opinion was considered?'

"Everything pointed to suicide, Boss. In the circumstances, his first answer seemed the most relevant, so I went with it."

"Very well then, it *might* have been suicide but it's looking more like murder to me."

"So, if we're taking the clock as Gospel, who tossed the flat?" It was Jill Hargreaves who spoke this time. "It couldn't have been de Grood because he was also already dead; there must have been someone else."

"Yes," Newman agreed, "and why all this sudden interest in the Professor?"

"Well, there's all the stuff the niece was on about, his work, whatever that was, and her trip to Brussels seems to figure somewhere," Gorman offered.

Newman chose that moment to announce he would be travelling to Brussels. "and what's more, you're coming with me," he told Gorman. "Get on to that Inspector…"

"Grenard."

"Yes, him, tell him we're coming on Monday and fill him in."

"Hinkley, I want you to keep an eye on the niece. I want to know what she's up to for the next twenty-four hours. Keep your distance, I don't want her to know you're there – take Burrows with you. Somebody is obviously interested in her, I'd like to know who."

Still without instructions, D.S. Hargreaves, was looking expectantly at Newman in that 'what about me' way but Newman answered her question before she could ask it.

"We've got three days before the trip to Brussels, I want you and Gorman to find this Weller character. He's up to his neck in something; let's find out what it is. Okay then – get going."

The detectives dispersed as Newman left the room.

11

Sitting with a cup of tea in the Selfridges mezzanine cafeteria, Sophia had a commanding view of the ground floor near the store's entrance. Her table was against the balcony rail and from her vantage point, she watched Gerald Hope enter the store and climb the stairs, a figure in dark pinstripe cutting through a multi-coloured swirling sea of fashion like a shark's fin. Not that she thought of him as a shark but the analogy amused her just the same. She waved to him as he stood at the top of the stairs scanning the diners.

"Sorry I'm late. I left as soon as I got your text. It took a while to get a taxi."

"Never mind, would you like a cup of tea?"

"No, I'm fine thanks," he replied, and sat down opposite her glancing around. "What made you want to meet here?"

"There are plenty of people around. I like to have people around these days."

Hope looked at her quizzically.

"Things have happened," she continued, "the type of things I was worried about when I saw you last – you told me not to worry – well, it turns out, I needed to."

Hope's face displayed a look of bemusement and then dismay as she told her story.

"When you left the office, you didn't tell anyone where you were going or who you were going to meet did you?" she asked.

Hope shook his head.

"Good. I'd prefer it to stay that way. Weller knew everything about me. How he did, I have no idea but if I'm going on with this, the less people who know what I'm up to, the better."

"I understand. I'll make the arrangements for Brussels personally, you'll be quite safe."

"I'm beginning to think I'll never be safe again. I'm half-scared out of my wits.I'm very tempted to take the money from this Weller or whoever he is, and disappear. It seems a hell of a lot safer than traipsing around Brussels knowing full well that there are people out there doing their best to stop me by whatever means."

"We don't know that for sure."

"Try telling that to Jake."

"Look," Hope leant towards her conspiratorially, speaking in a low voice to mask his words from the people at the next table, "Milo didn't come this far to give up; he believed in what he was doing. If you chuck in the towel now, the years he put in will be for nothing and, more importantly, his legacy will be buried by the very people he was out to bring to heel."

She looked at him for a moment, sighed in resignation.

"Yes, there is that but you have to understand, I'm frightened. I'll go along for now but if I feel the slightest bit uneasy in Brussels, I'll be on the first train back." She waited for her words to sink in then said, "Alright, tell me what to expect."

"The meetings are arranged. I spoke to Frans this morning. He fixed two meetings for you, both on Wednesday. The first one is at 8a.m. so I think you ought to go the day before. It's too risky relying on the train to get you there on time on the day – it might be delayed. I'm sure you know how Murphy's Law works."

"Are you coming? Your secretary said you might not."

"That's right, I'm afraid I have to be somewhere else that day."

She looked at him, anxiety showing in her face.

"And you think I can carry this off without you."

"You won't need me this time, Frans will look after you."

"If it's all the same to you, I'd rather not be there alone."

"I rather thought you would take Mr. Devan with you."

"If that's okay, you're paying after all."

Gerald smiled. "Oh, don't worry, it's all going down on the expense sheet. It'll come back later."

Sophia pulled a note pad from her bag, rummaged for a pen. Her misgivings were beginning to surface again. He's not coming, she thought, and I'm supposed to just waltz in and take uncle Milo's place. Sure enough, with Rick along for the ride she wouldn't be alone but what if there were trouble, the kind that saw Giles Edwards dead, oh yeah, that was no mugging, no coincidence, – or the kind of trouble which took Jake on a dive into the roof of a 2009 Ford Focus Zetec. Can Rick protect us both? She didn't let an answer have time to form or prepare a Hitchcock movie cameo.

"You'd better tell me about the meetings. Who are the meetings with and what should I be saying."

"The meetings are really only to introduce you to the main

players. You'll be seeing Frans before, of course, he'll collect you from the train and take you to your hotel. It'll be a chance for you to get to know him beforehand, he's a big shot, so be nice. Don't mention what's been going on in London though, he's more nervous than you are about this project and takes his security to extremes. It's been his concern from the start that big business will pay any price to prevent Milo's Scale getting into law. By 'price', he means monetary but wouldn't rule out other options. However, it might not help the day along if there's a suspicion your friend's fall was anything other than an accident; best not say anything about it." He gave a brief smile. "As I said, he takes his security very seriously which is how I know you'll be in safe hands."

Sophia rolled her eyes as much as to say, 'What the hell am I into here?' but then gestured for him to continue.

"Anyway, when you go to his office the next morning you'll meet his colleague, Jose Gabera; he's also a commissioner – together, they have been the driving force behind the project. They'll give you a catch-up session, everything Milo had discussed and who is promoting the formula and who's against it in the regulatory body etc..."

"Against?" Sophia cut in, "I was under the impression it was a done deal; I had no idea there would be resistance."

"Big business has friends too you know – not enough, as it happens but powerful, just the same. They shouldn't be underestimated."

Hope suddenly realised he should have been more careful with his words; Sophia's features were colouring with concern once more. "They'll lobby hard, that's all," he added, hoping to put her fears to rest.

There was a pause while Sophia regained her resolve.

"And the second?"

"The second is the main meeting of the day," Gerald began – relieved she hadn't been thrown off by his unguarded remarks. "You'll meet the main group of commissioners. They, along with Frans and Jose have prepared the submission to the Council of Ministers; they're the body of decision makers."

"I hope you realise I'm just a graphic designer not some great orator. The largest group of people I've addressed was at Michelle Grant's hen party and I'd needed a lot alcohol to do it."

"You won't have to make any speeches. They just want reassurance you're not going to duck out or do a deal with the opposition – the Wellers of this world."

"That's all?"

"I think that'll be all for the first time you meet them all. There is a chance they will ask you what you want from the deal."

"And what do I want?"

"Milo and I worked out an exact formula for this as well as a lump sum to be handed over on ratification. You'll need to come to the office to go over it before you leave."

"I'll come in on Monday."

"I'll go through the file with you but..," he hesitated for a moment, "but I'd like you to steer them off the subject; I think it would be better if I'm there when they start talking money."

"Maybe I should delay these meetings until you can come too."

"No, things have been held up too long already; these

people want reassurance now – I'll be with you when I'm needed."

"Okay, I'll do it but you'd better be with me next time because I assure you, my solo performance is a one day only gig."

"Understood, I'll call you later with a time for Monday."

"Tell no-one, please," she cautioned.

Hope nodded as he stood up.

"One more thing – Milo told me he had a flat in Brussels, you might want to check that while you're there."

"It's news to me but not a surprise. I'm learning Uncle Milo had a lot of secrets. Do you know where it is?"

"Not exactly, only that it's off the Place Jourdan. There must be some paperwork at his home somewhere."

"I'll look."

"Monday then," he said, and walked towards the stairs.

She watched him descend and quickly vanish into the mêlée below. It doesn't seem much of a big deal to him, she mused, but then again, his name isn't mentioned in Uncle Milo's will and nobody had threatened him in the way she had been – well, she hadn't actually been threatened but *something* was going on.

It had been a week since Walter had taken a razor to his beard, a drastic but necessary measure if he was to avoid recognition. He felt strangely naked without it and his face still detected resistance from the air with every movement – feeling it again as he changed position when Gerald Hope came down the stairs from the mezzanine. Hope was of no interest to him; Sophia Ferretti was Walter Nestrom's focus for today.

Walter felt a tingle of excitement he hadn't felt since the early days of his business when hacking the text messages of his competitors was his way of keeping ahead of the game. People were so naïve back then with no concept of security but thank god for it; the attitude had served him well but now, here he was… back on the shop floor, so to speak, ducking and diving. Despite all the new security gizmos introduced in the intervening years, he'd been surprised at the ease with which he'd tapped into Sophia Ferretti's phone and then those of her immediate circle.

Walter knew all he needed to know. Text messages had told of this meeting with her patent lawyer to discuss their next move – the audacity of it, he thought. This relative of Milo had the intention to profit from work which did not belong to her or Milo for that matter. The whole idea had sprung from work *he*, Walter, had handed to Milo as part of his thesis. Right now, she has a chance to accept what I'm offering or take the consequences. Milo hadn't seen sense and look what happened to him, Walter reflected. Much as he wished to take the credit for Milo's demise and the satisfaction it might have brought him, he could not; someone had 'gotten there before him'. There were obviously others who, maybe made aware by Giles Edwards of what the Professor was up to, had a more serious bone to pick with Milo – but this was no concern of Walter's. Walter had been cheated out of a final confrontation by the discovery of a very dead Milo staring from the last bath *he'd* ever take. In his fury, Walter had wantonly smashed up the place in an attempt to purge the earth of any remaining vestige of Professor Ferretti's plagiarism and banish the man from his thoughts. It hadn't worked though. Nothing would work until Walter had what was rightfully his.

Sophia Ferretti appeared at the top of the stairs. Walter half turned away, pulling the peak of his cap down to obscure his features. She would not have noticed him had he stood in the middle of the stairway; she was busy dialling as she descended, staring at her phone and oblivious to her surroundings. Walter wondered briefly who she might be calling but put the thought out of his mind; he had more pressing business and now was the time to act. As Walter fell in behind Sophia on her way to the Duke Street exit, he failed to notice the two men approaching him from his right.

That Morning, Hinkley and Burrows had kept their distance behind the 'Ferretti Girl', as Burrows referred to her, on her progress up Oxford Street from the Bond Street tube. The pavements were busy and keeping her in sight had not been easy. Ferretti had complicated matters by unexpectedly darting into several of the shops lining her route – each time emerging a few minutes later to continue browsing the windows.

Remaining undetected in these circumstances was proving a challenge but the detectives had devised a system which involved them splitting up when Ferretti entered a shop. One of them would hang back on the pavement while the other, followed the girl at a safe distance. They alternated roles to limit the chance of being spotted.

It was while Burrows hung around outside a shoe shop, just before Selfridges, that he noticed a smartly dressed man in his forties not far behind Ferretti as she went in. He seemed to be following her. Burrows picked up on him only because of the way he was dressed, expensive suit but topped off with a baseball cap. The picture was off somehow but it wasn't only the cap. Thinking on it, Burrows realised he'd seen the same guy popping up for the last thirty minutes – that wasn't right either. He took a few paces forward to keep the newcomer in sight just as Sophia Ferretti, followed a little way back by George Hinkley, emerged after the briefest scan of the shelves. Hinkley shot Burrows a questioning glance but grasped the situation as Burrows's gave a nod towards the man in the baseball cap.

Sophia Ferretti was held momentarily by the pedestrian light at the corner before crossing Duke Street and stepping into Selfridges through the side entrance. Her tail in the baseball cap followed a few paces behind. In turn, Hinkley and Burrows kept the same distance at *his* back. Inside the store, the detectives watched Ferretti climb the stairs to the mezzanine café. They hung back as the man, who it was now clear had a particular interest in Sophia, took up a position at the base of the stairs. He was feigning interest in the suitcase aisle.

From their position, the detectives could now see both Sophia, who, after a few minutes, had taken a table which overlooked the ground floor and her tail. He was still perusing but casting the occasional glance upward.

"What do you think, George?" Burrows asked, "Shall we pull him now?"

"Let's wait a minute; we need to be sure," Hinkley replied, nodding towards the focus of their interest as he continued, "He can't get up to anything for the moment."

Five minutes passed. The Ferretti Girl was cradling a cup of tea or coffee, they were not able to see which; her watcher remained near the base of the stairs.

"Hello, who's this?" Burrows remarked, as a tall man dressed in a pinstripe business suit, joined Ferretti at her table.

"I don't know but she seems to know him."

"This is getting more interesting by the minute."

Ferretti's visitor talked with her for about ten minutes and then left. Burrows and Hinkley watched him descend the staircase and make his way to an exit which led onto Oxford Street.

"Not a date, then," Hinkley remarked.

Burrows smiled in response. "Eh-up, we're on," he said, as Sophia rose from her table. Both detectives studied Ferretti's stalker as he changed position and gave his quarry sideways glances as she came down the steps.

George Hinkley turned to D.S. Burrows and said, "I think we'd better end this. He looks like he's getting ready for something."

"I agree."

Sophia was at the bottom of the stairs now and turning to the door where she had entered forty-five minutes earlier. She slipped her phone into her bag and picked up her pace. Her stalker in the baseball cap set off after her. She was at the door – he, immediately behind her, arm outstretched towards her neck. D.S. Burrows knocked him sideways just as Sophia, unaware of the drama behind her, pushed through the door and disappeared into the pavement throng.

12

Thursdays were always confusing for Rick; there was one lecture in the morning and the rest of the day was for library stuff and finding reference for whatever task had been set for delivery the following Tuesday, in other words, a half-day. It would have worked out better if this arrangement had occurred on Fridays and let the weekend start earlier. Nevertheless, he'd accepted the college's quirks and got himself into the habit of taking a light lunch at the refectory before returning to his flat by two. An hour spent topping up his research on-line and the rest of the day was his. Today, his regular routine was forced to accommodate, the meeting with Newman, causing him to miss his lecture and then, his lunchtime parley with Dr. Carter. Nevertheless, he was on track now, in sweats and jogging.

  During his recovery back home in Seattle, his appointed physiotherapist, a cute brunette called Joy who'd heard every pun there was to know on her name, so he needn't bother, had warned him against a sedentary lifestyle and had given strict instructions to keep his body moving. "I haven't spent eighteen months of my life getting your motor running again just so you can lie around and freeze it all up a second time." He'd taken this on board, diligently following a fifteen minute routine of daily exercise and, once a week, as part of the overall scheme, took a two mile run – five if he could manage it. This he squeezed in on Thursday afternoons.

Today was one of those when he was doing a two miler; too much was going on, added to which, Juliet had appeared asking favours. She'd taken it all in without a missed beat when he'd told her she was now Juliet Baxter.

"No problem," she'd said, as he'd relayed Carter's number and instructions to call, "and hey.. Rick – I owe you one." One what he wasn't sure but he'd bank it anyway for a rainy day.

He was on the home stretch, lost in the Heavy Metal pounding his ear drums from the player attached to his waist, when he all but collided with two men carrying a grandfather clock horizontally to a removal van as he rounded the corner into his street. The two men glared at him as he came to a skidding halt between the two of them and within a millimetre of the delicate antique they carried. He mumbled an apology and went around them but not before a momentary glance at the clock. It reminded him of Milo's clock and the forlorn way it had graced the floor on its side the day he found Milo dead, its pendulum hanging out of the inspection door like guts spilling from a carcass.

He got to thinking again about the time and date displayed on its face. It was something which had troubled him since it became obvious the Police were treating Milo's death as suicide. Unless someone had deliberately moved its spidery hands to confuse investigators, it showed the precise time and date the clock was upended. No, he didn't think it was a concern of whoever trashed the flat – that guy wasn't worried about confusing anyone. He was looking for something and in a hurry.

Of course, as far as the Police were concerned, there was no other person in the flat only Milo and it was he who broke the place up. Rick's assertion it could not have been Milo because, by comparing the estimated time of Milo's death told to Rick by D.I. Newman, with the time and date shown on the clock face, he was already dead when the clock stopped, had cut no ice with Newman. Newman had reiterated all the circumstances pointed to suicide and the date on the clock probably clicked over to the next day when it crashed to the floor. However, now there had been an incident at Sophia's and maybe, just maybe, the Police would take his theory more seriously. From what Rick had heard about Jake, he wasn't the sentimental type and definitely not the type to throw himself off a balcony for a woman. That fact alone should give credence to his view of events.

Still in his sweats and at his laptop, he loaded the pictures he'd taken of the scene before the Police arrived that Saturday. In the lounge-diner he'd taken two shots standing on a chair to capture an elevated view, each from opposite corners of the room. He'd have liked to have taken more but the knowledge the Police could arrive at any moment had forced him into cursory coverage only. Even so, the shots he took had done the job.

The picture of wreckage filled the screen. He zoomed into the clock face and the separate dials for day, date, month; Saturday, 21, March. Zooming out, he tracked to the right, across the empty bookcase and then the open drinks cabinet to the window. Vodka, something tickled the back of his memory. He filled the screen with the cabinet. There was one space where he knew the vodka bottle had once stood

– the memory was there, suddenly. It had eluded him these past weeks but the recollection of his observations, coincidentally playing back in the same order as when he'd browsed the bookcase on that first occasion in Milo's flat for tea, had dislodged the images from their hiding place. He'd been scanning Milo's books and was examining a 1948 paperback on the theory of probabilities; the text was beyond him, applying theory to queuing in telephone systems. Milo was boiling the kettle and rummaging in cupboards. He put the book back in the case and continued to take in his surroundings. Curiosity had made him open the drinks cabinet alongside the bookcase. Three bottles of red wine lay in a rack and a solitary unopened bottle of vodka stood next to a silver ice bucket at the back. He heard Milo set a tray down on the table behind him.

"I could offer you something stronger than tea if you'd like."

"No, thanks, tea's fine, thanks." Rick shut the cabinet. "Sorry for being nosey. Anyway, I don't think I could manage vodka at this time of day."

"Me neither, at any time of day for that matter. I drank too much of it on my twenty-first birthday; it seemed a good idea at the time but when it's your twenty-first, everything looks good after a few drinks. It took me a week to recover and now, even the thought of those few days it makes me retch." He was chuckling.

"I keep the bottle just to remind me never to get any more good ideas where vodka is concerned."

A smile played on Rick's lips as he recalled the mischievous glint in Milo's eyes. Vodka, it had been the element he knew was wrong about Milo's death and until now, the detail of the memory had been masked by a tangle of other seemingly unimportant fragments of information.

His mobile rang. Max looked up excitedly, woken from a curled doze at his feet.

"I'll be there in about thirty minutes," Sophia's voice was raised above the din of a passing truck. "Sorry I'm early. You are *at* home I take it?"

"Yes, and it's not a problem. Buy some milk when you pass the shop otherwise it'll be cheese going in your tea."

Rick's train of thought had been broken by Sophia's call. He scribbled a note to himself lest the jumbled ideas bumping around in his head were lost forever like those must-do things he often thought of on the verge of sleep and never remembered the following morning – a few key-words to put him right back there where sub-conscious notions wait for their moment to find form.

He showered, pulled on chinos and a sweater, barely having time to tie the laces on his shoes before his doorbell gave a short ring. Sophia entered using the key he'd given her. She was still staying at his; tonight would be the third night. He was in no hurry for her to leave and she didn't bring the subject up. He presumed she'd go back to her flat when she felt comfortable enough and that wasn't yet.

She kissed his cheek. "Honey I'm home," she said, grinning and handing a plastic carrier to him containing the milk. She put two paper carriers of her own on the floor and flopped into the sofa.

"Tuesday – is that okay for you?" She was looking up at him.

"Tuesday?"

"Brussels, I saw Gerald today – he's fixed meetings for Wednesday. The first is early, so we'd better go the night before. How do you fancy dinner in Brussels? Can you work that into your busy schedule?" she asked, a hint of sarcasm creeping into her voice as she remembered her own time as a student. Taking a couple of days off back then had never been difficult; someone was always willing to take notes for her in any lectures she might miss.

"Yes, I might be able to accommodate you."

"Very funny, now what kind of a hotel is this – where's the cup of tea I was promised? I…."

The muffled ring of her phone from within her handbag, cut across her words.

After rummaging and a glance at the caller I.D., she answered.

"Detective Inspector Newman …….., yes, it's me." Sophia looked across to Rick and mouthed the word 'Newman' simultaneously pointing at the phone.

Rick responded with an inquisitive frown as she continued.

"I see. No, that's okay – I'll be ready. I'm not at my flat though – I'm at Rick Devan's place………Half an hour then." She hung up and looked into Rick's eyes. "They've arrested someone. They think it might be Weller and they want me to identify him; a car's on it's way to pick me up. Will you come with me?"

"Of course."

*****

"I'm saying nothing until you let me call my lawyer."

"Do you need a lawyer?" D.I. Newman asked. He was

sitting at a table opposite Walter in a bare interview room. There were no windows to the street only a mirrored panel which overlooked them. "The reason you're here and not going about your business is because you chose not to explain yourself to my officers when they picked you up. At the moment, this is an informal chat but if you want to make it official….we can do that. We can take a D.N.A. sample and process you, get you into the system – it's up to you." Newman paused then said, "Now, what's it to be?" Walter lifted his chin, a grimace of acceptance on his face. He nodded.

"Good," Newman responded. "Now Mr. Nestrom, would you care to tell me why you were following Miss Ferretti." For a moment he was surprised to hear Newman call him by name until he remembered he'd emptied the contents of his pockets before they locked him in a cell. His credit cards and business cards would have given the Police all they wanted to know about him.

"I was *not* following her…….well, yes I was but not for any other reason than I wanted to talk her."

"From what I hear, you were about to attack her."

"That is a gross misrepresentation of my actions."

"Care to tell me what it was you *were* doing."

Walter hesitated. "I was trying to attract her attention. If your men had waited a second longer, they might have seen that I was about to tap her on her shoulder."

Newman looked sceptical. "Look, Walter, you don't mind if I call you Walter, do you?"

"Whatever," Walter gave a nod of as he spoke with a hint of an accent sliding over the word that betrayed his German origins. It always happened when he was agitated.

"Walter…we can dance around here all night. Just tell me what you want with Sophia Ferretti?"

"Her uncle," Walter finally replied, as Newman was about to lose his patience,"he was my tutor and he stole something from me. Now that he's dead, I believe Miss Ferretti is in control of it. It is my intention to make her an offer….a generous offer."

"Professor Ferretti hadn't given a lecture for at least five years and from my brief research on you, you've been running a business for the last ten years at the very least." Walter leaned forward a little, placing his elbows on the table and tenting his fingers. "It was a long time ago….twenty years or more – he took my idea from the thesis I handed him as part of my degree and patented it for himself."

"And you waited until now to come forward."

"Not at all. I have been expanding the idea over the years and was ready to file. As soon as I heard what Milo Ferretti was doing, I began proceedings to contest his application."

"How did that work for you?"

"I lost…..but I will pursue the matter through the courts if I fail to reach agreement with Miss Ferretti."

Newman considered Walter's responses then said, "Have you put your suggestions to her yet……say at the Coffee Shop at the Grosvenor House Hotel?"

"No. I have met her only once….at the funeral of her uncle. I didn't think that was the time to be talking business."

"Does the name Sam Weller mean anything to you?" Walter looked bemused, "No, should it?"

"It's not an alias you use from time to time?"

"Certainly not." Walter pushed his chair back and stood up. "Now, Inspector, I've answered all I'm going to. If you want to know anything else, arrange it with my lawyer. Unless you have a very good reason for holding me, I'm leaving. I'll expect an apology."

Newman studied Nestrom. His story seemed to have a ring of truth. "It's Detective Inspector, actually."

Walter tilted his head in a 'so what' way.

"Please... sit down for a little longer," Newman continued, rising from his chair as he spoke. At the door he turned back to Nestrom, "I'll be back in a moment. Would you like me to bring you a drink – coffee, tea?"

Walter sat back down with an air of resignation. "Tea – white with one sugar, please."

Gorman was in the corridor outside.

"The Ferretti woman just got here – she's with Devan. They're behind the glass."

"Okay, I'll be with them for a minute. In the meantime, take our friend a cup of tea will you – white with one."

Gorman nodded and Newman took the door to his left which led to the observation cabin. Its mirrored window gave a clear view of the interview room. Rick and Sophia were studying Walter through the glass.

"Do you know that man, Miss Ferretti?" Newman asked when the pleasantries were out of the way.

"No."

"He says he knows you. He says he met you at your uncle's funeral."

"No, I don't think so. There's something about him though. Who is he?"

"Walter Nestrom."

"Walter Nestrom! Well, yes, I did meet a Walter Nestrom at the funeral but he had a beard – a big bushy one. My patent lawyer told me about him and the trouble he was trying to cause. His objection to Uncle Milo's patent failed. Why is he here?"

"My officers picked him up; he was following you. He was behind you in Selfridges and lunging for you as you were leaving."

"My God – I had no idea. Just a minute, have *you* had me followed?"

"We've been keeping an eye out for you, that's all. Anyway, Hinkley and Burrows grabbed him before he touched you. By the time they'd secured him, you were through the door and gone into the crowd."

"Why on earth is he after me?"

"He says he was about to tap you on your shoulder to talk to you. He was going to make a deal with you for whatever it is your uncle was working on."

"Do you think he's the one who attacked Jake?"

"No, and judging from what you've said so far, I take it that this is not the man you met at the Grosvenor Coffee Shop."

"No, that's not Sam Weller. What will you do with Nestrom?"

"There's nothing we can do really. We'll warn him off and tell him if he comes within a hundred feet of you, he'll be arrested."

Sophia watched Walter accept a cup of tea from D.S. Gorman. "Tell him anything he has to say has to come through my lawyer."

Newman nodded and left the room.

"So, whoever Sam Weller is, he's still out there," Rick said, "but I reckon he's something to do with that guy in there."

They watched as Newman entered the interview room and spoke to Walter. Sophia winced as from a slap to her cheek as Walter stood up and turned to face the mirrored window with a look of utter contempt.

"He can't see us, can he?"

"No," Rick reassured, "he can't see us. I don't even think he knows we're here."

"He seems to know something. Maybe he's wrapped up in the thing at my flat with Jake and maybe he's not. Right now, I don't care – I've had enough for today. Let's go home."

Later that night, they sat opposite each other at a busy bistro in a cobbled mews off the Brompton Road. A scene from London's 'Swinging Sixties' era – soft light flickering from a candle set into a mountain of dribbled wax atop a Chianti bottle at the centre of the table, warming their features. It was a date of sorts Rick hoped. It certainly felt like a date. She was opening up to him and he was sure there was some connection between them. Several times he'd caught her studying him, their eyes locking briefly before one or other of them had broken the moment and turned away only to re-engage a few minutes later. He'd heard the whole Jake story – 'he had his eyes open – is doing better now, by the way' – and about her childhood, the death of her father and the impact it had on her and how it helped her cope when her mother died ten years later.

"You must think I'm jinxed – my parents, now Uncle Milo. I suppose if I obsessed over it, I might develop some kind of notifiable condition."

"Whatever condition you're in, I like it – I like it a lot." She smiled, touched his hand across the table and said,

"Flattery gratefully accepted."

Rick waited until the main course was over before he began voicing his theories about the circumstances of Milo's death. He figured that mischief and murder would be better discussed after a couple of glasses of wine, a tactic he'd learned from his father who'd always discussed difficult subjects either in the afternoon when senses had been lulled by the progress of the day or later, after alcohol had achieved the same effect. 'If you're going to get struck by the riposte,' he had advised, 'better the blade has been blunted first.'

Not that Rick was particularly concerned Sophia would run him through, more how dissecting the minutiae of Milo's death would affect her. However, when he moved on to the subject, she was more than willing to hear his thoughts.

"So, knowing of Milo's violent aversion to vodka, there was no way he drank it willingly, it must have been forced down his throat. It would explain the bruising around his mouth and on his neck if he'd been held in a grip."

"I don't understand why the Police didn't pick up on all this," Sophia observed, "when you take it all in, there should be no doubt – someone killed Uncle Milo."

"I think they made their minds up from the beginning and, not wishing to take their side, it did look like suicide at a glance."

"Mmm – you're more generous to them than I would be.

There were inconsistencies, the clock for instance – it stopped eight hours after the Police say he died. For him to have wrecked his flat he would need to have risen from the dead. Anyway, he loved his books far too much to throw them around the floor."

"The Police didn't believe the date on the clock from the start. They didn't tell me why they didn't, only that they had good reason not to."

"I'd say that since Jake got pushed off my balcony, they need to take another look. Someone pulled the place apart and if it wasn't Uncle Milo, who was it? I'd take bets it was the same guy who broke into my place."

"If Milo was murdered on Friday as the time of death indicates and the clock was tipped over in the early hours of Saturday, either the killer came back or it was someone else."

Sophia looked into his eyes and took his hand. "I think I've had enough murder talk for one night; let's go home."

In the cab home, she pushed up close so that he could feel the warmth of her body against him. Her cheek brushed his as the taxi took a curve and suddenly she was facing him, pressing her lips against his.

Max was waiting at the door as they reached it; he padded to the kitchen un-noticed by them in their haste. By the time he'd snacked, lapped at the water dish and made his way back, he found the bedroom barred to him. He cocked his ear at the sound of muffled cries from within.

The afternoon had given Walter a great deal to think on. He brooded in his hotel room, whiskey miniature in hand from the mini-bar. His arrest and informal chat with the

Police had been a total surprise; it just hadn't occurred to him to be on the lookout for a Police tail. The experience had shaken him up though. He poured the contents of the miniature into a glass and took a sip. Had his brush with the Police changed anything? No, not really. He was still mad at Milo, even more so with Milo's niece for going ahead with the Scale. No, nothing had changed. He would still pursue the matter but maybe a re-think was in order. It was another half hour of reflection before Walter picked up his phone and dialled.

13

The evening played out a little differently for Juliet. At seven thirty, she stepped into the lobby of the Dorchester hotel just one hundred and fifty yards along Park Lane from her own hotel. When she'd dialled Melvyn Carter's number at the allotted time, her call was picked up on the second ring.

"Dr. Carter speaking." The voice was confident and not what she'd expected at all. Her idea of him had been somewhat different; morose maybe – embittered over the passage of time by what ever incident had caused the dissolution of his business. She hadn't anticipated the upbeat individual on the end of the line. His voice told everything; she'd been wrong and little butterflies of foreboding telegraphed a message that this interview would be no walk in the park.

Juliet hadn't power dressed – light-coloured casual jacket, a dark skirt just tight enough to show her curves and a smart pair of high heeled shoes in black patent leather. And so, as instructed, she was here, half an hour later, crossing the lobby to the lounge and turning heads as she did so – some things don't change and long may they remain so.

Another surprise had been the choice of meeting place. She had expected to be summoned to the college at his convenience, not a five star hotel. Carter had suggested the Dorchester, explaining he had a dinner engagement there scheduled for eight forty-five.

"I can give you an hour if you're there at seven thirty," he'd said.

The lounge, of sofas and low tables mingled with potted palms dividing the seating into intimate nooks, was set out in an opulent high ceilinged walkway between the bar and restaurants. Couples meeting before dinner sipped cocktails. A few men in suits huddled across tables to wrap up business for the day. An unseen piano tinkled nondescript melodies and, looking around, she wondered how Carter managed such high tastes on a lecturer's salary.

"Juliet, Juliet Baxter?"

She turned around with a start to face a smartly dressed man in his late fifties. He was smiling.

"Sorry, I didn't mean to startle you. I'm Melvyn Carter."

"Not at all," she said, regaining her composure.

"Juliet…Juliet Baxter." She shook his hand.

He gestured to an enclave and they sat on opposite sofas, coffee table between them. A waitress appeared from nowhere and lingered at Carter's elbow. He ordered a gin and tonic.

"Can I get you anything?"

"Water please, sparkling with a slice."

The waitress scribbled the order and left as silently as she had arrived.

"This your first trip to London, Miss Baxter?"

"Please, call me Juliet. Yes, it's my first time."

"And is it everything you hoped it would be?"

"Pretty much but I've been working, so I probably haven't

seen all I should have."

"A pity, anyway, how is it you think I can help you?"

This was the tricky part. For the information she hoped to extract from Carter to have any credence at all, she would have to reveal her true identity to him. The next few minutes would either be the opening of a door that had been locked for ten years or the shortest interview of her career so far. The waitress arrived with the drinks just as Juliet prepared to speak. She watched while Carter signed the tab.

"Here's to you, Juliet......Baxter," he said, cheerily raising his glass.

"To you too." Juliet sipped at her sparkling water, lemon slice bobbing.

"You were about to say?" Carter was studying her with an intensity which unnerved her – as if waiting for only one answer. If it was the wrong one, she'd be on her way faster than travelling light.

"I have a confession to make, Dr. Carter; my name is not Baxter."

She studied his face for reaction but there was none. He remained silent, sipping his gin as if in thought.

"I know," he said, after a pause that seemed to drag on interminably. "You are Juliet Laskey from *The Seattle Times*. I'm afraid your friend, Mr. Devan is not that good at subterfuge."

Juliet was astonished how her cover could be blown so soon. "How did you know?"

"Oh, it wasn't that difficult; there were a few clues – the first being your colleague who spoke to my assistant. He didn't hide the fact he was from *The Seattle Times*. I wondered what the next approach would be if indeed there was to be one or if a substitute with the same background had been found but then Mr. Devan came along. When he approached me at lunch and said you were from his home town of Seattle, it wasn't a great leap to assume you were also from the *Times*."

"But you agreed to see me nevertheless."

"Yes, I can see why you might find that confusing but I was curious why it was me specifically you had to talk to… and even more so when I looked at the *Times'* website. I assumed, rightly as it turned out, that Miss Baxter was, in fact, Juliet Laskey. Given your stories are centred on business; I was intrigued to know how I could be of interest. Furthermore, there are very few circumstances which would cause me to pass up the opportunity to have a drink with a beautiful woman. I hope you don't mind me saying that."

She smiled, more out of relief than anything else that she hadn't been sent packing. "Why on earth would I mind?"

"Oh, you know, some professionals these days get a bit precious preferring to be regarded for their *brilliant* minds and not their good looks or some politically correct claptrap like that."

"No, you'll get no complaint here."

"Glad to hear it." Carter sipped his drink then set it down on the table between them and sank back into the sofa smiling the ad man's smile, arms outstretched along its back. "Well, we've done the intros and the dodging about, why don't you tell me how you think I can help you?"

How long is he going to keep that smile once I start talking, Juliet mused. She collected her thoughts and prepared the arrow.

"Sheldon Blane."

Carter's smile flickered momentarily at the edges then regained its composure. There was a pause. He lifted his eyes to an imagined spot in the cavernous ceiling space then brought them down to meet hers.

"Now there's a name I hoped I would never hear again."

"I take it you don't like him."

"To say I worship the ground that's coming to him would be an inadequate phrase to express my feelings towards Blane. There are no words, even for an experienced copywriter, to describe my disdain for the man." Carter leaned forward and took a gulp from his glass.

"I see. Do you mind if I go on."

"No, not at all, we've come this far; tell me."

Melvyn Carter sat impassively, as, for the next five minutes, Juliet briefed him on her style of reporting. She got onto the takeover of BBM which seemed to spark a reaction when she said the company's name in full, Buckley Blane Marketing.

"Sam Buckley was easy, a straight-forward rise in his field and no skeletons in his cupboard. Blane, on the other hand, has proved to be more difficult to flesh out. Former colleagues are reluctant to talk about him – I don't know why for sure but it seemed, without sounding melodramatic, out of fear."

"Why doesn't that surprise me," Carter cut in, making his words a statement rather than a question.

"His official biog in the flashy BBM brochure is missing a vital part."

Carter looked at her quizzically. "What part?"

"The part when he worked for you."

"Hardly surprising in the circumstances, a shit like Blane will always hide the bodies and if they're found, have a ready innocent to blame in such convincing tones that fools will chastise themselves for ever doubting him."

The smile was gone now replaced by a look of disgust.

"The circumstances… you said, 'in the circumstances'. Can you tell me about the circumstances?"

He looked at her then dropped his eyes to the floor. "She died, but I suppose you know that; we couldn't go on afterwards – it just didn't feel right."

"Marilyn, Marilyn Snell?"

Carter nodded and a wan smile returned as he seemed to reflect on some distant memory.

"So, what happened?"

"Sheldon Blane – that's what happened. Of course, we didn't find out until later…when it was all too late."

Juliet said nothing, letting the silence tug at Carter, waiting for him to continue with a story she felt sure he hadn't discussed with anyone for a very long time.

"We'd known each other at Oxford……Harry Gibbon and I," he said finally, in a voice so quiet it seemed he was mumbling to himself but it picked up volume as he went on. "After graduation, I went into marketing, he joined a P.R firm but we kept in touch. By the time we were in our forties, we were as far as we could go working for our respective employers and bored. Granted we were senior directors but the excitement was gone.

In 1994 we met Marilyn at a convention in Chicago. We all got on so well that what started out as a passing remark at dinner, became reality when we went into business together a year later. It was all very small beer to start with

– the three of us working from a walk-up in Old Compton Street. Three years later, we were picking up steady business and decided on a move to more up-market offices in Regent Street. We were into the bank for a hefty sum but it didn't worry us as long as the business covered the repayments – and it was managing fine."

Juliet was writing furiously on a notepad, paused for a moment to sip her drink then produced a small voice recorder from her bag.

"Do you mind if I use this?"

Carter signalled his agreement with a wave of his hand. She set the machine to record and placed it on the table.

"Please go on."

Carter drained his glass and returned it to its coaster.

"Well," he continued, "things were pretty good; work was coming in, we were paying our own salaries and those of eight staff."

"Was Blane with you by then?"

"No, I'm coming to that. Our clients were small to medium sized. We hadn't quite made it into the big time – but that all changed when we snatched the account of a burger chain – Rio's. They're gone now of course, bought up by one of the hotel chains but, back then, they were the darlings of the City and we handled their P.R. and ran their campaigns, sprinkling us with a little of their stardust. That's when we decided to groom an account manager; there wasn't enough time in the day for us to handle the work."

"Sheldon Blane?" Carter nodded. "We wanted someone to mould to our way of thinking. He was keen, good looking and smart. He left all the others behind.

Within three months, he knew every facet of our business

and was bringing his own ideas. We couldn't believe our luck."

"So, he was proving his worth."

"We all thought so but…." He hesitated.

"But?" Juliet repeated.

"I should have suspected something. Looking back, it was there for me to see but we were all caught up in our success, we didn't notice the snake amongst us."

"What was there to see?"

"Blane was twenty-five and bumptious back then. I put his manner down to the arrogance of youth. He wanted shares in the company and not a small amount. He reckoned he was outstripping Marilyn as far as bringing business was concerned and ought to be promised a partnership by the end of the year.

I reminded him that he had only been with us for a few months and began to explain that, with a few years' experience, all things were possible but he would have none of it. He said he'd give me a few months to think about it but he would have to move on by the end of the year if his status wasn't elevated. He didn't say it as a threat. That was the clever thing about him – he made it all seem like a pleasant chat. In other circumstances, I would have fired him but I couldn't. He was leading the Rio's account and was big buddies with their C.E.O. – a woman who constantly flirted with him and would, I felt sure, ditch us if not for Blane. Also, he was leading the pitches to our second big fish, a clothing chain.

Interest rates had risen by half a percent since we completed our structuring and business rates had gone up by a third. Everything would be okay for us as long as we kept all the clients happy and the bank in the dark about the precariousness of our position."

"How could you be in a precarious position? I thought money was flooding in."

"It was but we had high out-goings, the rent for a starter – it went up one third at review. More staff need more phones, more phones means bigger bills in big bucks; the list goes on. Anyway, like I said, as long as the boat didn't rock, we were fine."

Juliet looked up from her pad. "And Blane knew this?"

"In hindsight, yes, it never occurred to us to be worried about that kind of security. Harry and I had been around long enough to know the dangers though, we had no excuse."

Carter stopped speaking, his eyes reflecting some distant moment of torment. Juliet caught his attention with one of her 'keep going' looks.

"Oh, yes, sorry. The first inkling I had something was wrong came from Marilyn. It was a day in August; the 25th – I've had ten years to narrow down the facts of our downfall to the minute," he responded to the look of surprise on Juliet's face that he would know the exact date.

"She came in late that day; she looked dreadful – as if she'd been up all night. Her eyes were puffed up and her mood was pretty black. I tried to talk to her but whatever was on her mind, she wasn't going to discuss it. By lunchtime, she'd left. Then something else happened. A colleague from my old firm, Charlie Nash, dropped by to see me for a catch-up chat. He wanted to fill me in with the details of how he'd been head-hunted to a rival of ours, Chatwell-Blake-Barber, 'we'd be competing in the future', all in a jolly way, of course. As we were walking to my office, we passed Blane in the corridor. When we got to the office, Charlie asked me who it was we'd passed in the corridor – he'd seen him before, at his new place of work – not once, but three times. Charlie was curious to know if we had sent Blane to do some deal or other. I managed to brush it off somehow but the alarm bells had begun to ring, albeit, too late."

"Did you tackle Blane?"

"He denied he'd been there, of course, said it must have been a case of mistaken identity. A week later, he was gone. He'd been working for Chatwell all along. We couldn't prove it of course. Two weeks later, we lost the Rio's account then, the clothing chain – both went to Chatwell. We had to let most of the staff go; even the bread and butter work couldn't keep us. A short time after that, the bank came knocking. We'd already stopped taking salary and Marilyn was becoming very flaky; some days she didn't turn up to the office at all. She still wouldn't discuss whatever it was that was going on in her life. Harry and I were trying to keep the business from going under, so we didn't press her – we should have. We didn't see how close to the edge she was. In fairness, we were a little tied up."

The lounge was filling up and Juliet was forced to lean towards Carter to hear him above the chatter of the other parties around them. He brightened up suddenly.

"Another drink? Something stronger, maybe?"

"I'll stick with water, if you don't mind," she replied, anxious to keep his narrative going but he was already distracted, searching for a waitress and stretching up above the palms. Juliet looked at her watch. She only had another twenty minutes of his time. A waitress finally came over.

"I'll have the same again, please." He glanced at Juliet. "Sure you won't join me?"

She shook her head, "Please…continue."

"The final blow came on a Thursday. We were to have a make or break meeting with the bank that afternoon. We'd come up with a plan but had to give away shares to make it work. We weren't happy about it but there was no other option. Harry was on the phone when the front door buzzed. I remember the face of the Policewoman on the entry-phone monitor. There were no members of staff that day so I had to go down myself. She wouldn't tell me what she wanted until she was upstairs. When we were in the office, sitting at one of the desks, she told me. Marilyn had been found dead in her car. She'd locked herself in her garage with the engine running. A neighbour had heard the engine and become suspicious. He'd forced the door and dragged her out but she'd been dead a long time. I heard Harry drop the phone mid conversation; he was weeping." Carter's voice drained away, his eyes in an unfocused stare. Juliet waited as long as she dared; time was ticking on – he needed prompting. "Was there a note?" she asked.

He came to. "Of sorts, it was to Harry and me. It rambled a bit but the gist was she'd been having an affair with Blane. He'd dumped her in a particularly cruel way. The other factor was her home was about to be repossessed. She'd remortgaged to come in with us so, when her salary stopped, she couldn't make the payments. It was the first time Harry and I knew of her financial circumstances. She'd always led us to believe she had spare cash.

Blane had been using her, stealing her creative ideas from

her files and passing it on to Chatwell. When he'd got everything he needed and he knew we were onto him, he dropped her."

"The note went into that much detail?"

"No, like I said, it was rambling. No, we filled in the gaps quite by chance."

"Go on."

"After Marilyn died, we had no stomach to carry on. Everything seemed pointless – all the dancing around with the bank – the prospect of new partners etc..It was all too much. We decided to swallow the loss and move on. Harry and I both had money; we came to a settlement figure with the bank and paid them off in stages.

It was a couple of days before the office had to be handed back to the landlord. There was no-one to wrap the place up but Harry and me. So we did just that – lugging stuff into the skip. There wasn't much to salvage but on the last day we went to a back room to rip out the phone system and the CCTV equipment. It was the only saleable kit; the CCTV equipment was state-of-the-art with sound. Anyway, we did the phones first but then our take-out lunch arrived. We ate it watching the security tape in the machine, skimming backwards and forwards aimlessly. I almost choked when the cameras caught Blane and Marilyn; they were arguing. It got physical. She was throwing things at him – he was dodging until he pushed her on her desk and forced himself on her. She resisted initially but then she was part of the act. I got the feeling this is how it was for them. The time clock read ten thirty P.M. and the date was a week after he'd left the company."

"I don't understand. How is it you hadn't seen the tape

before and more importantly, they must have known they were on camera?"

"That's just it, no-one knew, only Harry and I – and it was either one of us who changed the tape when it needed changing which wasn't very often. It was set to activate out of hours only and worked on a motion sensor. The cleaning ladies were setting it off at the beginning but once we reset the timer to miss their time in the building, it hardly recorded anything. After a while, we forgot about it."

"I see. Please go on."

"When the sex was over, the argument started up again. Marilyn was accusing him of using her and he was agreeing, telling her she was too old for him anyway and he only had sex with her out of charity. He told her to look in the mirror then go and bother someone her own age. His only reason he'd been with her was to get her passwords and raid her computer for her work.
She slapped him and he slapped her back, knocking her to the floor. She got up and ran."

"And Blane?"

"He left a little later, after he had downloaded files from the system. We had no idea."

"When was it that Marilyn…."

"About two weeks later. I think it was the day she got the repossession order for her house. It was obviously all too much."

"Do you think she saw Blane after that night?"

"I really don't know but given the volatility of their relationship, nothing would surprise me. Women do unaccountable things for bad boys – present company excepted, of course."

"What happened to the tape?"

Carter looked at her as if deliberating. After a moment, he reached inside his jacket and pulled out a disc. "It's all here. Do with it what you will – if it stings that little bastard, all the better."

"You knew all along why I wanted to meet you."

"I had my suspicions. Now, I really must go. I enjoyed meeting you Juliet and please don't take this as anything else but a compliment – don't ever let the seamier side of life cloud those beautiful looks. Take it from me, I should know."

She smiled sheepishly for effect. "I'll try not too….and thanks…thanks for your time."

"Not at all."

She watched him weave his way through the palms then looked down at the disc she was clutching, a smile of satisfaction on her lips.

The Yale lock on the door to Sophia's flat presented no problems for Kierack; it had been the same with the door to the lobby downstairs – both opened in seconds. Forty-five minutes earlier, he'd watched her and Devan step from a taxi and head into Devan's flat. He'd observed from the shadows as the light from the first floor bedroom briefly threw a bright shaft onto the road outside. Kierack had caught a glimpse of Sophia before the curtains had closed and the window went to black. She'll be there all night, he'd thought, with some satisfaction and turned to make his way to her apartment in a different part of town.

Kierack stood in darkness for a few moments listening to the sleeping building then pressed his torch into life, playing the beam around the room. The place has been tidied since my last visit, he thought; the memory of it taking his hand subconsciously to his temple, rubbing where the glass bowl had struck him. He shone the light upward finally resting on the fitting at the centre of the ceiling. Standing on a dining chair, he removed the bulb and replaced it with one pulled from his satchel.

He returned the chair to the breakfast bar and crossed to the picture window with its view towards the City. Closing the drapes Kierack stepped into the kitchenette, ducking his head into a cupboard under the small hob set into a granite surface. He produced an adjustable spanner from his bag and located its jaws around the nut at the end of the steel mesh pipe feeding the appliance. Three rotations loosened its grip enough for gas to seep from the joint. Leaving the cupboard door ajar, he rose to his feet and silently slipped out of the flat, commending his work to Sophia for the very next time she entered and flicked on the light.

14

"What time do you have to be at college today?" She was standing naked in the bathroom doorway drying her hair with a towel.

"Ten thirty, why?" Rick was sipping coffee and throwing files into his rucksack.

"Could you do something for me before you go in?"

"Sure, but have we got time?"

"Not that," she said, playfully throwing the towel in his direction.

He went to her and placed his arms around her waist.

"Okay, tell me." He was looking into her smiling eyes.

"When we went to my place last time, I left a file on my bureau. Stupid, really, it was one of the reasons we went there. I forgot it and I need it for this afternoon. Could you pick it up and meet me at lunchtime – I'd go myself but there's a pitch first thing and I can't be late."

"Okay, but if I can't find it, I'll have to call you." His eyes drifted downward following the contours of her body.

"Pay attention!" she said, smiling seductively, "You can't miss it – it's a blue file on the bureau."

"Call me at twelve thirty to fix the place." She kissed his cheek and went to the bedroom.

Rick walked up to the lobby door of Sophia's building; it felt strange coming here without her. There was a silent space at his side where she should have been, digging his ribs – telling him to hurry up and put the key into the lock and to stop 'faffing around'. What a particularly English expression that was. It would draw blank stares back home. He turned the key and went to the lift with a sudden memory of Georgina Roe, his girlfriend in his last year before college. It was never true love but attraction and a kind of friendship – if that was possible. She had a key to her Uncle Mike's place while he was away in L.A. on business. She'd promised to feed the fish in his apartment on the Bay. It was a real bachelor's pad with cool electronics and a panoramic bedroom window looking out over the water. They spent one long Saturday afternoon there – Rick going for second base and her making sure he didn't get there. He still remembered the way he felt her uncle's presence in the place even though Uncle Mike was almost a thousand miles away. He had that feeling now, perceiving Sophia's presence as he rode the lift to her floor. It was the trigger for his film-flicker flashback.

That year had been a great year and Georgie was the icing but it had to end sometime and when *she* left for Berkeley and *he* for Boston, their time together was consigned to the file marked 'Memories'. He saw her once more, in the street a couple of years later. She had bloomed into a beautiful woman and was on a visit home to see her parents and her brothers. It was all a bit formal as she stood there with her mom and the shopping bags that said they'd had a day catching up but, as her mother turned to leave, Georgina gave him a lingering look. He smiled as he remembered the moment.

There were four flats on Sophia's floor and as with his apartment, the front door opened into a small hallway with another door at the end into the main living area. Light from the corridor outside lit the space as Rick went in leaving the door open. There was a faint damp smell and, as he approached the door at the end of the passage, he noticed a towel pressed against its base. He didn't remember it being there when they left the last time but he'd waited for Sophia in the lobby as she'd run back upstairs for something. He looked at the towel. Maybe it was to put this here – she must have had her reasons, he thought as he pushed the door open, gagging immediately. A rush of gas washed over Rick as he stepped into the darkened flat. He suppressed his instinct to turn on the light barely a millisecond before his hand hit the switch.

Newman's mobile rang. He recognised Rick Devan's number.

"Mr. Devan, how can I help you? It seems my days can't go by without hearing from you or Miss Ferretti at least once."

"I'm at her place at the moment; she asked me to come over and pick up some things. I think you need to come here. The place was filled with gas. I think someone has been in here."

"What have you done so far?"

"I opened the windows turned off the main valve under the sink."

"And what makes you think somebody's been there?"

"The gas pipe has been loosened enough to leak, the

curtains were closed – I know we left them open when we were here last."

"Have you touched anything else?"

"No."

"I hope you're phoning me from outside."

"I'm in the lobby but I think it's safe now; I got rid of all the gas."

"Stay there; do not go back to the flat. I'll be over as soon as I can."

Rick recognised the two forensic officers from a few days earlier; they were under the sink, examining the gas feeder pipe when he walked in. D.I. Newman had told him to remain in the lobby until his officers had established the flat was safe to enter. He'd been kicking his heels for fifteen minutes before the call came asking him to come up. It had been tough resisting the urge to call Sophia but thought it best to hear Newman's view before he worried her. There might be a simple explanation – he knew there wasn't one though.

Newman was in the middle of the room looking up at the light fitting on the ceiling as Rick entered.

"Ray," Newman called, to one of the forensics, "come over here a minute."

Rick followed Newman's gaze upward to the hanging lamp shade. A third of the bulb at its centre appeared darker than the remainder. As the forensics officer at the top of a step ladder gingerly removed the bulb, it became evident the dark area inside was liquid.

Newman frowned as he sniffed at a tiny hole in the brass bayonet where the liquid had been injected.

"Petrol," he remarked, "you were very lucky, Mr. Devan. If you had turned the light on, we wouldn't be having this conversation. This is a very professional job."

"Detective Inspector, I think we can all agree now that someone is trying to kill Sophia, shouldn't she have some kind of protection?"

"We've had someone keeping an eye on her for a couple of days now but we didn't expect this. We'll need to do more until we find who's after her and why. My officer reported her reaching work at about ten – she ought to be safe enough there for the time being."

"I'm seeing her at lunch. Is that going to be okay?"

"My officer will be around but I don't think whoever did this, will try anything today. If he's as professional as I think he is, he'll know he failed here. It would be too risky to try anything else so soon – he'll know we're watching."

"I wish I had your confidence. I haven't told her any of this yet. She's going to be very frightened – who wouldn't be?"

"Tell her at lunch not on the phone. My officer will make himself known to you both. There were two tasked, D.S Hinkley and D.S. Burrows but I had to pull Burrows off for a couple of days. Hinkley is a good man though."

"I hope so."

Across the street, Kierack watched the Police arrive from a non-descript hatchback. There were two forensics officers in a van and a plain clothes detective in an un-marked Ford saloon. When they had all entered the building, he started his engine and moved away slowly, disappointed that events had conspired against his plans. Brussels then, he thought.

Back at the company two-bedroom flat, Kierack studied the arrangements for his journey to Brussels. The ticket was valid for late Monday afternoon. That gave him all of the morning and some of the afternoon. If he was lucky, and there's no saying he would be judging by events so far, he could have one more try before the train pulled out. Leave her alone for the weekend – make her think I've gone away and then, out of nowhere on Monday sometime – a traffic accident. That might work, he mused.

15

"I know where Uncle Milo's flat is in Brussels; it's in Rue de Cornet. All the details were right in front of me in his desk drawer. I don't know why I didn't notice the deeds before. I must have handled them when I tidied up the mess after the Police had gone. You were right; it's off Place Jourdan."

Gerald Hope smiled his professional smile as he scribbled the address on a pad, tore off the sheet then turned to the file on his desk.

"I've got your tickets here; I hope I've spelt Mr. Devan's name correctly. You're booked on the 10.57 from London. It arrives into Brussels just after two. Coming back on Wednesday, you're on the 17.59. That service gets into London at about seven."

"Where are we staying?"

"The New Hotel Charlemagne in Boulevard Charlemagne – the rooms are pre-paid and any extras are taken care of. You won't need to pay for anything. The hotel is nearby to the Commission and Frans' office, so you'll have no difficulty getting to your meetings on time."

"Thank you. Not wishing to sound too paranoid, but who else knows about this?"

"Sophia, I told you I would take care of this personally. Just me, I'm the only one who knows the when and the where. I did all the booking on my personal laptop – it's not even connected to the office network."

"Sorry, I guess I *must* be paranoid after all."

He produced a bulging A4 envelope from a desk drawer.

"Here," he said, handing her the packet. "All the details are inside now, don't worry so much."

"I'll try not to."

He turned to the file in front of him.

"Okay, let's talk about royalties for a moment. Milo had some ideas but all were for discussion. What it boils down to is a system of licensing where the individual business sectors purchase the Milo Scale in the same way bar-codes are bought – the difference being that all products and services in the E.U. would be required by law to bear the Milo Scale and the fee for the Scale would be levied annually. It's proposed the E.U. will administer the charge and every sale will generate a royalty to you."

The magnitude and implications of her uncle's work began to dawn on her.

"Even if the royalty is a fraction of a percent, it'll run into millions – I hadn't really thought about it."

"You can see why there are people who are not too keen on the idea. Not only will it cost to gear up for the changes in the way companies market themselves and their products but it will force them to be more transparent in their pricing and marketing."

"What had you and uncle Milo decided?"

"We weren't sure of the royalty figure but we agreed on the down-payment from the E.U. – five million Euros and another three after six months. This would tide things over until the royalties came on stream. Although this seems a great deal of money, in the scheme of things, it's really not that much but Milo felt it was appropriate."

"I really don't know what to say, only I won't be saying anything about this in the meetings.That'll be for later when I know what I'm talking about."

"Good idea, just brush any question aside, however, remember what they ask and we'll be prepared for the next time."

"Okay. Unless there's anything else I need to know, I have to drop by my work today, they're beginning to forget my face."

Annabel could only hear snatches of conversation; the voices behind the door to Gerald Hope's office were muffled. It was a pity because his visitor was of particular interest to her. She'd have to work for her supper today, she thought, stealing a glance at the detective sitting on the sofa opposite. He was sipping the tea she had made for him. Annabel had been careful to appear disinterested in the conversation going on behind the door, smiling each time she caught him studying her and straining to catch stray snatches when he looked away. The voices grew louder and the door opened. D.S Hinkley set his cup and saucer down and stood. Sophia Ferretti stepped through shepherded by Hope. ".....call me tomorrow," Hope was in mid sentence. He saw her and Hinkley to the exit then walked back to his office, calling to Annabel as he passed her desk.

"Any messages?"

"Two, I've sent them to your screen."

"Thanks, could you come in for a moment?"

She followed.

The office was its usual neat self, the only clutter, two coffee cups and a plate of pecked-at biscuits in the centre of the desktop. Hope's laptop sat with its screen open and lit adjacent to the office's networked computer. No information was displayed only the cursor blinking in the start window begging a password. Hope was always careful to ensure his personal machine was in this state when not in use or unattended. He was completely unaware his password was known to one other – Annabel.

Good looks were not her only attributes; she'd been blessed with a keen brain and a photographic memory that made her school days a breeze. A glance was all it took to commit a page of text or diagrams or even a sequence of taps on a keyboard to her encyclopaedic mind. She entered university with starred 'A' grades from her sixth form but had been astute enough to know that nobody likes a smart arse and so had been self effacing in her success. She walked the same tight-rope at uni, modest about her undoubted abilities, carefully using her charms to get what she wanted and managing to be liked.

Gerald's password had just clicked into place without her noticing. She hadn't deliberately set out to discover it but, after her first week of work at the firm, subconsciously logging his key pattern on the many times she entered the room or passed his desk as he was logging on, it was there. It wasn't necessary for her to see the strokes close up, a letter here, a number there; her brain instantly compared each one to the rhythm of Gerald's keystrokes and logged the characters one by one until the sequence was complete in a virtual display tucked into a corner at the back of her mind.

She remained standing as Gerald bent to the network computer and hit a key. He studied the two messages she had sent earlier then cleared the screen.

"Nothing that can't wait; I'll be out at lunch until three." He reached into the top drawer and pulled out a small voice recorder. "There are a couple of letters on here for you. Could you get them out as soon as you can?

Oh – please take the cups out when you go."

"Yes, of course."

"See you later."

She nodded her reply as he left the room, lingering by the window, waiting to see him step out onto the pavement. She watched him pull on his gloves and hail a cab. As the taxi disappeared into the traffic, she turned back and settled herself into his leather chair and reached for the laptop. Her fingers slid over the keys with catlike agility. Moments later, she was in, scanning Gerald's private emails and recent documents, searching out the travel arrangements and hotel booking he had made on-line. Within minutes, the wireless printer in the corner was making a hard copy.

She retrieved the single sheet and went back to the desk. As Annabel returned Gerald's laptop to the position it had occupied before her incursion – careful to set it to its locked state, his notepad caught her eye. The top sheet was blank but light from the window caught the indentations of a note which had been scribbled large on the page that had been above but now torn out. Holding it closer to the light, she could easily make out the words, 'Milo's flat – Brussels'. She took down the address on the sheet with the other information she'd extracted and smiled inwardly. 'That's gotta be worth another five hundred', she thought.

D.S. George Hinkley signalled Sophia to remain in the lobby of the building while he took the precaution of checking the street outside. He scanned the pavements in both directions and beckoned her to follow. For Sophia, this was all getting a bit much. It had been two days now since the break-in at the flat and she was beginning to think that the threat to her personal safety was a case of mistaken identity or, at the very least, receding. She turned to the D.S. now walking at her side.

"Before I go back to work, I have to pick up something from Oxford Street; it'll only take ten minutes."

"Go ahead, I'm with you until I'm told different," Hinkley replied.

Fifty yards back, Kierack appeared from steps which descended to the vacant basement. Wearing a black beanie pulled down to his ears and concealed by a property agent's board, he'd watched first Hinkley and then Sophia, emerge from the lawyer's office and head off in the direction of Oxford Street. Crowds, traffic – perfect, he thought.

Sophia and Hinkley approached the junction at Cavendish Square, halting at the pavement's edge – waiting for the walk-light. Kierack was twenty yards behind now and closing the gap in the gathering numbers of office workers and sales staff filling the streets on their lunch breaks. The next crossing was at the other side of the square. The crowd bunched again waiting for the light. Kierack was at the centre this time, an arm's length behind Sophia. "Not yet," he whispered, inaudibly.

Sophia and George Hinkley were leading a crowd now as it moved on again then re-formed its phalanx, this time to cross Oxford Street itself. The group had doubled in size with Sophia and Hinkley perched on the kerb at the very front.

The noise from the busses and taxi brake screeches was deafening. A sixth sense told Hinkley to turn. He wheeled round to glimpse an arm with a massive hand, palm flattened at its end aiming for Sophia's back. He grabbed at it, deflected the blow but in so doing took the full force to his chest, hurling him into the road and the path of a speeding bus. It was over in an instant. Traffic came to a sudden halt against a background of shouts and screams.

*****

"Where's the girl?"

"Downstairs with Burrows and a WPC. She's pretty cut up."

"Anyone talk to her yet?" Newman's question was directed at Jill Hargreaves. She'd been alone in the incident room when the call had come about Hinkley. Newman and Gorman were already on their way to the Eurostar terminal at St. Pancras; she'd given them the news and they'd turned around.

"Not formally but she says she saw nothing – one minute he was next to her, the next, flying backwards into the road."

Newman threw his coat over the back of a chair and sat.

"Anybody else see anything?"

"Uniform took a statement from a postman coming off shift; said he saw a tall man in a leather coat reach across him towards Hinkley but lost his own footing in the crush. When he'd got his balance back, the man in the coat was gone."

"Did he see his face?"

"Fleetingly – but it won't do us much good; he said the guy had a beanie pulled down to his eyes and a scarf covering the bottom half of his face."

"What about CCTV?"

"There's footage of the incident but it's not that clear. It was caught by a single camera about a hundred yards away on the other side of the street – the nearest camera was faulty."

"Let me see."

Gorman came in and perched on a visitors' chair in front of the desk where Newman sat as Hargreaves hit the 'Play' icon. The flat screen monitor in the corner of the room came to life.

She hit the pause button and crossed the room to the screen.

"Watch this area here," she said, circling the blurred image of a tightly packed group of approximately fifty pedestrians at the kerbside. The detectives scrutinised the image but the distance from camera to subject, the angle of shot and sunlight reflecting off a shop window, prevented any clear recognition of individual faces. Jill Hargreaves walked back to her desk and clicked the mouse to advance the footage frame by frame. Newman and Gorman stared at the screen in horror as a tall figure in the third row, reared up in jerky movements and reached over heads with a flat palm strike which propelled the turning form of D.S. Hinkley into the road. The scene is instantly obscured by the red mass of a Routemaster.

"Poor bugger," Gorman grimaced.

"The bus blocks the view from here, Sir."

"What about other cameras?"

Hargreaves clicked the mouse and a new view filled the screen. She pointed again. "This is from the Cavendish Square end of Holles Street and this is our man I think."

A tall man wearing a long coat breaks away from a milling crowd at the top of frame and casually strolls down the street towards the camera position. His features are concealed by the combination of a black beanie and a scarf which covers the lower half of his face. Hargreaves paused the playback, freezing the frame before the subject could disappear from the camera's view.

"He fits the description given by the postman," she continued.

"Any more?" Newman's face was expressionless.

"Not yet, but everything from the north side of Oxford Street within a half mile radius, thirty minutes before and thirty minutes after the incident is being uploaded to an FTP address. We should be able to access it in about an hour."

Just then, Burrows came into the room.

"Can I have a word, Boss?"

The detective Inspector nodded for Dave Gorman to continue.

"Rick Devan's here to pick up Miss Ferretti. She wants to leave."

"Okay, I'll come and see her," Newman said, rising from

the desk. He turned to Jill Hargreaves. "See if you can get that footage any quicker. Oh, and Dave – speak to our friend in Brussels, tell him we've been delayed but we'll be there tonight on a later train."

Rick sat with his arm around Sophia in an interview room two floors down from the incident room. The door was open and a WPC sat across a plain grey table. Sophia sipped a mug of tea made for her by the WPC. The woman constable stood up as Newman entered closely followed by Burrows.

"Thank you, constable, you can go now."

The WPC nodded and left the room as Newman sat in the chair she had occupied.

"I'm sorry we couldn't have found somewhere less basic than this place but it's all we've got at the moment."

Sophia looked up into Newman's face.

"Is D.S. Hinkley dead?"

"I'm afraid so, he died in the ambulance."

Holding back her tears, she said, "He was such a considerate man, nothing seemed too much trouble."

Newman waited a moment and then said, "I know you've told the other officers but I'd like you to go over what happened just one more time – for me."

"That's just it – I don't know what happened – I was looking across the street, I was conscious of George next to me, it was a bit of a crush. I can't be sure, but thought he was turning around to look at someone behind him, then he seemed to go backwards into the road."

"Can you remember what happened next?"

"A lot of noise – people shouting; I froze – couldn't move,

I couldn't believe what had just happened. The ambulance came after about five minutes and I saw them lift George onto a stretcher; he wasn't moving. A Police Constable took a statement from me. I told him George was one of your men looking after me. Ten minutes later, a Police car collected me and brought me here."

"Okay, you'd better go home. Burrows will see you get there alright."

"I'll be at Rick's. We're meant to be going to Brussels tomorrow."

Newman's look was quizzical.

"I mentioned it to you last week – my uncle's business," she reminded him.

"Sorry; I remember now. I think I'd better organise someone to keep an eye on you while you're there."

"I don't think I'll argue with you Detective Inspector but I'm having second thoughts about the whole thing; someone is trying to kill me and I'm terrified."

"Burrows will get you home safely and check the place out before you go in. How are you going to Brussels?"

"On the Eurostar."

"Okay, Burrows will pick you up tomorrow and see you onto the train. Will that suit?"

Sophia nodded.

"Good – someone will call you later. One more thing, I'll also be in Brussels tomorrow on another matter. So, if you feel the need to call me, don't hesitate."

Rick had stayed silent for Newman's gentle questioning. He rummaged in his shoulder bag, pulled out a sheet of A4 and handed it to Newman.

"Here, it's *our* itinerary. Gerald Hope arranged it. He

assured Sophia no-one else knows the details, so we should be okay once we're on the train."

"I'll let you know what's been arranged when I know it." Rick and Sophia stood up and went to the door followed by Burrows.

"Call me when you get there," Newman called after Burrows.

16

When Newman got back to the incident room, Jill Hargreaves was studying what appeared to be more footage from street cameras.

"The website's up, Boss."

"Show me."

"This shot picks up from the last one in Holles Street." Hargreaves was standing by the monitor; she gestured to Gorman to advance the clip. "This is from the corner of Cavendish Square – here's our man now." Her finger underlined the same tall figure they'd followed in the previous sequence. "He crosses the road into the square then ducks into the underground car park; we're trying to get the footage from the company but it's taking time."

"Is there anything of him leaving?"

"Not that we've seen yet, Boss."

"What about before – before the incident? Ferretti said they walked from Gerald Hope's office in Wigmore Street. It's about half-way down so I reckon from there up to the lights at the junction at the end of Harley Street then across the square and crossing into Holles and then to the kerb of Oxford Street, would take about ten minutes. Take a look at the route from fifteen minutes before; I'll be in my office when you're ready."

Kierack descended the main ramp into the car park, careful to pass behind the cameras viewing the entry barriers where drivers halted to pull their tickets from the machines. There was another camera angled to take a wide shot of the same area but it wasn't working – and not by coincidence. When he'd parked his car, two hours earlier, Kierack had made his way back to the entrance on foot and, out of sight of the attendants chatting in a kiosk at the exit, had used his height to reach up and pull the output cable from its socket rendering the device blind. His action had gone totally unrecorded.

The car park was built around a central core encapsulating a staircase to ground level and although there were many cameras, their positioning, at intervals on the wall of the core, was such as to prevent them from covering an area of about ten feet at the rear of each of the preceding cameras in the chain. It was a lapse that Kierack had been quick to notice during a previous visit on unrelated business and he'd earmarked the location for a time he might need to use its weaknesses.

When he'd driven in and parked to be in time to observe his target and her minder enter the lawyer's office, a trilby hat was atop his head securing a latex mask in position. He wore a smart jacket with a collar and tie. He did not turn to face the ticket machine to collect his ticket, presenting only a profile to the camera which recorded all entries. On leaving the car, he'd carried his coat over his arm. It wasn't until he was down the stairs of the vacant basement, two streets away, that he removed the hat and mask replacing them with his beanie and scarf. He'd pulled on his overcoat and waited.

Now he reversed the procedure but this time in the blind spot behind the camera at the entrance. He faced the wall, slipped off his coat, pulling the hat and mask from its deep pockets. When the cameras picked him up, they registered a character far removed from the casual assassin hunted by the Police.

Newman sat on a swivel chair next to D.S. Gorman facing the flat screen set up in the corner of the room.

"Okay, let's see it."

Hargreaves clicked on the 'Play' icon and then paused the action almost immediately.

"We've edited an eight minute sequence from a half-way point in Wigmore Street. There *is* another camera, but it's too far away." She clicked the mouse and jerky images filled the screen. "Here's George and Miss Ferretti."

The rear view of D.S. Hinkley and Sophia entered the bottom of the picture and moved up as they progressed along the pavement. An identifying highlight circled their image, distinguishing them from other pedestrians. "And here's our man now;" she continued, "he's about twenty yards back." She pointed to the ghostly image of a tall figure wearing a long dark coat, purposeful in his pursuit, held within a second highlighted circle. The gap between the circles closed a little as George and Sophia reached the junction at the top of the road. Their stalker hung back, maintaining his distance. "He keeps away until they get to the other side of the square."

Two cameras later, and the front view of a group of pedestrians became visible as they gathered kerbside waiting to cross the road separating Cavendish Square from

Holles Street. Hargreaves paused the frame again. The picture was much more defined than previous footage. The facial features of D.S. Hinkley and Sophia were clearly discernable at the fore.

Newman studied the picture. "Where's he gone?"

"Next frame, Sir." Hargreaves advanced the footage a frame at a time. "Here," she said, pointing to the head with a beanie pulled down to the wearer's eyes. "He's two rows back. We can't see his face though. He keeps that damn scarf up the whole time."

"Okay, keep going."

The images began moving again at their flickering gait.

"Right here, it changes to the Oxford Street shot we saw before."

The three officers watched again passively as the re-run of George Hinkley's last conscious moments played out in stop motion.

Ernst Kierack stared at his reflection in the full length mirror fixed to the wall of the flat provided for him by his employer. It was modern and centrally located and, up until the time Kierack took it over, was occupied by a senior executive who had left to run the Hong Kong office. The only changes Kierack had made were to the guest room. It was now a small gym with weights and a Multi-gym exerciser to accommodate his punishing daily work-out. His body was a taut mass of muscle and he was going to keep it that way. On the company books as 'Security Advisor', he enjoyed all the privileges of senior management without the claptrap.

He straightened his tie and smoothed his fair hair. He wore

a charcoal grey pinstripe suit tailored to fit his solid six foot three frame and teamed it with a blue shirt. His black size eleven lace-up shoes shone. He turned to catch his profile and put on a pair of clear, black rimmed spectacles. Despite the expensive tailoring, the power of his body was evident. He turned again, checking his look. Could he pass for a salesman selling stationery to the university or did he still look the man he really was, the disaffected son of a Stasi agent from Berlin who had run with opportunist gangsters when the Wall came down. Hmm... pretty good, he thought, I think it'll do.

The journey to St. Pancras took twenty minutes. The cab dropped Kierack at the entrance with forty-five minutes to spare. He travelled light, one small bag with a strap slung over his shoulder. He passed through the ticket barrier and dumped the bag on the rollers at the x-ray machine, emptying his pockets of change into the tray provided, then stepping through the metal detector arch. He collected his belongings as soon as they emerged from the machine and ambled into the waiting hall. It was a tranquil expanse of thick carpet and bare redbrick walls lit with hidden downlights. Two attendants sat at a long information desk made for five. A coffee bar and restaurant lay thirty feet to his right. Kierack looked around him, surprised at the small number of waiting passengers – he'd expected to be lost in a crowd.

He picked up a cup of coffee from the stand and glancedat the departure screen. The boarding light was blinking and simultaneously, glass doors slid open allowing access to the escalators which led up to the platforms. On the platform, the train seemed to stretch to the horizon. Stewardesses stood at the entrances of each of the carriages waiting to assist. As he stopped momentarily to check his ticket for his carriage number, by chance, he glanced behind him. There were two men coming towards him in a hurry. He recognised one of them immediately. It was the detective he'd seen from his car outside the Ferretti girl's flat. There was no way they were here for him. He was unknown to them. 'Police business in Brussels?' he wondered. He stepped away from the train and allowed them to pass, standing near to a waste basket making an exaggerated performance of draining the dregs from the paper cup. The two detectives boarded the train without taking notice of him. Kierack crumpled the cup and tossed it into the basket, boarding behind them.

He hung back in the corridor between the carriages and watched the two policemen through the glass door match their ticket numbers with their seats, stow their bags in the rack and sit opposite each other across a folding table. The carriage was almost empty save a party of four women and a family of three at the far end. He checked his ticket and then his watch – three minutes to go before the scheduled departure time. If anyone else was coming, they'd better be here soon. He looked at his ticket again; his seat was two carriages away. There was a hiss and the doors closed.

Waiting for the train to move and keeping the spot where the detectives were located in his peripheral vision, he let the glass door to the carriage slide open and stepped in. He stopped just short of the detectives and made a show of checking the number on his ticket and then the numbers above the seats, feigned recognition of his allocated place and seated himself in the vacant seat across the aisle in the same row as the policemen. Ernst Kierack opened a copy of the Evening Standard scooped up on the way to the platform and appeared to be lost in its content.

Newman looked across at D.S. Gorman who was folding his coat.

"Have you got Grenard's number in your phone? I thought I'd call him – find out what he's doing about looking after Ferretti and the American."

"I spoke to him just before we left. He'll be calling before five our time."

"Well he'd better hurry up, it's almost ten-to now," Newman said impatiently.

Gorman's phone rang. He looked at the incoming caller message.

"It's him. Hello Inspector, yes, we're on our way. Yes, yes, I see. She will be there tomorrow – there are two of them; she's bringing a friend. They will arrive at two in the afternoon." There was a pause then Gorman spoke into the phone again. "Can you spell the name please? Merriel." He was writing as he was speaking. "Serge Merriel – one of your detectives – thank you, Inspector; I'll pass this to Miss Ferretti. See you in about ninety minutes."

Gorman hung up and slipped his phone into his pocket.

"Well?"

"He's sending one of his detectives to the station to pick them up," Gorman replied looking down at the note he'd taken. "Detective Merriel, he'll be at the barrier when they leave the train."

"Okay, I'll call the Ferretti girl."

Kierack found it bewildering how people using mobile phones on trains always spoke loudly as if they were on some international call made in the years when volume was necessary to be heard. The most sensitive detail could be overheard several rows away without any thought of privacy. The same could not be said of *both* policemen sitting across the aisle. Kierack had rightly identified Newman as being the superior officer and noticed he was the most cautious. When Newman called the Ferretti woman, he'd cupped his hand around the mouthpiece and had made it difficult but not impossible for Kierack to follow the conversation. It was the second policeman who helped the most, filling in the gaps when his boss looked to him for confirmation during his call.

Ernst had been unlucky with the Ferretti woman so far but finally, something was going his way. Until now, he had no set plan to achieve the Boss's wishes and had been pondering his options. Any solution must be clean and point to an unfortunate accident or a random mugging. It was just like the old days in Berlin. The excitement was always in the creation of a plan and the primary question the same – how to get close to the mark? On this job, the question had answered itself. Scouting the location and picking a spot that would afford him a clear escape route would not be necessary and the 'how to get close' had just fallen into his lap.

"Call me if there's anything you're not happy about; we can have someone here in minutes."
Rick and Sophia nodded in unison.

"Okay then," Burrows went on, "I'll see you in the morning."

As the Yale snicked into its cradle, Rick turned the key in the Chubb for good measure. They sat in silence for a moment each end of the sofa, Sophia re-running the last few hours in her mind's eye. Rick, staying silent until she was ready. Finally, Sophia spoke.

"I know I said I'd keep on with all this but I'm having serious doubts again. I'm a nervous wreck. I can't go on like this forever – worried I'll be under the next bus or my flat might explode – I'll go mad. What if they never catch whoever's behind it?"

Rick went to her and put his arm around her.

"Why don't you call Gerald Hope – tell him you need to delay?"

"I've already had that conversation and the outcome will be the same."

They fell silent again. Rick thought for a moment.

"Maybe the only way is to sign up with the E.U. right away," he said finally, "make it too late for the bad guys to do anything about it. If you sign up, they'll have no reason to keep after you. I've a feeling that if you sell out to this Weller character, they may still want you out of the way in case you change your mind."

She nodded her head slowly with sceptical eyes.

"I keep thinking that I'm in a bad dream. I'm just a graphic designer for God's sake – I'm not cut out for this dancing in the dark. Neither option is appealing as far as my safety goes."

"We have to minimise the danger and keep the Police with us the whole time – if they'll do that."

"Okay, let's wait for Newman's call. Maybe he'll have organised something we can live with." They both smiled at the pun.

Rick's thoughts turned back to Sophia. Her call to Gerald Hope didn't really produce anything. Hope would try to bring things forward but had thought it would take a few days for his man to arrange and Sophia would probably have to return to Brussels next week. She was coping so far and a call from D.I. Newman with the name of the detective from the Brussels Police who would meet them from the train, seemed to give her comfort. Also, D.S. Burrows would now accompany them on the train and hand them on to the Belgian detective. Initially, Newman had thought that once they were on the train, they'd be safe but, after thinking about how determined Sophia's faceless pursuers seemed to be, he'd changed his mind. Burrows was due to pick them up in the morning at nine and he was thankful for it.

Before he slept, Rick thought of Juliet. How was it, the mere sight of her name still had the power of a cattle prod in the ribs? He put it down to that 'unrequited thing' poets droned on about.

17

On the lower level, inside the Midi Station, Ernst Kierack was seated in one of the food outlets along the main concourse nursing a cup of coffee. He had deliberately ignored his employer's instructions to find a place to stay in La Chasse and found a small guest house eight minutes' walk from where he now sat. He felt more comfortable remaining off the radar until the job was done. If nobody knew his whereabouts, the less likely it was that he could be sold out. His boss hadn't shown anything, up to now at least, to indicate he might do such a thing but Ernst was sure if push came to shove, the instinct would be to look after number one.

The place was busy with lunchtimers from the surrounding offices who dropped into the station not because it was the best cuisine in Brussels but because it was quick and convenient. There were other eateries in Place Horta, an expansive cobbled area enclosed by high buildings on three sides and accessed directly from the station, but they were more formal and took time.

Kierack was early, reckoning Merriel, the Belgian detective whose name and description had been so conveniently provided by his travelling companions on the Eurostar, would be too. He had spent time getting a feel for the location and its exits. He judged that Merriel intended to collect his charges from the barrier, take them down the stairs, then the escalator to ground level and through the exit which led on to Place Horta. Merriel wouldn't bother parking in the station's multi-storey, he was on protection duty – he'd park on the cobbles next to the taxis for a quick getaway.

Kierack drained the last from the paper cup and crumpled it into a bin as he stepped out onto the concourse. He didn't wear a suit today; he was less formal in a sports jacket and tie with dark trousers. Almost jaunty in his manner, he crossed to the chocolate shop at the foot of the escalator, passing a two Euro coin to the assistant in exchange for a bar of marzipan covered with dark chocolate.

Kierack stepped out onto Place Horta and, as he'd predicted, immediately caught sight of an unmarked black Peugeot pulling onto a raised area adjacent to the taxi rank at the end of the pedestrianised zone, the cluster of aerials on its roof betraying its identity. He took a bite of the chocolate bar and found a bench seat with a clear view of the car fifty yards away.

The air was fresh and the white puffs of breath from passers-by were caught in the light of a winter sun that was never going to climb high. Heels clacked on the cobbles around him mixed with snatches of girl-talk and executive banter.

It was a few minutes before the driver emerged. What was it about policemen; he could spot them anywhere in any country. Was it a look or the way they gave off some imagined ownership of the street around them or maybe it was Kierack's line of business that had tuned his radar? He studied the man who was locking the car from the key fob. This would be detective Merriel. He was of medium build and in his forties, Kierack judged. He had dark hair and his left cheek bore a scar that ran from his chin up to the bone beneath his eye – a battle scar maybe. To Ernst, the detective looked fit and handy. Timing would be a key factor if he was to take him – surprise would be the only way. The old feelings returned, the rush of the unpredictable – the tingle of anticipation in his fingers. Merriel passed within a few feet of his position on his way to the station entrance. Ernst rose and followed at a safe distance as Merriel took the escalator to platform level. He watched Merriel familiarise himself with the 'Meet Point', check his watch and then look up, searching, Kierack hoped, for directions to the toilets; the preferred plan depended on it.

He had been here two hours earlier as the early train came in from London. Chauffeurs held up clipboards emblazoned with the names of their expected charges, standing like rocks in a fast running river as the mêlée of passengers streamed either side of them.

There was only one toilet facility nearby. It was at the end of a wide but quiet corridor and not supervised by a warden collecting coins for its use as the other facilities on the main concourse. It was out of line with the flow of passengers heading for the escalator to the ground floor exit and, from Kierack's observations, little used. The passage curved to the left, obscuring the entrance from the Meet Point one hundred feet away. Just before the toilet entrance, a janitors' room was set into the wall. Kierack had slipped the lock, finding the room empty save a tall cleared out metal cabinet and a few discarded rags.

Merriel, checked his watch for the second time and headed in the direction of the toilets, a solitary silhouette against blue tiled walls. Kierack followed silently. As Merriel reached a point level with the door of the janitors' room, Kierack called out to him in the best French he could muster.

"Detective Merriel? I'm Detective Sergeant Gorman from London."

Merriel stopped and turned.

"I was hoping to catch you. I have a message from Detective Inspector Newman regarding the people you are collecting."

"Yes, I am Merriel," he replied cautiously.

There was a gap of fifteen feet between them and Kierack kept up a brisk pace, closing the distance in long strides. Merriel glanced down as the tall, well built man approaching him at speed, appeared to accidentally drop a large envelope which slid towards him. The word 'Merrial' was written across it. Merriel stooped to pick it up, noticing his name had been misspelt. He'd averted his gaze for a split second and rose to glimpse the blade in the extended hand of his unexpected messenger. He parried the blow but the knife sliced his upper arm. He was off balance and fell hard on the tiles, groping for his gun. He was not quick enough to avoid a kick to the side of his head which carried such force it spun his body on the polished floor like a Catherine wheel. In an instant, Kierack was on him, gripping his chin with one massive hand and his crown with the other, giving a sharp twist. The neck snapped with a loud crack. Kierack kept pressure on Merriel's windpipe until the detective's legs ceased their scrabbling.

There were voices in the corridor behind him and the sound of approaching footfalls. In short order, Kierack pulled Merriel's lifeless body into the janitors' room and shut the door quietly behind him. He held still for a moment, listening to the voices of a man and woman pass by and fade as the couple went into the wash room, the woman's heels clicking on the tiled floor.

Merriel's wallet held his Police I.D., two credit cards and fifty Euros in notes. Kierack checked the trouser pockets, locating the keys of the unmarked car on Place Horta and several Euros in change. He pocketed the wallet in his jacket – the keys and change into his trouser pocket along with the detective's gun and set about hauling the corpse to the cabinet.

It had been Newman's first time on the Eurostar. He hadn't known what to expect but had been pleasantly surprised at the smooth organisation. The seats were comfortable and the snack he and Gorman had taken at the stand-up café-bar two carriages away, had been appetising – something you couldn't say about most railway catering, he mused.

One of Inspector Grenard's men had been waiting for them at the barrier as they left the platform with the Inspector's apologies. He'd been called out. A car would pick them up at nine the next morning.

They'd spent the night in a three star hotel a few minutes walk from the station, Grenard's idea, apparently to save time. Newman was disappointed they had been unable to get on with things but he presumed Grenard had more pressing cases than his. He couldn't complain, his own arrival had been delayed by Hinkley's murder.

Gorman was cradling a second cup of coffee at a window with a street view in the small reception area. It was just before nine a.m. and the two detectives waited to be collected. Gorman had carried his cup through from the dining room in the hope he might be able to down it before the car came.

"How many of those do you get through in a day?" Newman asked, shaking his head disapprovingly.

"I lose count after the first five."

"You must be a quivering wreck by the end of the day."

"No, but I get a hell of a headache if I don't get my fix." Newman was still shaking his head when he saw a car draw up and a uniformed officer get out.

Twenty-five minutes later, they were shown into a third floor conference room at Police Headquarters in rue Marché au Charbon. Gorman showed his pleasure as a flask of coffee was brought in unbidden. He gave Newman a sideways glance. The room was carpeted and a long oval table with cushioned chairs placed around it, dominated the space. The street-side wall was of glass from waist high to the ceiling. A video projector hung on a bracket from the centre of the ceiling facing a screen on the wall at the end of the room.

The door opened and a tall man in his forties with black hair streaked with grey entered followed by two younger men each carrying folders which they set down on the table.

"Detective Inspector," he said, holding his hand out to Newman. "I'm Grenard and these are Pieters and Delfic."

"Pleased to meet you," Newman said in reply and then,

gesturing to Gorman, "This is Detective Sergeant Gorman,"

Grenard shook Gorman's hand.

"Please – sit."

Pieters or Delfic, Newman wasn't sure which was which, served coffee all round and produced a plate of doughnuts from a side cupboard.

"I'm sorry I didn't meet you, we had a murder on the other side of town. You know how it is, I'm sure."

Newman nodded, he knew how it was alright – it was what had kept him single. Despite some near successes, in the end though, it was always the job that killed it. It was the uncertain hours and the ditching of plans made long in advance. The women he'd known just weren't prepared to put up with it but he knew many officers who had wives who obviously had. How did *they* manage it?

"I think the best way to open," Inspector Grenard began, "would be if we tell you what our investigation has uncovered so far and then, you follow with events in London."

The Inspector looked at Newman with an expression that sought approval.

Newman nodded.

"Good," Grenard continued. "Luc de Grood, let's talk about him."

The Inspector gave a hand signal to Pieters who opened his file and spread its contents on the table in front of him. Newman had identified him finally, noticing the name on the folder.

"On Tuesday, March 24th we received a call from Jean Fochet, the janitor of the Lanse building in Rue de Cornet.

He had discovered the body of Mme. De Grood. She was in her bath with her wrists cut."

Newman was impressed with Pieters' English; it was a hell of a lot better than Newman's French which ran to greetings and goodbyes only.

"How long had she been dead?" he asked.

"About a week, her killer had made a crude attempt to make Mme. De Grood's death appear as suicide."

"How did the janitor come to be in the apartment – did he have a key?"

"Yes, he had a key. It is a condition of the building that the janitor has a key for emergencies and in this case, it turned out to be helpful."

"Yes, I see but what made him go in?"

"The meter reader."

Newman's expression was questioning.

"Every month, a meter reader from the electricity company calls to read the meters in the building," Pieters continued. "In new buildings, the meters are on the outside of the apartments but the Lanse Building is old, built in 1910. The meters are in the kitchens of each apartment. Mme. De Grood always made a point to be in but if she had to go out, she would tell Fochet and he would accompany the reader."

Gorman, who up to this point had listened silently, savouring a cup of coffee, looked up at Pieters.

"What do we know about Fochet? Is he a suspect?"

"It was the first thing we thought of. He found the body, what was he doing there – all that kind of thing but we struggled to find a motive. He's been working there for ten years since leaving the Army. He was honourably discharged after an accidental shooting on exercise where he was wounded. He has a first class reference from his commanding officer and several commendations. It would seem out of character."

"Is there any chance we could speak with Fochet? You can never be sure.." Gorman began but Pieters cut across him.

"Forgive me, Detective but there are reasons we believe it more likely that Luc de Grood is more of a candidate for the crime. In any case, Monsieur Fochet has taken a few days to visit his sister in Lille; he'll be back at the end of this week. But to go back to Luc de Grood – over the last five years, there have been seven call-outs to domestic incidents involving the de Groods. All the calls came from the wife but when it came to the formalities, she always refused to press charges. De Grood was a salesman for Jensen valves. They make valves for the oil industry. The valves are not the kind of thing you'd find in your kitchen. A Jensen valve can sometimes be the size of a small car. From what we understand from Fochet, de Grood was away for periods of a week or more visiting clients around the world.

"So his wife was alone in the flat during the day?" Gorman enquired.

"No, she had a job at a veterinarian clinic about five minutes' walk across Place Jourdan but in the evenings she was at home. According to Fochet, de Grood was a jealous man."

"I'm sorry to interrupt, Detective Pieters, but how would he know that?" It was Newman this time.

"I'm coming to that, Detective Inspector. Fochet was slow

to admit it but de Grood paid him several times to let him see the building's security footage. The building is old but the tenants paid for a digital system a year ago. The entrance is monitored and there are two cameras in the corridors on each of the four floors. The comings and goings from the elevator and anyone in the corridors entering or leaving the apartments is caught on the system. Apparently, the arrangement developed from an occasional request, when de Grood would sit with Fochet in his basement flat to skip through the footage captured during his absences to Fochet making a disc of the feed from the corridor outside the de Grood flat for every period Luc de Grood was away on business."

"What was de Grood's explanation for wanting the discs?" Newman again.

"He was quite open about it – he didn't trust his wife. He wanted to see if she'd had any visitors while he was away."

"Oh, I see." Newman pondered out loud. "He must have spent hours in front of a screen."

"Fochet says he could have saved him the trouble; nobody ever went into the apartment while he was away, only his wife. He tried to reassure de Grood but he was having none of it."

"Something must have happened for him to go ape-shit. He must have seen something on one of the discs."

"Apparently, it didn't take much," Inspector Grenard interjected. He signalled to Delfic. Delfic pushed his chair back from the table, flicked a wall switch and the blinds closed, dimming the room to half-light. He went back to his seat and pointed a remote control at the DVD player atop the side cupboard from which the doughnuts had been produced. He hit 'Play' and an image of a corridor with the entrances of the four apartments on the floor where the de Groods had theirs, appeared on the wall behind Grenard.

"We checked the footage for the week preceding the death."

"And...?" Newman asked.

"No-one, other than Mme de Grood, went into the de Grood's apartment. However, *she* did go into one of the other apartments."

Grenard had grabbed the attention of both English detectives. He nodded to Delfic again and the screen showed movement. The figure of a woman suddenly appeared from a doorway on the right of the picture. She crossed to the door opposite and pressed the entry bell. The door itself was only partially visible. The camera was positioned to catch movement in the corridor and so captured the doorways side-on. D.I. Newman studied the jerky footage of Mme. de Grood waiting for the door to open. She took a step back as a man appeared in the doorway. His back was to the camera and he stood half in and half out of the apartment. After a few moments of conversation, he ushered her inside.

"Who's the neighbour?" asked Gorman.

"We don't know for sure. The apartment was rented by a lawyer, Jens Calder. He's a partner in a firm here in Brussels but we haven't been able to contact him; he's on leave in Kenya with his family on a bush safari. He left the day after we estimate Mme. De Grood was killed. When we called his mobile it was out of area but I suppose that was to be expected if he is in the middle of nowhere."

"Is he a suspect?"

Grenard thought about the question for a moment.

"Not yet…but there's something not quite right about the arrangement – he has a wife and two children but they have never been here according to the janitor. His colleagues at his office know nothing of the apartment; they say he has a house in the suburbs."

"Maybe he took the flat on behalf of a client," Newman offered. "Do you have a shot of him?"

"Yes," replied Grenard, turning to Delfic and giving him a nod. "This next sequence was taken by the cameras in the entrance lobby."

When Detective Delfic had changed the disc, he pressed the play button on the remote. The screen came to life again with jerky frames of figures coming into the building as well as those leaving. The picture quality was good with the screen split in two; one half displayed a long shot of the hallway the other, a close-up of the door. The facial features of every person entering were captured in reasonable detail. Gorman was about to remark on the high quality when a new sequence of images took his words away.

"Hold that frame. Now go forward one frame at a time." Delphic adjusted the remote to the single frame setting and set the pictures rolling forward frame by frame. A man in his seventies was captured coming through the door. The camera caught a partial profile. He was looking down to put his keys into his pocket. As the series of still pictures progressed, the man's head began turning towards the lens, capturing his features in close-up.

"Stop right there," Gorman commanded excitedly and threw a glance at Newman.

Inspector Grenard gave the English detectives a puzzled

look.

"Gentlemen, do you know this man?"

"He's now the reason we're here," replied Newman. "This is Professor Milo Ferretti or was, I should say – and this little video says we've found our link and at least one part of my case is finally coming together."

Grenard lifted his eyebrows, quizzically. "One part of your case?"

"Yes, one part, the other looks as if it might be something else altogether. I'd better explain – if that's alright with you gentlemen and you've done with Luc de Grood?"

"Yes, yes, please enlighten us," Grenard replied. "The floor is yours."

Newman took the next fifteen minutes going over the circumstances of Milo Ferretti's supposed suicide and the events surrounding the Professor's niece, including the murder of his officer.

"We thought it was all connected but, from what we've learnt from you today, the evidence points to de Grood being the Professor's killer. Now all we have to do is find out who is after Sophia Ferretti."

Grenard stood up. "I think now would be a good time to break for lunch and then we'll go to the Lanse Building – give you a chance to look around. It might help."

18

Sam Buckley rose from his desk as Sheldon Blane came into the room. He gestured to Blane to sit on one of the three black leather sofas surrounding a coffee table. The comfortable meeting area was where Buckley liked to discuss matters in a more informal manner than he would do if he were in the boardroom. Francesca, Buckley's P.A., stood expectantly in the doorway, her tall figure almost in silhouette against the sunlit walls of the outer office.

"Can I get you a coffee, Sheldon?" Buckley asked.

Blane shook his head.

He turned to Francesca. "Thanks, Franky. I'll call if we change our minds."

When he was sure the door was closed, he made his way to the sofas and sat down opposite Blane.

"Which is it, Sheldon, seven or eight days to go?"

"Eight but I'm working on making it sooner."

"Have we given them everything – are they happy now?"

"If there's anything more they could possibly need, I can't imagine what it might be. It seems as though their man, Allsop, has trawled through every piece of paper and file covering the last six years and more. Some of the stuff was already archived and had to be shipped back to the office."

"So, is he done?"

"He says so."

There was a pause, then Buckley said, "I had a call this morning…. from an American journalist."

"Oh?" Blane was surprised Buckley should mention it. The pink sections had been calling since the announcement of the takeover.

"This one's a bit different from the run-of-the-mill; she's a feature writer for the financial section of *The Seattle Times*."

"Okaaay," Blane drew the word out, still wondering why this should be significant.

"I've seen some of her work; it's very thorough and she has a reputation for digging deep into the main players and the impact takeovers have on the market. She hasn't indicated she has any agenda, just that she is writing a feature on the takeover by Reimer and, as Reimer are a Seattle based company, it's of obvious interest to her readers. As far as I can gather, her piece will feature the C.E.O of Reimer and his deputy and then, of course, you and me."

"Well, she can dig away; she'll end up with a hole and nothing in it."

"Look, I'm just being devil's advocate here. You know how they are. They offer you honey then shove an assegai up your arse. I'm just being cautious, that's all, it's my nature – we're so close now, I don't want anything to go wrong."

"Nothing's going to go wrong, Sam. I think you're over reacting. This journalist – what's her name?"

"Juliet Laskey."

"Okay then…this Juliet," he continued, "she's probably

going to write something positive – a feature to oil the wheels."

Buckley paused for a moment then forced a brief smile.

"I hope you're right. What set me off was something she put together about 'Steamers' six months ago."

"The clothing chain – didn't they go under?"

"Yes," Buckley replied, "and thanks, in no small part, to Ms. Laskey."

He'd got Blane's attention now.

"If you believe the management of Steamers, they had a blip in their cash-flow, nothing serious just a temporary shortfall. They'd organised cover with their bank who'd insisted they take in a partner for extra confidence. Everything was done and dusted. All that remained were the signatures. This is where Juliet Laskey came in. She'd been following Steamers for a while and thought the problems went deeper than their C.E.O. was letting on. She'd also had a tip from an insider who'd told her all was not well and the manufacturing had been moved to India and there were child labour issues. She went on to prove at least some of their product did not conform to the labour laws. The deal with their bankers went out the window and their prospective partners denied they'd ever been in a deal."

"Yes, I remember now. So, that was her. Well she'll find no child labour here. If we can survive the scrutiny of that ferret Allsop, we can welcome Ms. Laskey with open arms."

"I've always been proud of what we do here but you know how some of these types are when it comes to big numbers and golden goodbyes for the execs, they get pimples on

their arses and put some kind of undertone on the thing."
Blane was smiling.

"When is she coming in?"

"This afternoon, to see *me*. I said I'd let her know when you could fit her in. Call Franky with a time, can you."

"I'll look in the diary…and don't be concerned; I'll handle Ms. Laskey and I'll be checking for pimples."
They laughed in unison.

"I think I'll have that coffee now."

Just before two, D.S. Burrows stepped onto the platform at Brussels' Midi station. He looked up towards the barrier and spotted a tall man standing amongst a group at the gate. Burrows had a curious sense of déjà vu as he fixed his gaze on the man who was a clear head and shoulders above those around him. He was holding a small placard with the word Ferretti written across its face in felt marker. Hardly discrete, Burrows thought, but made no more of it than a difference in culture. He shook off his unease and signalled Rick and Sophia to follow him onto the platform.

The journey time had passed quickly enough. It was broken by a visit to the restaurant car where all three of them stood at high tables chatting and drinking coffee. Sophia had taken a call from Gerald Hope. Frans Helder would now meet them at their hotel at seven thirty and not at the station as planned – he was stuck in meetings. Sophia was jumpy about it at first and had Newman not arranged for a pick-up by the Belgian Police, she'd have told Burrows they'd be joining him on the first train back to London but, as they were to have their very own Police escort for the whole of their stay, she let the thought go.

They descended from the train and tucked in behind Burrows in the swell to the gate, the wheels of their overnight bags rattling on the hard surface. With a minimal gesture, Burrows caught the eye of the tall placard carrier who crumpled the card and tossed it into a waste bin before heading over.

Burrows held out his hand. "Burrows, D.S. Burrows, you must be Merriel."

"Yes, I'm Merriel." The tall man produced an I.D. and held it up briefly before returning it to his pocket. "I'm very pleased to meet you," he continued, in an accent Burrows couldn't quite place. "This must be Miss Ferretti and Mr. Devan?"

Rick and Sophia nodded in unison.

"Good, shall we get going – I presume you want to go to your hotel?"

"Yes," Sophia replied, as she turned to D.S. Burrows. "Thanks for babysitting us. Have a good trip back."

"I will. You've got my number, so if there's any problem, call me." He looked up at their new guardian. "Good to meet you – take care of them."

"Oh, don't worry, I will."

Burrows took one more look at the party of three then turned and walked off in the direction of the information desk.

Kierack reckoned he had three hours before Merriel would be missed. The pressure of time and the unknown sent a squirt of adrenaline through him. This is what his job was all about – stalking the unseeing and then the kill – the anticipation sent his heart thumping. He looked into the rear-view mirror; both his charges were content and taking in the city as he drove with gloved hands through honking traffic to the hotel in Boulevard Charlemagne. He'd explained in matter-of-fact tones that Police regulations required them to sit in the back seats, omitting to tell them, of course, that he could lock them in there at any time if he so wished – Merriel's car was fitted with rear door locks operated from the driver's seat to contain the more lawless of its passengers. That was not part of his plan though, not yet, anyway.

The girl had asked him to get them to the hotel then, after they'd checked in, take them to an address on the Rue de Cornet. *This* would be where his plan would play out. He'd already been there preparing for the visit he knew his targets would wish to make, thanks to intelligence provided by the Boss. How the guy had come up with the information, he had no idea but it was right on the money.

What *had* been a surprise was to find Police crime-scene tape across the door of the flat opposite. There was no Police presence however, and he put it down to an old on-going investigation or that someone had simply forgotten to come back and tidy up. Ernst wasn't unduly concerned and had set about his work disabling the CCTV system. There was no reply from the janitor's flat. He had his story as an interested future tenant ready to trot out but didn't get the chance because the janitor seemed to be on vacation. One look at the mail piled in the janitor's box in the lobby confirmed this. It was of no consequence; he'd located the recorder behind a panel with no more than a filing cabinet lock. Kierack disconnected the machine from its power source after removing the disc. There'd been one tricky moment, the sound of a tenant inserting a key into the front door from the outside. He'd ducked down behind the counter as she passed by unaware of his existence.

D.S. Geoff Burrows had found a window seat and as the light faded outside, he dozed. After three efforts to call both Newman and Gorman and hearing the 'out of area' message, he'd worked out that neither of the detectives had thought to remove the bars on foreign networks before leaving London. It was no big deal though, he merely wanted to confirm the handover. He woke pondering the situation; he ought to tell *someone*. Fumbling in his coat pocket, Burrows found the scrap of paper where he'd noted Grenard's number.

There were about thirty minutes remaining before the train would enter the tunnel and his phone would lose signal. The number rang as soon as he dialled it, there were no bars on *his* phone. He was put through.

"Inspector Grenard?"

"No, I am his assistant. Can I help?"

"This is Detective Sergeant Burrows. I was trying to find my colleagues."

"Ah yes, Inspector Newman and.."

"Their phones don't seem to be working. I wanted to inform them I handed over the passengers to Merriel."

"They are at lunch, I'm afraid but I can pass the message."

"Thank you."

"No problem. He didn't frighten you then – Merriel." The assistant's voice betrayed some inside humour.

"Sorry, I don't understand."

"We joke with him about his scar. He sometimes calls it his Frankenstein mark."

"Where, where is it – his scar?" Burrows was suddenly frantic.

"You can't miss it. An old knife wound across his face." Burrows stayed silent, the wind knocked out of him.

"The Merriel I met, had no scar."

"If there was no scar, that was not Merriel."

"You need to get them to call me right away. I'll be in the tunnel soon – right away please." He sank back into the seat and closed his eyes, running the scene at the station over and over. He froze the action at the point he'd taken that first glance up the platform to the gate – the moment of his uneasy déjà vu when he spotted Merriel or someone, as he now knew, posing as Merriel. It wasn't the man himself who'd sparked something, it was the grouping – him amongst the group, head and shoulders above the others. With a sickening feeling rising from his stomach, Burrows remembered where he'd seen a similar image, at the traffic light in Oxford Street – Bob Hinkley's murder. The grouping was the same with a towering figure at its centre. He dialled Sophia's number; it rang but she didn't pick up. As he hung up, his mobile trilled almost immediately – a local number he didn't recognise.

"Burrows?" It was Newman.

"Sir, I'm sorry…, he showed me I.D."

"You're sure it wasn't Merriel?"

"Merriel has a scar across his face; whoever it was, he sure as hell had no scar. It's worse sir."

"Go on."

"I think it's the same guy who got Hinkley."

There was silence at the end of the line.

"Did you try the girl?"

"She's not picking up."

Another silence, then, "I'll call you later." The line cut.

19

It wasn't necessary for them to check into separate rooms but for appearance's sake, they had done so. The rooms were adjoining and the door between was unlocked by 'Housekeeping'. Sophia had dressed casually in a short jacket over a roll neck sweater, jeans and trainers when she'd left home that morning, anticipating once they'd checked out Uncle Milo's flat, they might have time for a look round before the shops closed and the meeting with Frans Helder.

They freshened up and headed to the lifts.

"He doesn't say much – our protection officer," Rick observed, as he hit the button marked 'Lobby'.

"You're right, he's not the greatest when it comes to chit-chat but I suppose babysitting two tourists isn't exactly his idea of Police work."

"I think he'll get pretty fed up if he has to follow us around all day."

"We don't have a choice; I'll be glad when we're back in London."

"Yeah, you're right. It's not exactly a carefree atmosphere."

The doors opened onto the lobby, busy with a group of Japanese tourists milling while they waited for their guide to check them in. As Rick and Sophia crossed to the exit,

Sophia plucked a 'What to do in Brussels' leaflet from a stand at the 'Guest Relations' desk.

"Just in case we get bored of *other* things," she smiled mischievously.

After a brief scan of the parked cars dotted along the entrance ramp, they spotted their ride; Kierack was sitting in the unmarked Police car twenty metres away. He rolled the window down and waved to attract their attention.

"Are we ready to move?" he asked, with all the geniality he could find as they drew near.

They nodded.

"Do you know where Rue du Cornet is?" Sophia was fumbling in her handbag for the keys to the apartment and her address book. She found the book and flicked over its leaves as they climbed into the back seats. "The Lanse building," she said finally.

"Don't worry, Miss Ferretti, I know exactly where it is. We can be there in a few minutes."

Rick and Sophia sat in silence taking in the city from the rear of their chauffeur driven Police car. Kierack negotiated the traffic around the European Union headquarters and down Rue Froissart, turning before Place Jourdan into Rue du Cornet. A tranquil street of town houses for well-off professionals, Rue du Cornet boasted tree-lined pavements and the convenience of adjacent shops and restaurants in Place Jourdan. The Lanse building was a little way up on the right, a cream painted period building with the obvious signs of recent renovation. Parked cars prevented Kierack from leaving the unmarked Police vehicle right outside. Instead, he pulled up on the opposite side of the street.

"Okay," he said, "we're here."

Sophia looked up at the building through the car window wondering what she would find inside. How much of Uncle Milo would be there if anything. Maybe it was just a crash pad and there would be the bare minimum – only what he needed to eat and sleep. I'll soon find out, she thought, as she opened the car door.

Kierack followed them as they crossed the road to the building entrance. He glanced up and down the street for any sign of the Police who had taped up the door of the flat opposite the Professor's. There was no-one, the only movement, a scrap of paper caught in a gust – skidding along the pavement.

Sophia had two keys. She guessed the entrance key first time and pushed into the lobby. There was a caretaker's counter on the right but there was no-one manning it. She walked over and peered behind. There were shelves but they were empty save a pad with a ballpoint attached. She took out the pen and lifted the fly-leaf, blank.

"It's flat five – second floor I'd guess."

She hit the button once they were all in the lift. Kierack stood at the back, his pulse going up a gear with the anticipation of the coming drama.

Deep carpet turned their footfalls to muted thuds as they left the lift for flat number five, halfway down the corridor. Sophia inserted the key and pushed open the door.

Rick followed her into a small hallway. Kierack kept back a few paces and quietly closed the door behind him. Sophia ignored the cloakroom to her left and went into the lounge. The floor was covered from wall to wall in deep pile grey-blue carpet. Two leather easy chairs with matching sofa were positioned around a low table. Other than a few magazines scattered on the table, there was no other sign of occupation. The blinds were open and a hatch on the far wall gave a view to a kitchenette lit from an unseen window.

"This must be the bedroom," she said, pushing a door to her right.

The curtains were open, the room filled with dull afternoon light. A fitted wardrobe was let into the facing wall, its wood effect laminate matched the headboard and side tables of the double bed. She slid back the door; it was empty save a few wire hangers. The bed was stripped. Sheets, pillow cases and duvet were neatly folded in a pile with two pillows at the centre of the bed. A table lamp was placed at the side of the mirror on a dressing table but there was nothing personal, no ornaments or pictures only a few coins in a shallow steel dish about the size of a dinner plate on one of the bedside tables. Rick guessed it was where Milo emptied his pockets before retiring.

He looked around the room. "This is more of a place to stay than a home. There's nothing here but the bare essentials." Sophia nodded her agreement and noticed a roll of thick black duct tape on the bedside table next to the dish. She was about to examine it when her phone rang in the depths of her handbag.

"Don't answer that."Kierack commanded menacingly.

She turned, bewildered to see him pointing a pistol, elongated by a fat silencer, at her chest.

"Now, sit on the bed – you too, Mr. Devan."

Hesitantly and in disbelief, they did as ordered.

"Who are you? Are you going to shoot us?" Sophia clung

to Rick, trembling.

"Never mind who I am, just know you've caused me a great deal of trouble over the last few days – and no, I'm not going to shoot you if I can help it – far too many clues for the forensic team. I have something different in mind involving gas and an explosion. Now, Mr. Devan, please pick up the roll of tape and tape Miss Ferretti's elbows together behind her back."

Rick stared at him. "You're the guy – you set Sophia's flat to go up."

"This time there'll be no mistake – now, get on with it." Kierack waved the gun at him.

He slowly picked up the roll of tape, looked into Sophia's terrified eyes then back to Kierack eight feet away. Whatever Kierack had planned for them didn't involve them ever leaving the flat. If he was going to do something, it had to be soon. He looked around for something, anything to use as a weapon.

"Forget it; I'll have a bullet in you before you can take a breath. Now, tape her up." Kierack stepped forward and brought the barrel of the gun down hard against the side of Rick's head, sending a blinding stab of pain across his skull. A warm trickle ran down his cheek to the corner of his mouth, salty to the taste. He clutched his head – it hurt like hell – swayed as he got to his feet, picking up the roll of tape and leaning over Sophia.

"Play along," he whispered, as he gently brought her arms behind her back. He tried to make his words sound conspiratorial as if he had a plan, anything to give her hope.

"No talking," Kierack snapped, brandishing the gun. "Any more, and you'll feel this again."

He looked up at Kierack who had stepped back again.

"Okay, okay, I'm doing it."

Then, two things happened. One, by accident, the other by providence. In his nervousness, Rick dropped the tape. It rolled across the floor to Kierack's feet. Kierack, suspecting a ploy, stepped aside, raising his arm, threatening to strike Rick again but a loud rap on the front door knocker caused him to turn his head to the direction of the sound. Rick didn't hesitate. He pushed Sophia aside, dived for the steel dish, upending it and spinning it hard towards Kierack in one movement. Kierack got off one wild shot before the steel Frisbee struck him squarely under his chin sending him reeling. Rick leapt up and tore the lamp from the dressing table, crashing it against Kierack's skull – sending him to the floor and his gun out of his hand.

"Run," he shouted to Sophia.

She was already bolting for the door as Rick followed up his attack, grabbing the dressing table chair and bringing it down repeatedly on Kierack who was scrabbling for the gun. Rick kicked it to the corner of the room then gave another kick to the side of Kierack's head. The guy just wouldn't stay down. Rick needed to go and now. He ran for the bedroom door, slamming it behind him and turning the key – anything to delay their would-be assassin who was already getting up.

As Rick sped out the front door, he passed a bemused woman holding a clipboard. Whatever she was selling, there was no sale here today, he thought, as he made for a door marked 'Sortie' at the opposite end of the corridor to the lift, hoping to God it concealed stairs to the street and Sophia.

"Little bastard," Kierack mumbled as he struggled to his feet, clutching his neck. The force of the dish had pushed his Adam's apple into his throat, momentarily cutting the air supply to his lungs. As he stooped to retrieve his gun, blood from a head wound plopped in blobs to the carpet. He felt unsteady but, after a moment of wooziness, stood up and his senses began to return. He went for the bedroom door, shooting out its lock and near tearing it from its hinges in his haste.

In the corridor outside and coming close to knocking her over, Kierack brushed past the woman canvasser who had almost certainly been the individual guilty of distracting him by rapping so damn hard on the door – he should shoot the bitch for that alone.

The door to the emergency stairs was slightly ajar but closing slowly against the resistance of a hydraulic ram, telegraphing Rick and Sophia's escape route. He pushed through and took the stairs three at a time then stood out in the street scanning left and right for any sign of them – nothing. The light was fading as he ran down to the end of the road and stood at the corner of Place Jourdan, scrutinising the pedestrians in the square. Then a glimpse of them – they were running into a street leading off on the other side. Keeping his pistol under his coat, Kierack cut across between the parked cars and chased into the street after them.

There were no pedestrians to hinder Rick and Sophia. They slowed and glanced back at their pursuer then darted off as he gained on them. Ernst could see the pavement was blocked ahead of them by commercial refuse bins, waiting for the night collection. They would be forced into the road.

Traffic was very light; only one car had passed in the last few moments. He veered into the road, sliding to one knee and taking aim at the point he expected them to emerge from the parked cars lining the street.

Suddenly, the world turned over and the pain of a thousand blunt hammers striking as one, seared into his right side. His brain held the frozen image of his quarry staring back down the road at him in amazement, then he was flying into blackness.

Rick and Sophia stood motionless in the road blessing their luck. They'd stepped out to avoid the refuse bins blocking their path and had glanced down the road just as Kierack had jumped out from behind a parked car thirty yards away. He'd gone to one knee and was taking aim at them but, in his passion for the kill, was unaware he'd stepped into the path of a speeding sports car which had no time to avoid him. The impact had sent him spinning through the air before he landed on the roof of a car parked on the opposite side of the street.

The driver of the sports car got out as inquisitive bystanders, who had been drawn out of the square by the sound of screeching tyres, began to gather. A car was wailing its alarm and flashing hazard lights and attracting onlookers. Kierack's body lay motionless cradled by a cavernous dent in its roof.

Rick took Sophia's hand. "Let's get out of here," he said, in a low voice.

They began to walk cautiously back down to Place Jourdan on the opposite side of the street. The sound of distant sirens persuaded the pair to pick up their pace. Rick's head was throbbing and he put his hand to the wound. It had stopped bleeding but his hair was matted with dried blood.

Sophia turned to him. "I need to go back to the flat. My bag's there with my passport, credit cards – all that; I think it'll be safe enough. She gestured towards Kierack. "I don't think he'll be going anywhere for a while. We could see to that while we're there," she added, pointing to the wound on Rick's temple.

"It's okay for the moment but you're right about our friend over there; he could be dead but if he's not, I don't think he'll be chasing us any time soon. Let's get your stuff and go back to the hotel; I can clean up when we get *there*."

"I'm thinking London."

"Whatever you say."

20

On the second floor of the Lanse Building, Milo's door lay open. Rick pushed it wide and beckoned Sophia to follow.

The interior was gloomy in the dying daylight. Sophia made to flick the light switch.

"Don't touch it," Rick shouted, knocking her hand away. "We don't know what he's done in here; it might be something like the set-up at your place. Let's do what we have to do in the dark and get the hell out."

She nodded.

They went directly to the bedroom. The door was a mess, shot through at the lock and torn from one of its hinges. It groaned as she forced it open. Her handbag was where she'd left it on the bed – the spot where not long ago, she'd expected to die in a gas fuelled inferno. The thought sent a shiver through her and she began to shake uncontrollably, tears running down her cheeks. Rick put his arms around her and wiped her face with the palm of his hand.

"It's over now, the guy's history. In a few hours, we'll be back in London."

"How do we know he was the only one, there might be another one."

"We don't, so let's not hang around to find out."

She stepped over the wreckage of the table lamp, spying

the steel dish where it had fallen from its delivery to Kierack's neck.

"That was one lucky shot," she said, a faint smile doing its best to break through."

"Luck didn't come into it. Now, let's go."

She scooped up her bag then stopped suddenly; there were noises in the next room. They kept silent, expecting Kierack to burst in like a recurring nightmare.

"Anyone there?" a hesitant voice called out.

They relaxed, instantly recognising the Estuary tones of D.I. Newman. First Rick then Sophia trod through the wood splinters littering the floor in the doorway to be met by Newman, D.S. Gorman and three other men Rick didn't recognise. Newman shook his head.

"If there's trouble anywhere these days, I run into you two."

"Believe me, Detective Inspector, we're pretty fed-up with it too," Rick said, holding his hand up to the gash on his head which had suddenly begun to throb again. "How did you know where to find us?"

"Burrows called – he thought you might need us; he found out, quite by chance, the man who met you wasn't who he said he was – and there was a call from one of the neighbours. Apparently, he'd let a woman conducting a survey for the municipality into the building. She'd gone back, banging on his door, saying she'd been almost flattened by a man with a gun."

Newman gestured to Grenard. "This is Inspector Grenard. He's the boss around here and these are two of his best men. Now, do you want to tell us what's been going on?"

Rick went over every detail since leaving Burrows at the

Midi Station, explaining their escort had given them no cause for them to suspect he was anyone other than Detective Merriel from the Brussels Police. He rounded off his account describing how their would-be assassin was sent on an upward trajectory in Rue Gray, about ten minutes away.

Sophia cut in. "Let's say we've seen enough of Brussels and we're on our way back to London."

"Miss Ferretti, I know…." Newman was interrupted by the ring of Detective Delfic's phone.

The detective's conversation was brief. He hung up and looked up at Grenard.They exchanged a few words in French then Grenard turned to Newman, grim faced.

"Detective Merriel has been found murdered at the Midi Station. It's too early to say for sure but the officer on the scene is of the opinion that Merriel was strangled. He was found by one of the cleaners in their chemical store."

Grenard turned back to his detectives and gave instructions in French. Rick heard Rue Gray mentioned but the discourse was too fast for him to follow. One of them left, the other pulled his phone out and began dialling.

Newman noticed blood seeping between Rick's fingers as he held his hand to his head. "I think we'd better get that seen to. Is there anywhere nearby?" he asked Grenard.

"Yes, I'll send Delfic with him in a moment but I have a few questions, if you can manage a few more minutes."

Ernst Kierack woke, opening his eyes slowly to a regular beep coming from his left. He made to turn towards the sound but there was some kind of brace holding his head in a fixed position. The smell of medical cleanliness filled his nostrils as his senses came back on-line and with them – pain, pain everywhere. He was in a hospital room. That much he could determine but had no recollection of how he got there. The bed had been set to hold him in a half sitting position which allowed him to take in some of his surroundings. There was little furniture – a night stand with a substantial water jug and tumblers resting on it, one metal-framed chair and a wheeled table of the kind that could slide over the bed for meals – a sink in the corner and, in his direct sight, a defibrillator. They must be expecting trouble, he thought. The walls appeared white but it was difficult to tell; the blinds were closed and the room was lit by concealed lights which were dimmed. In his peripheral vision, he could distinguish a drip of some kind travelling down a clear plastic tube into his left arm and a bell-push lying next to his hand. There was a cap clipped to the forefinger of his right hand; a wire ran from it but he was unable to see where it went. He had been stripped and dressed in a hospital gown and felt a little vulnerable in his nakedness – something he wasn't used to.

Whatever it was in the drip, it wasn't enough to kill the pain. He needed something stronger and pressed the bell-push. As a nurse entered a few moments later, light from the corridor outside spilled into the room and Ernst caught a glimpse of a uniformed guard, a Police officer maybe, silhouetted in the open doorway standing sentry. The nurse said something in French. Kierack shook his head, feigning incomprehension. He could understand her but his French required effort and he wasn't in the mood for effort.

"Deutsch?," he asked.

The nurse shook her head.

"English?"

She nodded. "You're back with us," she said. She was slim, in her early fifties and not unattractive with dark brown hair tied up under her cap. She wore spectacles with tortoiseshell frames that went with her hair.

"I need something for the pain." Kierack screwed up his face in a wince signalling agony to a much higher degree than he was actually feeling; he needed a big hit to get out of the place without the pain bringing him down before the cops did.

"I'll see what I can do. You're a very lucky man you know."

Kierack's expression questioned her idea of luck.

"Your x-rays just came, only a fractured rib and a bruised collar bone. Yes, you were lucky.....I think it was your muscles that saved you." She gave a knowing smile that said that she, along with others, had checked him out under his gown while he'd been comatose.

Kierack pointed to the brace restraining his head. "This is luck?"

"Just a precaution in case your neck was broken – but you're okay there; the doctor will be in to take it off soon. You'll have one big bruise though."

"Where are my clothes?"

She looked at him questioningly over the top of her spectacles. "They are in the closet but you won't be needing them for a while," she said, in an all-knowing tone. "You must rest. I'll be back with something for the pain."

He held up his hand with the pulse monitor clipped to his forefinger. "Can you take this off please; it's irritating me. I'll be fine without it."

"I think I can do that for you."

She flicked some switches on a machine out of his vision and removed the clip from his finger. The beeping stopped.

As she went out, he caught another glimpse of the guard at the door. This time, he was looking in and talking into his radio, calling the big boys, no doubt. Pretty soon, they'd be all over him like a rash, asking all kinds of questions he wasn't going to answer. Time to ditch his assignment and leave; it wouldn't be sensible to keep after the girl. If he got away now, they would have no idea who he was or where he came from – he'd been careful to deposit his passport with his suitcase in the left-luggage locker at the station after leaving his lodgings that morning. His gun was somewhere in the street but even if they found it, there'd be no prints. The other gun, the one he'd taken from Merriel, was still under the seat in the detective's car where Ernst had placed it ready for the unexpected. No, there was nothing to link him if he went now. A quick change to his salesman persona and he'd be a ghost on the next train – and not necessarily to London.

The door opened; the nurse was back.

"One of these and your troubles will vanish," she said, approaching him with a pink pill between her thumb and forefinger. He recognised the killer of all woes – Pethadine; he had a bottle of the stuff back at his flat for emergencies just like this and, in his younger days, had flown with it for recreational purposes. You don't need a woman when you've got one of these little babies, he thought but remembered it should be taken with the wariness of its silky ways snaking into your head and whispering messages of both euphoria and paranoia. On Peth, you can't trust either emotion. She handed it to him and then went to the night stand, pouring water from the jug into a glass tumbler and holding it close. "Here, take it with this."

Kierack swallowed the pill held between her thumb and forefinger, chasing it down with the water sucked through a straw. The nurse was studying him as he drank. So cordial, he thought. She seemed not to worry that there was a Police guard on the door. He wondered if she would be so relaxed if she knew his occupation. She clearly didn't and, he conjectured, neither did the Police; they hadn't put it together yet or there would be more than one man on the door. He was just someone of interest because a passer-by may or may not have seen him with a gun.

The nurse took the tumbler away and returned it to the night stand. "Give it five minutes and you'll feel better. I'll leave one more over here." She was giving her professional smile. "I'm going off shift now. The night nurse will be in later but if you need her before, call her with the bell."

His Police guard eyed him again as the nurse went out, craning his neck for a better view as the door closed. When it was firmly shut, Kierack pulled the drip from his arm then set about removing the frame from his head. It unclipped with ease and he sat up with his legs over the side of the bed. The move was too quick. Pain shot through his torso and the room swayed on a drunken wave of nausea. He clung to the bed frame to steady himself and paused to allow the blood pressure to equalise in his head. His surroundings began to stabilise and he carefully dropped his feet to the floor. A lightning bolt of pain crackled up his spine as he took a controlled step forward, his knee joints feeling like they belonged to some clanking robot in need of oil. He made it to the closet and gripped the door frame. His clothes were neatly folded, gloves on top. The contents of his pockets, including his phone, were tipped into an instrument dish on an adjacent shelf. His coat hung from a hook at the side.

Dressing was more difficult than walking but by the time he got round to his shoes, the drug was kicking in and he carefully eased his coat on then his gloves. Ernst slipped the paper tub containing the second Pethadine pill into his pocket. Using the towel at the sink, he wiped down any surface he might have touched then cracked the drapes and looked down at the rain soaked car park two storeys below, glistening in the yellow light from streetlamps.

The window was out of the question as far as escape went – the only way out was past the cop on the door. The drug had given him a feeling of wellbeing and the pain, although not gone, had been pushed back to a dull ache. Escape would need to be quick, hold the element of surprise with noise kept to a minimum and contained within a close area of the room.

Grabbing the jug and two glasses from the night stand, he tipped the water into the sink and took up a position behind the door. Simultaneously, he threw the glass tumblers at the floor at the base of the door and let out a piteous low moan.

The cop was in the room in an instant and could not sidestep as Kierack brought the jug down hard on his skull.

There would be CCTV in the corridor and Kierack took the only part of the officer's uniform that would be of use and, moreover, the only article that would fit – his cap. Pulling the peek as far down as possible, Ernst Kierack slipped out.

21

"I know you've been over it already, but I'd like you to tell me again – everything from the moment Burrows left you." Newman knew he might be pushing it but thought it was worth a try.

Sophia gave him a tired look and sighed irritably. "Yes, I've been over it with you twice now. Nothing's changed."

They were sitting in Rick's hotel room, Newman and D.S. Gorman on chairs with their backs to the window facing Rick and Sophia – close together on the bed. Inspector Grenard was down in the lobby checking at the reception desk for CCTV records covering the earlier part of the afternoon.

"I just want to pack up and go home," she continued.

"I quite understand but you're going to have to stay at least a day until Inspector Grenard has finished taking statements; one of his officers is dead, remember."

"Yes, and because of me. I need to get away – I don't feel safe anymore."

"You told me someone is coming to meet you at the hotel this evening," Newman continued as Rick put his arm round her.

"Frans Helder?"

"Yes. What time is Mr. Helder coming to see you?"

"Seven thirty was the arrangement but after all that's happened, I don't think I'll be up to small talk with an E.U. commissioner."

"I think it would be just the thing to keep you occupied. D.S. Gorman and I will be nearby at all times. From what I understand, you came here to meet Mr. Helder. As you can't go back to London, you might as well do what you came to do."

Rick turned to face her. "I think he's right. We're here now; we might as well get it over with as well as the stuff tomorrow. The next time they all want to see you, get them to come to London."

"Okay," she said, after a pause but with an undertone of, 'if anything else goes wrong, you will all pay dearly'.

Newman looked relieved; the last thing he wanted was a battle of wills with her.

"So, let's hear it one more time."

Inspector Grenard sat in the duty manager's office along a corridor behind reception. The Duty Manager, Charles Marcel, tapped his keyboard until his screen broke into a chessboard of flickering thumbnails displaying the recorded feeds from the hotel's security cameras. He tapped another sequence and the fifty-inch flat screen TV fixed to the wall opposite his desk, came to life with the same images but now larger and more discernable. Inset into each, was a small set of numbers indicating time and date. Marcel gave a sweeping gesture towards the display.

"Take your pick. I can enlarge and play any of these."

On the way to the hotel, Rick had described to Grenard how the man posing as their Police escort had waited for them in the car outside the entrance while they checked in

"I need to see the entrance and the ramp up to it. "

Marcel tapped the keys again and the screen split into two.

"This is the same view from different angles."

The picture on the left of the screen was from a high angle and gave a three-quarter view showing the tops of vehicles but also their registrations. The faces of guests as they arrived were only partially visible but would be caught by other cameras in the lobby.

Marcel pointed to the right side of the screen. The angle was much lower, shot from a camera fixed only a few feet from the ground at about the window height of an average saloon car.

"The camera is concealed in a lighting bollard at the edge of the down-ramp. It's a fairly new addition to monitor general activity around the entrance."

"Miss Ferretti says she checked in at about two thirty – can you confirm that?"

Charles Marcel rattled on the keyboard again.

"Fourteen thirty-eight to be precise."

"Okay then," Grenard said, directing a nod at the TV screen, "let's see the footage on these two from ten minutes before."

The time and date counters spun their numbers as Marcel jogged the frames until the time on both read fourteen twenty-eight. He glanced at Grenard who nodded his instruction to hit the 'Play' button. Immediately, the two frames, displaying alternative views of the same scene, came to life. The quality was good and the motion fluid with cars arriving and dropping their passengers before moving off and passing within a few feet of the bollard camera.

As he watched, Grenard became hopeful of capturing an image of Merriel's killer. He leaned towards Marcel without taking his eyes from the screen.

"How concealed is the camera in the bollard? he asked.

"Very – unless you know it is there, you wouldn't see it." Suddenly, Merriel's car came into view. Grenard craned his head closer to the screen as Sophia stepped out of the rear door on the hotel side and Rick from the other. Sophia stooped and ducked her head back into the car through the open door; seemingly talking to the driver whose door and window remained shut. Grenard cursed under his breath. After a few moments, Sophia withdrew her head and shut the door, striding into the hotel with Rick at her side. The car pulled away but stopped tight into the curb opposite the camera in the bollard. The driver's window was in clear view but rolled up. Behind the reflections on the glass, Grenard could only make out the ghostly outline of the man behind the wheel; he cursed again.

"Can you fast forward at double speed?"

Marcel obliged and the figures milling in the hotel entrance portico jerked back and forth amongst a constant flow of cars dropping guests and seemingly pulling away at high speed. The only object which stayed rooted like a stone statue, was Merriel's unmarked Police car with its driver's window firmly shut.

"Okay, freeze it there."

Grenard had spotted Rick coming out closely followed by Sophia; they didn't see the Police car immediately and were looking about them.

"Go at half speed now."

Grenard held his breath as he watched the driver's window of Merriel's car inch downwards in slow motion. A hand appeared – waving to Rick and Sophia and then the face of its owner; calling to them.

"Freeze it right there. Can you go in closer and give me a clear shot of him?"

"Just a moment." The Duty Manager moved a joy-stick and tapped his keyboard.

"Got you, you bastard," Grenard exclaimed, as the grainy features of Merriel's killer filled the screen. "Can you copy that shot?"

Marcel nodded.

"Good. Email it to this address, please." Grenard had scribbled across one of the Duty Manager's Post-its on the desk in front of him. He flipped open his phone and hit the speed dial for Delfic. One ring and it was picked up.

"Yes, Boss."

"There's a photo coming over to you now; it's our man. Run it through the system – see if anyone knows him. Have you traced which hospital they took him to yet?"

"The V.U.B, Pieters is on his way over there now."

"Get him some help; this guy's trouble and I don't want to take any chances."

"Understood."

22

Rick took Sophia's hands in his and forced a smile.

"Are all your weekends-away this challenging for your companions?"

"Not in this way….but challenging all the same," she replied, returning his smile and savouring the light moment. Newman and Gorman had gone to the lobby to meet up with Inspector Grenard, leaving them alone in the room, although two officers remained outside the door. This was as alone as they would get for a while. Sophia broke the moment, picking up and sipping a cup of coffee made from the room's DIY.

"Rick, what do you think," Her face suddenly showed the stress of the day, "…..about the whole Scale thing? Should I cut my losses and sell to the Wellers of this world – or should I tough it out for the real big bucks and possibly wind up dead in the process?"

"You've asked me this question three times before in different ways; it doesn't change the answer – you and only you can decide. If you are genuinely asking my opinion, I'd say keep on with it for all the reasons I've given before and even more so now."

"Why more so now?"

"Because they tried to kill us – I'm pretty sore about that

by-the-way. We got one of theirs though, so I reckon they're pretty pissed too. Once you've had your meeting, there's nothing they can do to stop Milo's Scale going through. If they're going to delay things, they have to do something before tomorrow. As we now have a genuine Police escort, I don't think anything will happen to us."

"I hope those are not famous last words." She cracked a smile and took another sip. "Seems a lifetime ago when I didn't have to look over my shoulder; I don't think I'll miss the feeling if we ever get out of this."

"We'll get out of it and you might find life dull."

"Listen, I long for dull." She leaned over and kissed him then looked at her watch. "We've got fifteen minutes before Helder; I need to freshen up." She drained her cup and went to her room through the connecting door.

The lift doors opened onto a lobby full of noisy guests milling about in their eveningwear on their way out, waiting to be called to taxis or biding time with partners before dining at one of the hotel's fine restaurants. Through the crowd, Rick caught sight of Inspector Grenard and Newman talking to a tanned athletic looking man near the reception desk. The conversation looked intense and Rick took the tanned man for Frans Helder and the subject of the conversation, the afternoon's events. Dave Gorman stepped out of the lift first, nodding for Rick and Sophia to follow. He'd rapped on their door five minutes earlier informing them Helder was downstairs and he'd take them down.

Sophia turned to Rick as they fell in behind Gorman. "Do you think that's our date?"

"No doubt about it. I think it's showtime."

They made their way through the throng to the reception desk. The two detectives and Helder stopped talking and faced them as they approached; Frans Helder's hand was extended.

"Miss Ferretti, I'm Frans Helder. The Inspector was just telling me of your ordeal today."

Sophia shook Helder's hand. He was a good-looking man in his late forties and spoke with an accent which added to his charm.The tan, she guessed, came from ski slopes featured in the photos she'd seen in Gerald Hope's office. He was easy in company and had an air of being at home on a yacht, executive jet or private island – there was nothing economy class about this guy. He was a real smoothie but his face was open and he looked her straight in the eye so, he was probably one of the good ones.

"Not quite the welcome we were expecting but the Inspector assures me we're safe now." She smiled and gestured to Rick. "This is my friend, Rick Devan."

Helder shook Rick's hand. "Shall we go somewhere quieter, the bar, maybe?"

He led the way. Grenard's phone rang.

"I'll catch you up," he called after them and put the phone to his ear. "Yes, Pieters, what is it?"

"He's gone, Sir. When we got here, the officer left to guard him was unconscious in the room and there was no sign of him."

"He only had one guard?"

"When he was admitted, they weren't sure what the risk was. A witness to the accident said he thought our suspect was holding a gun when he was hit by a car. It wasn't found at the scene so it wasn't clear if he was dangerous or not.

The witness could have been mistaken – it was late afternoon and not the best light conditions. The officer on guard wasn't one of ours; he was part of the hospital security team. The hospital had called it in and was waiting for someone from us."

"And?" Grenard said, impatiently.

"It wasn't prioritised; the dispatcher put a call out in the normal way. There were two patrolmen on the scene when I got here. They were dealing with a traffic accident nearby when they got the call and didn't leave until they'd finished up. When they finally got here, they found the guard."

Grenard let out a long sigh. "Dust the place for prints and see if there's anything else there we can use – CCTV. We need to find out who he is. Oh – and put out an all points with the photo; maybe we'll get lucky."

The bar could accommodate fifty people or more and was lit by concealed spots throwing pools of light onto tables and clusters of easy chairs. A breathy saxophone weaved its dusky tones through a relaxed atmosphere in contrast to the lobby's bustle. D.I. Newman and Gorman sat at the bar, backs to the counter drinking nothing stronger than Coke and keeping an eye on the party of three they were there to protect. Rick, Sophia and Helder were grouped at a corner table in comfy chairs. Grenard had parted from the detectives, leaving the number of his personal mobile and gone back to his office.

"I'll leave on a morning train," Newman said, taking a swallow and nodding in the direction of their charges. "You'd better tag along with them all day tomorrow until they've finished their business and giving statements. Just bring them back in one piece, please."

"No problem, Boss."

"Let me begin by saying how sorry I am for the ordeal you have endured today; it is unimaginable that someone would go to such lengths to prevent our meeting." Helder was leaning towards Rick and Sophia who were opposite. His expression showed genuine concern and although he leaned towards both of them, his eyes were holding Sophia's. Sophia remembered what Gerald Hope had said about worrying Frans Helder unnecessarily but things had gone way past saving Helder's sensitivities; she would dictate the rules from now on and he'd have to put up with it.

She held his gaze for a moment then said, "Yes, well I hope it's behind us now. I'll do what is required of me tomorrow and get back to London as soon as possible. I'm only still here because I don't want to let my uncle down."

Helder nodded his understanding.

"Your uncle was a man of vision. If he had survived to see his ideas put into practice, he would have received the gratitude of all Europeans. It is such an important law that we will pass; the everyday lives of millions will be rewarded with a new clarity, one that cannot be clouded by double-talk. Milo was passionate about this."

"Yes, I understand the importance but, when Gerald told me about my uncle's work, I didn't realise there would be people willing to kill me to prevent it getting to law. It's very frightening and I am tempted to take the money I was offered and forget I ever heard of 'Milo's Scale'."

"I too, was shocked when the Inspector told me what had

happened to you but….and I know this is easy for me to say, you must hold on for just a little longer. After all, you now have twenty-four hour protection. If you give up, it won't just be Milo you will let down but all those people he hoped to help."

She glanced at Rick. "We're here now, so we'll get on with it. In the light of what's gone on today, I'd like you to combine both meetings to one; I want to leave by midday. Please contact Jose Gabera and the other commissioners and tell them of the new timetable. If they can't make it, they'll have to come to London or talk to me by Skype."

"I'll see what I can do. Now, let's run through the agenda over a drink – what would you like?"

In the cab to the station, Kierack tried to hide the effects of his injuries. Even with the drug, climbing into the rear had been a study in controlled movement to avoid a grimace or anything that might attract unwelcome attention from the driver. He needn't have worried though; the driver had his mind elsewhere – bobbing his head in mini jerks to the rhythm of some beat or other pumped to his ears through headphones. Kierack held a deadpan expression as the driver's eyes flicked up to the rear-view mirror from the road at random intervals out of habit. It was dark though and Kierack's features were lit only fleetingly through the rain spattered windows by reflected street lighting or passing headlights, not long enough to be scrutinised or catch an occasional wince as the wheels of the cab passed over a pothole or a bump in the road.

Luck had been with him so far. Despite his brief visit to the hospital, time was also with him; it was only five forty-five on a very long day. He'd picked up a cab almost immediately and estimated he could make it to the station with time enough to retrieve his bag, change to embrace his salesman character and have the option to catch the Eurostar he'd booked or any other train out of town. They'd be looking for him now, he thought, but it would take time for them to get their act together; he had a window of about half an hour.

There had been tighter situations. What was happening now was *nothing* to worry about. What about the trip with Horst in Berlin; that was one on which to reminisce – he'd *really* thought it was all over *that* time. They were in a Mercedes saloon they'd jacked at a junction. Horst was driving and Kierack was pressing his hand to a bullet wound in his shoulder as sirens screamed behind them. Yeah, he'd resigned himself alright – but then, as had happened so many times in his life, fate had stepped in and something good happened. Not good for Horst, he caught a stray bullet in the back of the head which shot his brains onto the windshield, but good for Kierack. The bullet in his shoulder, although burning with the fire of a branding iron, had sharpened his senses. In one action, he'd reached for the door handle and Horst was out and Ernst was grappling the wheel with his good arm. In the rear-view, he saw the two pursuing blue-and-whites collide as Horst's spinning corpse fell into their path. Ernst smiled at the recollection and looked up as the cab pulled into the drop-off at the Midi Station.

He gave a reasonable tip to the cabbie, not too little or too much – nothing to make him remarkable enough to stick in the cabbie's mind for an inquisitive detective to pull out when it was his turn for a grilling. The driver barely looked up, his head still jigging to the beat in his ears.

Through the drizzle, Kierack could make out flashing blue lights at the far end of the entrance bay; he kept his distance and headed for the lockers and the adjacent washrooms. When he came out, the old Kierack was gone, replaced by a bespectacled businessman in a pinstripe. There were more Police now and he was beginning to think he'd misjudged his timing – pretty stupid to go to the very place they might look for him. On the other hand, they didn't know who they were looking for – just a tall guy in a long coat. The long coat had gone – wrapped in a plastic bag and ditched in a waste bin at a cafeteria as he sipped a cappuccino from a paper cup, taking in the lay of things.

The main ticket office had a cluster of blue uniforms but not enough for a manhunt. Maybe this was the normal compliment or maybe there was something else going on; there just didn't seem enough urgency in the way the officers were going about their business for there to be something specific – and the blue lights outside, a mugging maybe. Still, no sense in tempting fate; he wouldn't chance the ticket office but take the Eurostar to London. His boarding pass was already in his possession so there was no need to check in with anyone, just slip it into the auto barrier and he would be on his way.

The pain in Kierack's ribs was still holding off – just. In thirty minutes or there abouts, he'd need the other pill. He patted his pocket to reassure himself the little life-saver was there, crumpled his coffee cup into a bin and gingerly slung his bag over the better of his shoulders, joining the swell to the gate.

On the platform, hostesses stood at the first door of each carriage for the length of the train, checking boarding passes and guiding any confused passengers. He passed by several of them and ducked into an unattended door, walking the interior to his pre-booked aisle seat. As he sat down, it suddenly occurred to him his phone had been silent for the entire time since he woke in the hospital and that was surprising – the Boss never left him alone for more than a few hours. At the point of flipping it open, the reason became apparent; someone had turned it off during his down time. Pulling his clothes on, there had been other things on his mind – like the cop outside the door not to mention the pain engulfing his entire body; checking his phone hadn't entered his head.

The screen lit up with a dozen missed anonymous calls as his thumb pressed the phone into life – not anonymous to him though. All of them came from the same source – his employer's pay-as-you-go throw-away phone which had the single purpose of maintaining contact with his security advisor.

"Where the hell have you been?" the Boss's voice was angry and agitated in equal measure.

"It's good to talk to you too, Sir."

"What's been going on – is it done?"

Kierack let a silence hang for a moment then said, "There were problems."

"Problems? What kind of problems?"

"The Police are looking for me but they don't know where to look and even if they did, they don't know who I am or what I look like."

"Jesus Ernst, you're becoming a liability. Did the job get

done?"

"Like I said, there were problems."

"So, no, in other words."

Kierack didn't answer.

"Okay then," the voice at the other end of the line continued. "Did you get away clean?"

"I'll tell you in a couple of hours – I'm on the train."

"Forget the girl and Devan; I've moved things up a few days. It's too late for them to screw the deal now anyway. Call me when you get in; I may have another little job for you."

Kierack closed his phone, settled into his seat and closed his eyes. The Boss was clever and had looked after him well, knowing by doing so, he would always be sure of Kierack's loyalty. It explained why Kierack let him speak to him in what others might regard as disrespectful tones. In the past, Kierack might have broken a man's arm if there was any suggestion of disrespect – in fact, he *had* broken bones without compunction for lesser transgressions. ,His boss was different though; he was a very ruthless man and not frightened to dip his hands into the blood of others – blood that he'd spilt in the first place. No, the Boss was not a man to be trusted fully because where there was one Ernst Kierack, there could easily be another – with orders to remove the first if he got out of line.

23

It was seven thirty Tuesday night. Juliet was at her window table in her room at the Hilton overlooking Park Lane and beyond it, Hyde Park. She scrolled down her piece on Buckley; it was okay and that was the best she could say about it. As predicted, Buckley's history was unremarkable and reflected the character of a man with modest ambitions who had methodically trodden a road to the top. Nothing wrong with that, the guy had made it on his own terms and very soon would be cosseted in the comfortable security that only millions of dollars can bring. There was no edge though – no one killer deal that had set him on his way. His story made interesting – run-of-the-mill interesting – reading, but that's all.

There was a rap at the door.

"Juliet, it's Jack."

She went to the door and let in *The Seattle Times'* London stringer.

"Can I get you a drink, Jack?" she asked, as she ushered him to a chair.

"No, thanks, I'm driving home after this."

Juliet crossed to her laptop and hit the save button then settled herself into the easy chair opposite her visitor.

"So, Jack, what's new?"

"I've been digging and I might have something of interest."

"Oh?"

"Yes, concerning your Mr. Blane."

"Go on."

"Seems he has some kind of scary security guy. Nobody at the firm seems to know much about him only that he's big, German and bad. Rumour has it that Blane had a car accident once – his fault apparently – but when the guy that he ran into tried to claim from him, the fella wound up in the hospital with injuries similar to that of arms being broken by a big bad German."

"Do we have a name?"

"Better than that, we have a name *and* address. His name's Kierack, Ernst Kierack. Blane found him in Berlin a few years ago."

"How did you get all this stuff?"

"I had a hunch and went looking for a job at Buckley Blane's human resources department. They had three vacancies, one in the department itself. I asked if they were replacing someone or increasing the numbers. Turns out they'd fired someone called Doug last week. It wasn't difficult to track him down with a couple of phone calls back to the department from a pay-phone posing as a debt agency."

"And?"

"Douggie Raymond was very helpful after I'd plied him with a Caramel Macchiato at Starbucks and fifty pounds. He used the WI-FI in there to get into the system at his old office; they hadn't changed the protocols which he said was ironic." Jack paused for a split second and then continued in what Juliet took to be a take off of Douggie, "They were so damn smart in giving me the bum's rush because of their

258

'oh-so-diligent' security where I.T. was concerned – catching me out with some porn site or other but forgot to lock me out of the system when they fired my arse, – his words not mine," Jack added.

"So what makes a security guard so interesting?"

"No, no – this guy's not some Wells Fargo hick; rumour is, and it's only rumour – no actual evidence you understand, that he's a 'problem remover' is how Douggie Raymond put it. He's not someone you want to get on the wrong side of. Douggie only ever saw him at the office once when the guy picked up his I.D. tag – once was enough apparently. He was a man of few words with hands the size of trash-can lids. What made him more interesting was what happened to his file. Blane's P.A. – another one you shouldn't cross, by the way – went down to H.R. and asked for it. She never took it back and when the computer logs were routinely scanned at the end of the week, all reference to Kierack was gone."

"So if the file was removed, how was … Douggie able to hack something that wasn't there?"

"He had a little private file he kept in the system for quirky things – you know, childish boys' stuff and anything that amused him. He can't explain why he did it but he had an urge to save Kierack's file. When the real file disappeared from the main system, he was more curious and decided to keep it in his own cache in case it was worth something later. Turns out he was right. Mind you, he was so pissed with his old boss, he'd have given it up for free but I didn't think that would be quite right."

"Okay, getting back to this Kierack character – he doesn't exactly seem the type to give interviews."

"Well, yes," Jack agreed. "That's what I thought at first but there's been a lot of speculation in the Buckley Blane ranks that the takeover might mean a whole raft of them losing their jobs. It's just possible this Kierack character might be pissed with his boss. I would hazard a guess, if anyone knows where the bodies are buried, it's going to be him."

"That may be, but I think we'll keep him as a fall-back; I don't need his kind of trouble right now."

"Okay, understood but what about this for an idea. Raymond says the guy doesn't come to the office. What does he do all day for his money as 'security advisor'? – that's what Douggie says he's down as on the books. I could keep an eye on him for a day or so; see what he's up to – maybe we'll get something – unless you've got somewhere better for me to put in some time."

"No, I haven't. Go ahead – keep an eye on him; don't get caught though. I don't think he'll be a happy boy if he sees you. "

"I can look after myself."

She gave him a 'Don't let me have to visit you in the hospital' look.

"Okay, okay – I'll be careful."

"We understand each other then. Now, you'd better leave me to get on with my notes; I'm seeing Blane tomorrow afternoon."

"Good luck."

She smiled. "You too."

Jack had left his car in the underground car park beneath the Hilton and was back behind the wheel at a little after eight. His wife was expecting him at home in Ealing at nine, a journey of twenty minutes at this time of night at worst. As he slipped his ticket into the slot at the exit barrier, he checked the time again on the dash. His curiosity was getting the better of him and there was definitely time; he could swing by Kierack's address – it was only a couple of streets away after all. He could check its location and the surrounding side streets for places to duck out of sight, should circumstances dictate when he started observing the guy for real, and still be home without getting the silent treatment from his wife.

No more than five minutes later, he was pulling up at a red light at the junction of Bond Street and Brook Street. He turned right into Bond Street on green. There were no parking restrictions after six thirty and both sides of the street were lined with the vehicles of revellers on a night out. He was lucky though and found a spot at the curb almost immediately. There weren't many pedestrians on the pavements, those that were – couples mostly – had wrapped themselves in warm clothing glancing into the lighted shop windows arm in arm.

Jack's breath floated on the cold night air as he stepped onto the pavement, damp from the earlier rain, and began walking up Brook Street, casually scanning the buildings on the opposite side of the road as if he was interested in the architecture. He didn't look directly at the block which he knew to be Kierack's – one never knew who might be watching him watching. Instead, he stopped and turned, studying the building's reflection in the department store window at his side. He rubbed his hip; the damp weather had brought on his aches as it always did.

As he was about to return to his car, a taxi pulled up at the traffic lights thirty yards from him. A giant of a man climbed out of the back. Judging from the way he moved, he seemed to be in some kind of pain – every action evidently causing discomfort. Was this Kierack? The guy ticked all the boxes of the description given by Douggie Raymond and his features appeared to match the bland I.D. portrait image Douggie had also pulled from the personnel files. It was difficult to tell at this distance. It would be one hell of a coincidence if it was – what were the chances? Jack half-turned back to the window, not wishing to take the risk of ignoring an adrenaline squirting gut feeling that this was indeed him.

As the man made steady progress up the street, Jack felt exposed as if caught in the beam of a spotlight at a Broadway show even though Kierack – he was sure this was Kierack now – was on the other side of the road. He didn't think Kierack had seen him. He sure as hell hoped he hadn't; his surveillance plan would be canned before it started. He had to make a move – and now. Kierack had reached his door and had his back to Jack. He was pressing a key to the lock. Jack took the opportunity and walked up the street away from his car, casting a look back at Kierack who was beginning to turn around. Jack quickened his pace, trying to ignore the ache in his hip.

Kierack wasn't sure if it was the downer effect of the Pethadine as it wore off or a sharpening of his thought process – again a side effect of the drug as it left him – that was bugging him about his brief conversation with Blane as the train pulled out of the Midi Station earlier. That bit about 'becoming a liability' was starting to get under his skin like an itch from a mosquito bite. The more he scratched at it, the more it grew in his mind and pretty soon it was going to be a bee sting, and if he didn't figure it out, it would grow to an open wound.

The journey had been uneventful and careful to move with the crowd, he cleared the exit barriers at St. Pancras unchallenged. Climbing into a black cab was easier than the saloon model that had whisked him away from the hospital in Brussels a few hours ago.

The pain was returning now, telegraphing its messages with every jolt in the road and sudden swerve made by the oblivious driver. He reached into his pocket for his second dose of Pethadine and worked enough saliva into his mouth to swallow the pill By the time he stepped onto the pavement at the corner of Bond Street and Brook Street, the wave was washing over him but not cleansing him of the growing doubt and the feeling of something not quite right in his universe.

There were few pedestrians, only a few window shoppers gazing into the department store on the corner. He made careful progress up to the lobby door of his building. There was no need to conceal the effects his injuries had on his careful steps along the pavement; there was no-one here to notice him. As he inserted his key, he caught the reflection of a man on the other side of the street who seemed to steal a glance at him. Ernst turned around in a way that would keep the stretching of his torso to a minimum but, by the time he'd made the turn, the man had begun to walk off up the street. Kierack thought he detected a limp in the man's gait – an old injury, maybe. He was covering it well, but it was there alright – was he covering something else? Kierack watched for a moment longer and turned back to the door when the man reached the next corner and disappeared from view.

In the lift, the drug worked its magic, pushing the pain away to the dull ache he'd become accustomed to over the past few hours. The feeling of wellbeing returned and he chastised himself for his mental ramblings over Blane and what he might be up to. He tutted and shook his head at his own paranoia. Blane had promised him two hundred thousand Dollars when the deal went through and there was no reason to suppose anything had changed. The guy had always wired all the cash he'd ever needed and wired it to him without hesitation. There was no cause to mistrust him – anyway, what would Blane have to gain by getting rid of him now? – and yet…that word he'd used, 'liability'. Kierack brushed the thought aside again as he reached the third floor, stepping from the lift with his bag slung over his shoulder despite the aches.

There was no fresh milk in his refrigerator. He made black coffee, took a sip, set the cup down and went to the windows overlooking the street three floors below, to close the drapes. His night was mapped out – coffee, then sleep. A contradiction to most but it worked for him.

As he reached for the pull-cord, he glanced down at the damp tarmac, starting as he glimpsed the guy with the limp. He was walking back down the street. This in itself was unremarkable – it was the 'oh so' casual glance at Kierack's building as he went by that set the bells ringing.

Kierack's favourite movie of all time had Kierack's favourite actor of all time in its starring role. The movie was Ronan and the star was Robert de Niro who, as a CIA man having a pre-operation chat with another agent, utters a line that resonated with so many situations in Kierack's line of work. "When there's a doubt, there is no doubt!"

The axiom had served Kierack well in the past – saved, he *should* say and now, as he watched his watcher walk to a parked BMW at the junction with Bond Street and climb in, there was a doubt – a doubt about Blane.

24

Sheldon Blane was in the office early Wednesday morning. There were thirty hours to go before the deal was signed off and the unstoppable process of wire transfers would commence. He was confident but at the same time unsettled by feelings he couldn't quite nail down. He went over everything one step at a time beginning with the Ferretti girl. There was a slight chance she could cause a problem if, after her meetings in Brussels, the commission decided to press ahead and release their intentions immediately but that would be a break with tradition; in the few dealings he'd had with the E.U., they had procrastinated beyond belief. He wasn't sure what had transpired between Kierack and the girl because Kierack hadn't called in yet. He was sure however, that whatever had happened would have encouraged Ferretti to have a few thoughts about his offer – for all the good it would do her now he'd moved the timetable up.

His morning, from nine until twelve, would be taken up with some to-ing and fro-ing with the ever irritating accountant from Reimer, Ted Allsop. The prospect of a three hour meeting with the man irked him but he kept his thoughts on the end result. The meeting could possibly be concluded in two hours if it were not for the other party expected to be present – Buckley. His inane interjections always led discussions on irrelevant sidetracks which led nowhere and wasted time. Bite my tongue, Sheldon mused, this time next week, it'll all be a bad dream and I can forget about these arseholes forever.

The intercom buzzed.

"Yes."

"Miss Laskey is holding. She's asking if you mind her bringing a photographer this afternoon."

"Put her through." There was a click as he kept the call on speaker-phone. "Good morning, Miss Laskey."

"Good morning."

"My P.A. tells me you want to bring a photographer. I'm quite happy with that."

"Thank you. He only needs to stay for ten or fifteen minutes to take a few shots of you and then he'll leave us to get on with the interview. I find contemporaneous pictures give dimension to my stories."

"Fine, see you at two thirty."

"I'll look forward to it."

He cut the line. Pleasant or irritating, he mused – the afternoon could go either way. He was so close now and if he didn't handle the interview well, this woman could unsettle what was a done deal in all but the signatures. He'd have to schmooze his way through – take her for a drink maybe, when the interview was over.

The untraceable mobile rang in his pocket.

"Yes Ernst; what took you so long – you were going to call me last night."

"I was a little ill."

"Nothing serious?"

"No, nothing I can't handle."

"Good. There may be a job for you late this afternoon. I want you to wait at your place until I call you."

"Okay, but I'm not at my place right now. What time do you need me there?"

"From three onwards," Blane replied.

"Okay, I'll be there."

The conversation ended.

Kierack closed his phone. This was exactly what he'd expected – an instruction to stay put and wait for Blane's clean-up guy to come over and shoot him through the spy hole when he went to answer the door. Well screw that, he had some of his own plans and they included a similar surprise for Mr. double-crossing Blane.

He was sitting up in his bed and feeling the full force of his injuries. The pain convinced him it wasn't the drug giving him ideas – it would be okay to take another dose. He reached over gingerly to the bottle of pills on his night stand, popped one of the pinks and flushed it down with black coffee. If Blane wanted him to be at the flat at three, it would be from that time forward, play would begin. Well, Mr. Blane, we'll start the game a little earlier, he thought.

Jack recognised Juliet's cell number as he picked up.

"Yes, Juliet."

"I need you this afternoon; you're going to be the photographer."

"I knew I was good for something. Tell me the when and the where."

"Buckley Blane at two thirty. You don't have to stay long

– just show your face, take a few shots then leave. I want Mr. Blane to know I'm not alone in London; after what we know about him, I think it pays to be cautious. He needs to know I'm expected somewhere else after the interview and there would be questions if I was a no-show."

"Hey, Juliet, I didn't mean to freak you out about the guy; I'm sure you'll be quite safe – this is London and he's an adman not the despot leader of a Third World state."

"You're absolutely right but humour me."

"Okay, I'll get there a bit before you – check the place out. I was just about to start my stake-out but I guess that's off my agenda today."

"Yes, forget about it until later; my need is greater."

"I'll see you there."

Rick woke early. Sophia was still asleep, her deep breaths barely audible as he crept out of bed and made for the bathroom. It had been a long twenty-four hours. He looked in the mirror and stared back at himself, thankful his Frisbee skills had allowed him to see this day. However, a nagging feeling told him the adventure – if he could call it that – was not over yet.

He shaved and showered then slipped through the connecting door into his own room to dress. He called room service, ordering breakfast for two from the bedside phone. His watch still had London time – it was just after seven. Helder had managed to combine the meetings and they would gather in Helder's office at nine thirty. A car had been ordered to pick up Rick, Sophia and D.S. Gorman at nine in front of the hotel. Knowing how long it took Sophia to prepare herself for the world, he reckoned now would be the time to wake her.

He took a step towards the connecting door when his phone signalled the arrival of a text. In the silence of the room, it almost made him start and, in the space of a millisecond, he asked himself who would be texting at seven A.M. and answered before he'd completed forming the question, Juliet – who else? Now graduated to that title of 'Paid Reporter' with the subtitle of 'I don't care what time it is or what you're doing, I have an important story to write so answer my questions'; she'd been a quick study and fallen true to type.

The message consisted of two words, 'Call me'. That might be difficult right now seeing as the first lady he'd really cared about in a long time was asleep in the next room. He slipped the phone back into his pocket and went through the connecting door to where Sophia lay asleep. He bent over and kissed her cheek. She stirred and opened her eyes, smiling at the sight of him.

"Are you coming back to bed?"she asked, pulling him on top of her.

"You only said that because you know we've got to get a move on."

"There's always time if you make time."

"I know how long it takes you to get ready and by my calculation, we've just got time for you to do that and maybe, just maybe, have a cup of coffee before the car rolls up at the front of the hotel."

"Killjoy."

"You have no idea what it takes for a guy to say no to a beautiful woman."

"If you say so," she said, sliding out from under the covers and then standing naked in the doorway to the bathroom. "Sure you won't change your mind?"

"Go, before I do and we have D.S. Gorman banging on the door telling us the car's downstairs and asking where the hell are we."

"Ookay," she said, drawing out the word and stepping into the bathroom and closing the door behind her.

He waited until he heard the shower running then went back to his room. Juliet had said, 'call me' and he was thinking of doing just that – he didn't want her calling him at the wrong time when it would, A. be difficult to talk and B. warrant an explanation as to who it was he was having a somewhat stilted conversation with. He thought about that for a moment. Why should it be stilted or awkward? He couldn't explain it – it just would be, that's all. So better to get it over with right now, find out what the hell it was that she wanted and hang up before the last drip of steaming water hits that sensuous body in the shower next door.

"Juliet, you asked me to call."

"Hey, Rick – thanks for calling back. I wasn't expecting you to call so soon."

"What can I say, I'm just too dependable. So, tell me, what's up?"

"Are you back in London?"

"Not yet but I will be this afternoon."

"Good. Can you join me for a drink later…as a way of thanking you."

"For what?"

"Melvyn Carter, he came through for me. I don't know for sure, but I think what he told me will shake something loose."

"I'm glad it worked out. Anyway, where and when did you have in mind?"

"There's a great bar downstairs at the hotel here. Say about eight?"

"Juliet, there's just one thing…I'll have someone with me. We are sort of…"

There was a pause but then Juliet broke it suddenly.

"Of course, bring her."

"I hope it's okay with you."

"It's fine. See you in the downstairs bar at eight."

As Rick hung up, he felt Juliet had been caught off-guard but his train of thought was broken by a knock at the door of Sophia's room.

"Room service."

He crossed to the door of his own room and silently cracked it enough to have a view of the corridor and check it was a waiter outside Sophia's door and not some other giant from the stable of 'Hitmen-R-Us. The guy looked like a waiter and he held a pad not a 357 Magnum. Rick studied the man's body language for twenty seconds then went back and let him in. Breakfast had arrived and not more of the trouble he'd been suspecting.

Juliet put her phone down on the pillow next to her, disappointed. She'd found herself thinking of Rick in unguarded moments since their meeting in the Mezzanine Lounge a few days before. The instant he'd appeared, she'd been reminded of what had attracted her to him that day of the interview. He was still cute in a smouldering sort of way and she'd had a real struggle to keep her mind on the job in hand. It should have been no surprise to her that he would be with someone – someone who had seen what she had seen in him.

As she padded to the shower, a tiny feeling of rejection began its weave of witchery. In the cascade of hot water and shampoo, she tried to reason it away but it would not leave her. In a few months, she'd be married; what was she thinking. She knew what she was thinking. She was in a foreign land, a long way from home and, at the back of her mind, was the fantasy of one night with Rick before she said 'I do'. It was just a fantasy, wasn't it? But there was another truth. It was a fantasy until it played out the way her subconscious had planned it – a drink, dinner maybe but then, back to her room for a never to be repeated night of confirmation she was doing the right thing to leave the past behind and marry into her future. There would be no consequences, her subconscious assured her of that. But, in a one-minute phone-call the plan – she could now admit it was a plan because there was that rejection thing swirling in her stomach – had been swept away as sidewalk leaves caught in a gust of Autumn wind.

25

Fran's Helder's office was several floors up at the Berlaymont building in the European district. It was spacious and overlooked Schuman Square, at the end of Rue de la Loi. It wasn't really a square but a traffic island at the centre of a group of E.U. administration buildings – the chauffeur had pointed this out to Rick, Sophia and D.S. Gorman on the drive over. The Berlaymont was a huge building of cruciform design with four wings spanning from its central core and the place of work for thousands of civil servants – more information from the driver who was determined to give them the tour spiel.

A man Sophia took to be Jose Gabera, was already there talking with Helder as they entered. He stood with his hand outstretched to greet them. Frans came out from behind his desk, striding over and planting a kiss on each of Sophia's cheeks in the European way. The ritual, as carried out by Frans Helder, was a little too enthusiastic for Rick's liking but he reasoned they'd be leaving here in a couple of hours so no need to get worked up.

"Jose Gabera, Miss Ferretti," Frans said, making the introductions.

"So pleased to meet you, Miss Ferretti," Gabera said, in accented English, shaking Sophia's hand warmly.

"Please....call me Sophia."

Rick took Gabera's hand, introducing himself.

D.S. Gorman hung back at the door. "I'll be in the outer office," he said, retreating. Sophia turned to him, nodding her thanks.

"Please, let's sit," Frans said, gesturing to sofas in the centre of the room.

As the party settled into their seats, a secretary handed coffee around.

Jose Gabera spoke first.

"Let me first thank you for coming today despite the distressing events of yesterday which Frans told me about; we appreciate your dedication very much."

Sophia gave a brief smile which, she hoped, would hide her desire to be gone from this place right now. "I'm trying to forget about it," she said, picking up the cup on the table in front of her and taking a sip. "Are we expecting any of the other commissioners to join us?" she asked.

"No," Frans answered, "it was short notice for them to change their schedules but we reached a compromise."

"And?" Sophia pressed.

"We conference-called with Gerald Hope late last night," Frans continued. "We agreed on a form of words for you to sign. The other commissioners obviously wanted to meet you but they accept there are changed circumstances and quite understand your desire to return to London. Their reason for seeing you was to impress upon you the real need for the legislation Milo's Scale would bring about but, if you agree to sign the declaration of intent, all the boxes will have been ticked. The document confirms your intent to come to an agreement with the Commission to launch your uncle's formula. It's only a declaration of intent and is predicated on the clear understanding that you will not ratify any agreement until your monetary conditions have been agreed. However, by signing this today, and after we've dealt with a minor hiccup that has appeared on our side, you will allow us to announce the project to the world."

"A hiccup, what hiccup?"

"The commissioner from the Netherlands has suddenly raised an objection; we are in the process of talking him round. We can go ahead without him but would prefer our decision to be unanimous."

"When do you expect to make the announcement?"

"Early next week, if all goes well with our persuasion." Sophia turned to Rick. "What do you think?"

"Seems okay, but you'd better talk to Gerald first."

Frans Helder had anticipated this reaction."He's expecting your call," he said, signaling to his secretary who was waiting at the door, to put a call through to Hope.

To Sheldon Blane's surprise, the session with Ted Allsop had gone very well. There were no last minute hitches only formalities. Sam Buckley had turned up at eleven with nothing more than mild interest in the proceedings until that was, to his and Blane's total astonishment, Ted Allsop produced the final contract for signature. Blane observed it had already been signed by Reimer's C.E.O. and deputy some days previously. He hadn't been expecting to sign until the following day. Within five minutes, the signatures were on the paper, dated and witnessed by Hennie, who added glamour to the occasion by appearing, when summoned, in a close fitting Armani suit with a skirt showing her thigh through a side slit.   .

"Seems like we have a deal," Buckley said, when they were alone.

"Seems so," Blane beamed.

"From five tonight, we're no longer captains of this ship."

"And not too soon," Blane added. "I was surprised the deputy C.E.O. guy….Watson, wasn't here."

"He was supposed to be. Evidently he was delayed but he'll be here with his team tomorrow."

"Well, he'll need to learn fast because when the handover period is done, I'm on a flight to sunnier shores. After the last few months, I need it."

"Three weeks and we can say goodbye," Buckley mused. "Though I think they may be calling for a few months to ask where the paper clips are kept."

"Don't kid yourself. They won't know you once you walk through that door for the last time. They won't want to…and good luck to them – it's their baby now."

"You're right, of course. I'll just have to forget it was ever mine; it'll be hard for a while."

"You'll get over it. Anyway, I'll see you at the end of the day; I have to prepare for my guest – Juliet Laskey."

Sam Buckley took the hint and rose from his chair. "Oh, yes, the formidable Miss Laskey. It still matters what she writes, so be nice. I know that everyone has signed but we don't want it to be un-signed because Juliet Laskey says something's not right. It's not over until the money's in the bank."

Blane nodded his understanding.

"See you later," Buckley called from the door.

Sheldon looked at his watch; it was midday. He got up from the sofa at the meeting nook and went around and sat at his desk. There was something he'd planned for the next day but as things had moved on, he'd decided to do it now despite Buckley's warning that things could still go awry. It was something for Hennie but also a little insurance for himself.

Hennie had stuck his moods and rages, given him as good as she'd got, had never wavered in her loyalty and obeyed all his instructions – whatever they had been. In the last twelve months, she had helped in some vital housekeeping – editing, he called it, before the Reimer execs began their trawling. She'd removed files from departments throughout the company at the dead of night, purged hard drives and shredded anything *he* deemed negative.

It was his life policy never to let anyone near or give more than sixty percent access to the truth of any situation for fear of undermining his position but with Hennie, he was comfortable giving more than he would to any other. She was a kindred spirit somehow and had been unbiased counsel; what's more, she was well aware of her powers to turn him on with an itch he knew he should never attempt to scratch. Tomorrow, she would leave Buckley Blane. Blane would be moving out of his office to make way for the team from the States. He wouldn't need an office to accomplish the handover and he wouldn't need a P.A. Tomorrow would be the last time he would ever see her.

She had indicated her intention to take a few months off before looking for something to suit. He didn't imagine for one moment that she would have any difficulty. He'd made sure she had been awarded a generous severance package from the company but he felt it a requirement to reward her personally with something more than cheap words of gratitude. In a few hours, the payment for his shares would hit his account, of that, *he* had no doubt, and Hennie had some hand in that. He leaned to the side drawer, pulled it open and withdrew a cheque made out to her for the sum of fifty thousand pounds. She wouldn't talk about her time at Buckley Blane but, if anyone asked, he reasoned, fifty thousand would cloud her memory.

He pressed the intercom. "Hennie, can you come in here for a moment?"

There was the usual click and a few seconds later, she stepped in, the two top buttons to her blouse were undone; the jacket to Hennie's suit was hanging in the outer office. Her lipstick was pillar-box red, freshly glistening with gloss.

"Please, sit," he said, gesturing to the sofas and coming out from behind his desk. She said nothing, keeping the expression of dumb insolence he liked so much as she sank into the soft leather – her eyes never leaving his.

He sat opposite her.

"I don't want this to sound patronising – you've known me long enough to know that's not my style but your level of dedication to me – I didn't expect it frankly. I had planned to give you something tomorrow to show you how much I have valued you over the last four years, a parting gift – but as we completed the formalities today, there's no sense in waiting."

He handed her the cheque. Her expression did not change as she studied it.

She put it down beside her; her lips parting almost

imperceptibly. A full thirty seconds passed.

"I also planned to give you something," she said finally, "but I planned it for today. I arranged your diary accordingly."

Blane was mystified.

"You have nothing until two thirty," she continued.

Blane sat in silence as she went to the door and turned the key in the lock.

She worked her seductive walk to his desk and, with one sweep of her arm, brushed its surface clutter to the floor. She turned to face him, placed her hands on her thighs and slowly lifted her skirt. Blane swallowed, catching his breath as the tops of her stockings were revealed. Her skirt was above her waist now – she wore no underwear. He was on his feet but under her spell. She slid sideways onto the desktop parted her legs and brought her knees up, digging her stilettos into the leather inlay. Her head was facing him, cheek pressed against the hide – eyes locked with his.

"Now, fuck me," she oozed.

*****

Kierack could see the entrance to Buckley Blane from his window seat in Starbucks across the street. His surroundings were noisy with the clatter of cups and babble of late lunchers. The coffee was black and strong and hurt to swallow despite his pink pills. He rubbed his throat where the steel dish had impacted and cursed the man who'd spun it at him. Never let me see *you* again, Devan, he thought.

He'd been busy since his call to Blane. There was a

confirmed reservation in the name of Erik Neiman, one of his three identities, on a late flight to Paris – his bag and a change of clothes were already at Paddington in the left luggage locker for the fifteen minute Express ride to Heathrow when his work was done.

His plan ran through his head again; he couldn't afford a slip – Blane was as ruthless and as dangerous as *he* was but Kierack had surprise on his side. There would be chance for Blane to explain himself, of course, but it wasn't likely to alter the outcome; there was too much evidence to deny his duplicity. He checked the time on the wall clock – ten after two. If things were going to happen, it would be about now.

Almost as he had the thought, a figure caught his attention on the pavement.If there had been any doubt in Kierack's mind about Blane's intentions, it was swept away in that moment. Maybe he wouldn't give him a chance to lie his way out after all. Walking towards the entrance of BBM was someone Kierack recognised. The limp was more concealed but still there to a trained eye. "My friend from last night – come to get your orders or your cash?" he whispered to no-one, as he watched the man who had been tasked with killing him, disappear into the building.

Kierack could picture the scene in Blane's office – the two of them discussing the hit. Blane's new man telling Blane how he'd done the recon and how it was going to be and Blane saying he didn't need to hear the details only the result. "Oh, and one other thing – no trails please – here's the cash, half now, half when it's done."

Yes, the scene up there was so familiar – but this time they were discussing *him*; it was new for Kierack to experience the role of the hunted, albeit momentarily. He smiled to himself; they were up there and unaware *they* were the hunted now.

It was just after three when the focus of Kierack's attention emerged from the building. There was no need to follow – he already knew the man's destination; he'd let him wait there for a few hours. The effects of the painkiller were receding and he held off taking another dose to gauge the level of pain he'd be forced to endure if, as he knew he would have to sooner or later, he stopped popping the pinks. He had enough to last a week but no good would come of taking the stuff for more than a few days and anyway, he needed his wits about him for his next task. He drained the last of his second cup and carefully shouldered his satchel.

Blane lived in an exclusive Kensington block. Kierack had been there on two occasions, once at Blane's invitation to fit a security device and once, without Blane's knowledge, to fit two additions of his own. These were, a high definition pinhole Webcam disguised as a power socket which he'd substituted for an existing wall socket and a bug in the landline which transmitted the numbers dialed and live conversation to a voice activated, online recorder. Kierack liked to know the sort of person he was working for and so a little spying on his employer would give him the measure of the man. He'd studied Blane's movements without his knowledge for several weeks. The man kept to a routine – the office before eight and back home never before eight in the evening. Kierack had gathered as much intelligence as he could to give him an edge if ever he needed it. He needed it now.

Blane, in clichéd style, kept a wall safe behind a hinged painting. It took only a few days for the high definition camera to record Blane's finger punching in the combination. On Kierack's only official visit to the flat, Blane had paid him in notes taken from the safe and, it was a fair assumption, a balance resided there. Either way, whatever it contained today would be leaving with him as unpaid dues.

His cab pulled up to the block and he swiped the cloned card to let him into the lobby. Five minutes more saw him in Blane's kitchen under the sink locating the gas feed pipe and working on his signature dish; he didn't want to be searching for the feed later when time might be tight. Ernst produced an adjustable spanner from his bag, set it to fit the collar holding the pipe in place and left it there. He went to his bag again, carefully removing a plastic box and setting it down on the breakfast bar. It contained one of his special light bulbs.

He crossed to the safe, removed the glove from his left hand and punched the combination, wiping his fingerprints from the keys with the glove as it clicked open. There were packs of fifties amounting to fifty thousand Sterling and fifteen thousand in U.S. Dollars. Tucked beneath was a loaded Luger semi-automatic pistol. A spare clip, also fully loaded, lay next to it. The money, the Luger and two gold Rolex watches went into his satchel.

"Is that it then," Sophia said, resting her head on Rick's shoulder as the Belgian countryside sped past the window.

"Is that the end of it or is there more to come – what do you think? Is Poirot over there," she nodded towards Dave Gorman who was dozing with his head against the window, "going to be following us everywhere forever?"

"I can't say for sure but maybe there'll be a few more twists before we can say it's over."

"I thought you'd say that. So we're stuck with the escort for a while yet. I could do with a night off."

Rick had been waiting for the opportunity to drop out Juliet's invitation for a drink at her hotel; the right moment hadn't presented itself until now. He didn't want to get into his history with Juliet but reckoned he could wing it as long as, when the three of them met up, Juliet didn't drop a passing remark which betrayed more than 'just good friend' status in the way women do when claiming prior ownership or subtly point scoring against each other. He could go alone, of course, but he didn't want to. He'd decided to chance it.

"Me too," he agreed. "We can do that tonight if you like." He paused for a beat, then continued. "I heard from a friend over from the States – she's asked me – us…for a drink at her hotel if we were back."

"She," Sophia said, with exaggerated scepticism.

"Yes, Juliet is someone in the newspaper business I knew a while ago."

"And what about our friend over there?"she nodded in Gorman's direction again. "Is he coming too?"

"I hope not but we'll have to see what his boss says. If he has to follow, he has to follow. So, what do you say – are you up for it?"

"Absolutely, we could go on for dinner somewhere later

– I can't be doing with your spag-bol again."

"Is that a judgement of my cooking skills?"

"No, just the repertoire – you need to learn how to make another dish."

"Okay, it's a deal – plan your outfit."

Rick checked the time, about an hour to go. A woman in her fifties took cautious steps in the aisle carrying paper cups of hot drink in each hand and a pastry squashed under her arm. His nostrils caught the fragrant whiff of coffee as she passed. Sophia was sleeping, head occasionally lolling forward with the movement of the train. He pulled out his phone, hit the text icon and sent a brief message to Juliet, 'We'll see you at eight', making it clear he wouldn't be alone. How things have changed. Only a few weeks ago he'd have been controlling heart palpitations at the very notion she was calling him. It didn't seem that important any more – there were still one or two palpitations though…..if he really got down to it.

Reflecting on the meeting at Helder's office, he was left with a feeling of anti-climax; it had been brief and was over in about forty-five minutes. Sophia was relieved to sign her letter of intent to the commissioners after a brief conversation with Gerald Hope and be out of there. Detective Inspector Newman persuaded the Belgian Police to let them return to London. They'd made it to the station in time to board the eleven thirty train. It had been twenty-four hours of high speed, on-fire drama of the kind he would hope never to repeat unless, of course, it was Sophia dragging him through the hoop. There was a text beep from his phone; 'I'll be waiting', it read.

26

Juliet's cab dropped her outside the offices of Buckley
Blane Marketing at around two twenty. As she came out of
the lift on the tenth floor, she spotted Jack sitting on a bank
of seats outside a glass walled office at the end of the
corridor. He had a camera slung over his shoulder and was
drinking tea but set it down and rose to greet her the
moment he saw her.

"Juliet, right on time."

"How long have you been here?"

"About fifteen minutes, long enough to ride the lift with
the woman from H.R. who interviewed me for a job – not
a hint of recognition. I think it says a lot about their H.R.
department."

"Okay, are you ready?"

"Yep. We go through the glass door to where the rather
attractive lady is behind the desk. She's the P.A.I was
warned about but I'm not sure I believe my sources. She
was very pleasant and even brought me a cup of tea."

"Let's get on with it."

Juliet had a knack of picking up on the internal mood of
companies within a few minutes of entering their doors.
She had a stock of seemingly innocuous questions she

would ask random employees on her way to reception – and at reception itself, there were a few more specifically targeted probes. The responses gave her a picture as clear as a psychometric questionnaire employed in any of the world's best H.R. departments. It was ironic because generally, she didn't rate psychometric tests. Her judgement, albeit a generalisation, was they might indicate a candidate had the potential to kill his grandmother but not any use in judging if he would be good at the job for which he'd applied. Psychometric testing might have some use somewhere on the planet but not in her universe…and yet, here she was deriving answers to apparently unconnected questions, the very same method psychometrics were founded upon. At the back of her mind might have been the fact she had never taken a test of any kind she couldn't ace yet had been scored low in an aptitude test by her high-school careers officer, Barbara Wilson. Not that Juliet was immodest, but the conclusions drawn from the test were clearly wrong; she'd made a career and made it in a big way. However, if there was one thing the experience with Barbara had taught her, it was there's an exception to every rule. So, even though Juliet had a reputation for being right, there was also the possibility she could be wrong.

Steamers, the company whose downfall she was most associated with recently was a company where she'd got it right. Paradoxically, she hadn't set out to cause its collapse, quite the reverse, in fact. The head of their P.R. department had contacted her with a story of positive growth. He invited her to the headquarters to meet the C.E.O. and hear of their expansion plans. Fatefully, on the day of her visit, their P.R. executive was delayed in traffic and she had been left waiting for twenty-five minutes in the reception area of the open plan office. She had used the time gainfully; eliciting vox pops from passing members of staff. One of them had pressed a scrap of paper into her hand with a phone number and the words 'Call me' hurriedly scrawled across it.

The interview itself hadn't gone well. The C.E.O., initially charming, became evasive to the point of irritation when pressed on the most basic questions regarding the detail of the financing for their expansion. Suddenly, she'd felt the session was being brought to a swift close and the planned interview to be followed by lunch, ended before it had started with the C.E.O. saying he'd been called away. What should have been a feel-good story was rapidly starting to feel bad.

Later, back at the office, she'd called the number on the scrap of paper pressed into her palm. The stories of staff cuts and child labour in India hit the fan. Steamers' house of cards began to tumble without a friend to catch them.

The atmosphere at Buckley Blane was as far away from that at Steamers as the Earth is from Mars. The offices were bright and filled with easy-going staff of obvious talent. There was a manned coffee bar at the back where employees took their breaks. Looking around her while the receptionist called upstairs to announce her arrival, Juliet felt the energy of the place. Whatever Blane might be, he knew how to motivate his workforce.

Jack held the door for her as they entered the P.A.'s office. It was spacious; panelled in walnut veneer and expensively carpeted. A window ran down one side and the spaces between the vertical blinds showed a sliced view across the City.

As they entered, Blane's P.A. rose from her seat behind a sleek desk which displayed a small centrally placed plaque reading 'Henrietta Lawson' on its surface of inlaid leather. Juliet guessed she was about thirty and it was instantly evident why she'd got Jack's vote. Ms. Lawson was tall and striking. Her hair was short and precise, highlighting her cheek bones and full red lips. Her suit was clearly expensive, drawing the eye to her breasts and following every curve of a body with no surplus. Her dark brown eyes locked with Juliet's instantly.

"Miss Laskey," she said, greeting Juliet and flashing a quick smile at Jack, "I'm Hennie, please follow me; Mr. Blane is expecting you."

"Thank you."

As Hennie led the way, Jack turned to Juliet with a 'see what I mean' grin lighting up his face.

Hennie pushed through a door set into the wall at the side of her desk and stepped to one side as Juliet and Jack went in.

Blane's office was expansive but surprisingly free of the usual trappings of a high-flyer. There was a comfortable meeting area with leather sofas and a large flat screen television – its sound muted – tuned to Bloomberg but there were no executive toys on his desk or modern paintings hanging on the walls. This was a place of work with no distraction, that is, if you didn't count the sensual Ms. Lawson.

Blane had his back to them with a phone to his ear as they entered. He was silhouetted against a window which spanned the width of his office – a distance of some thirty feet. The glass was tinted and in panels from floor to ceiling. Vertical blinds were pulled wide, giving a breathtaking view across the Thames as if from an airship. He put down the receiver and turned towards them when he heard the door.

"Miss Laskey," he said warmly, reaching to shake her hand. "I've been so looking forward to meeting you."

"Please, call me Juliet."

"Very well then, Juliet."

He turned to Jack.

"Jack Tennant," Jack said, before Blane asked."

"Jack's here to take a few pictures," she explained.

Blane nodded. "Can Hennie bring you both something to drink – coffee, tea or something else?"

They declined and Hennie left the room as Juliet seated herself on one of the black leather sofas.

"If we could get the pictures out of the way first, I can let Jack go."

"Of course," Blane said genially and positioned himself by the panoramic window with London as the backdrop for Jack's shots. Juliet studied him for the first time as he posed there as if he owned the view. Sharply dressed, he was an attractive man with a bad boy edge. She guessed every click of the shutter would produce a money shot.

After a few minutes, Jack was done with the set-up by the window.

"I just need a few of you with Juliet and I'll be finished," he said, gesturing for him to sit on the sofa opposite her. For a few minutes more, Jack kept shooting informal frames as Blane began to chat with Juliet across the low table that separated them.

"Okay, Juliet, I think I've got everything you need. I'll get going if that's okay with you."

She nodded.

"See you at four thirty," he said, making for the door."

As the door snicked behind Jack and the room momentarily fell into the deadened silence which only comes with expensive wall to wall heavy pile, Juliet glanced at Blane. He was relaxed and, she conjectured, confident in his ability to bat away any curve balls she might throw. It wasn't her intention to do a hatchet job although there were those who wished it, Melvyn Carter for one. She calculated Blane had his fair share of skeletons and digging them out could put a bit of colour into a two-a-penny takeover piece.

She'd researched Reimer's reasons for the acquisition of BBM and despite their official line, knew it was the expertise and client base surrounding what was known inside BBM, as the Creative Numbers Unit or the C.N.U. which drove their desire. The principal function of the C.N.U. was to create schemes that were nigh impossible to penetrate, barring consumers from knowing the true worth of any product or service on a comparison basis with others. The practice was widespread but BBM had turned it into an art-form with blue-chip clients spanning continents. By absorbing BBM, Reimer would instantly become the global leader in the craft.

Juliet noticed Blane giving her the 'once-over' as she pulled her notes and a small recorder from her attaché. She held up the recorder. "Do you mind if I use this? It helps me to remember when I can't read my own scrawl."

"I don't mind. Please, go ahead."

"I was keen to meet you," she opened. "The word is you're the one who brought about the takeover."

"That's not strictly true. Reimer had been dancing around us for some time but only made some serious overtures about eighteen months ago. I merely took their interest to a natural conclusion."

"That's not quite the way I heard it but I'll accept your modesty on the issue."

Blane smiled.

"I have most of what I want on the deal," she continued, "but I like to fill my pieces with background on the personalities involved and their histories, aspirations, that sort of thing. It gives more depth to my stories. The cold facts are always interesting but usually, only to the business world. Since I started at the *Times*, I've managed to broaden the reader profile of the Business Section. I'm telling you this at the beginning so that you're not mystified by my questions."

Blane gave his genial smile. "I've read your work, Miss...Juliet, so, ask away."

"Is there anything off limits?"

"No, were you expecting there to be?"

"Not at all. From the little I've read about you, it would surprise me if there were."

From Sheldon Blane's experience, attractive women are wary of other attractive women and usually for competitive reasons. It would have been interesting to have seen Hennie's reaction when the lovely Miss Laskey flounced into her office. He was confident Hennie would always behave as the consummate professional but he knew her well enough to detect the friction which would have undoubtedly been sparking under the façade of her smile.

Yes, Juliet Laskey was a stunner and had a record of stunning several C.E.O.s with her charms before picking motives and careers apart by catching them out in a lie. Mindful of Buckley's advice, in this instance, he'd be careful. She obviously had something she was expecting to floor him with – why else the 'off limits' probe. I'll think on my feet, as I always do, he thought, but whatever it is she has up her sleeve, it better fire real bullets because, where the deal's concerned, that train's leaving and I'm in the First Class section – hell, I *own* the First Class section.

"How was it you teamed up with Sam Buckley?" she asked.

"We got chatting at an industry dinner; it sort of went from there. His company was doing well enough but I had a few ideas he liked and he felt we could push the game up a bit if we were together."

"What kind of ideas?"

"It's difficult to make a list but to summarise, we began to change the emphasis of our campaigns."

"That doesn't really tell me anything."

"Okay….let me put it another way…."

She gave him no time, cutting over him.

"Would it be anything to do with the C.N.U.?"

Blane's eyelid flickered almost imperceptibly as she delivered the question but she saw it.

"To suggest that was the main thrust of our business would be to suggest we only had one idea; no-one is interested in a one-trick pony – least of all the City. We major in several areas and have a wide diversity of international clients who would testify to the fact that we excel in all of them." He held her eyes in his as he continued – his smile never far from his lips. "And that's what Reimer saw in us."

It was her habit to pull out a niggling prod right at the beginning of her sessions to see if feathers could be ruffled enough to destabilise her subject and steer him or her into departing from the prepared script. It wasn't working here though. I'm not going to rattle Mr. Cool with any questions about the takeover, she thought with wry amusement. Although she'd caught his slight discomfort, irritation maybe, at her C.N.U. question but still he came back quickly with an answer already cooked and wrapped.

"I only mention it because it's the rumour floating around – the C.N.U. is what Reimer really wanted and the clients who went with it." She waited but there was no response from Blane. He'd given his answer and there was no more. He's done this many times before, she thought, angry with herself for not learning the first time.

"Well let's take up a different topic."
Blane was confident in a 'bring it on' way.

"Let's talk about you," she said, "Sheldon Blane – from the beginning."

"Oh, I don't know if I can remember the beginning."

"Anything to get us started – your parents, for instance."

"I was brought up by an uncle. I was orphaned when I was nine. He had a market stall – it was where I discovered I had a head for figures. The rest is pretty boring – school, university and then the world of work."

"If you had a head for figures, how did you end up in marketing and not accountancy or something in the City?"

"It wasn't so much the maths; it was how it could be

applied to consumerism which interested me. Marketing seemed the natural path."

"Okay, I get that – so tell me about your first job, Chatwell-Blake-Barber wasn't it?"

"You've done your homework, I see."

She tilted her head in confirmation.

"I read the Press Pack that Reimer gave out when they announced their intentions."

"Yes, Chatwell-Blake-Barber was where it all started. I…"

"So your time with Melvyn Carter doesn't really count?" she cut in.

There was a pause. Blane's expression changed briefly as he appeared to be considering the question. Juliet had hoped she had landed a blow to open him up but it had shown only marginal effect. True, it hadn't bounced off – his genial smile faded a little but it soon returned as the answer to the question she now realised he had undoubtedly anticipated, maybe not quite so soon but anticipated nonetheless, was delivered fresh from the oven.

"You really *have* done your homework; I'm impressed."

She smiled and tilted her head again in the same gesture of confirmation. You have no idea, she mused, holding her smile and preventing him from reading her thoughts.

"I'll answer your questions relating to Melvyn's company but it will have to be off the record. Do you agree?"

Juliet nodded. It wasn't what she wanted but it would have to do for the moment. At the very least, she might get something she didn't know.

"Very well then," he continued. "My time with Carter Gibbon was only brief and it was a period I'm not that proud of so I prefer to forget it."

"Weren't there three partners in the firm – wasn't the full name Carter Gibbon Snell? Did you also forget about Marilyn Snell?"

This one landed. The name Marilyn Snell took the smile clean away, momentarily replaced by a cold stare but as quick as it had vanished, the smile crept its way back.

"As I said, I…" he began.

"There are people who say Marilyn Snell took her life because of you," she cut in, desperate to follow through with another to the body. "Because of what she'd allowed you to do and the collapse of the company as a result of it – do *you* feel responsible in any way?"

In the five-second silence which followed, Blane's composure cracked only momentarily before returning to a deadpan expression and finally, forming a humourless smile. Nothing is going to draw him out she concluded; there'll be another set piece coming any moment.

She decided not to wait.

"I'm not making any judgements, you understand," she continued, "but I'd like to hear your views. And there's the DVD, of course – I'd definitely like your views on that."

For Sheldon, this was rapidly turning out to be one of the most interesting interviews of his life. In the past, he'd spent his time covering tracks and dodging bullets. Had this been two days ago he'd have been more concerned, to put it mildly, more likely calling Ernst for one of his clean-ups before any nasties hit the ears of the Reimer execs – but not today. If all this is about his character and not the company, there'll be no damage. It might even boost his reputation as a ruthless operator. Today, there's no need to break a sweat. Today, the Dollar equivalent of thirty-eight million in Sterling would hit his account at any moment and so it was a day to enjoy. Today, Juliet Laskey does not have the power to upset me. The mention of Marilyn Snell was a bit of a surprise though but Juliet was good, something from left field was to be expected. I'll wager there's more though; she's got that look one sees in the eye of the hunter about to deliver the kill shot. She thinks the disc in her hand has the means to slot it.

Juliet brandished the DVD given to her by Melvyn Carter holding footage from the security cameras he'd come upon quite by accident. "Do you have a player?" she asked.

Blane leaned towards her, took the disc and went to his desk. He picked up a remote control and pointed it towards the flat TV on the far wall which was silently displaying Bloomberg's market report. A panel opened below the screen revealing a player, its disc tray ready to receive. He inserted the disc and returned to the sofa.

Juliet glanced first at the TV, then back to Blane to catch his reaction as the drama unfolded on the screen but there was no reaction, none at all. He sat impassively as Marilyn Snell's voice rose first in anger then passion and finally despair. Juliet said nothing while the disc played on, glancing at him from time to time. Blane's countenance changed momentarily at the sight of himself stealing data from the company main-frame but it was only a fleeting shift, as if something was of mild interest to him.

The sequence ended with picture and audio going to white noise. Blane let it hiss for a second or two before hitting the 'off' and turning to Juliet. She met his gaze.

"It's not part of my story," she said, "…the disc – it's just something that came up on the way…I'd be interested to hear what you have to say."

"About what?" Blane was still polite and seemed surprised at the question.

"About Marilyn Snell's suicide, the collapse of Carter Gibbon & Snell and your part in it all."

Blane took his time before speaking. Juliet could almost feel the cogs turning to the correct setting inside his head, like a jukebox plucking a record from a rotating stack. He had an explanation for everything and even though there was genuine surprise on his part when the footage began to roll, she now knew there was no shaking him.

"As I said, it's a period I'm not proud of but before forming your opinion, there are factors to be taken into consideration."

Juliet looked at him sceptically. "I'm listening."

"Take Marilyn for instance, she had a few issues before I ever came along – Harry Gibbon for one."

"Oh?"

"There was something broken between them when I arrived. I admit I took advantage of her vulnerability and used her to get information but like I told you, I'm not proud of it. When it was time to leave, I broke it off the only way I knew. The way I broke it off with Marilyn might seem cruel but tell me you haven't, sometime in your life, dumped someone in a way that makes you ashamed when you think about it. My excuse is I was young, ambitious and arrogant. To paraphrase Dylan, I'm older than that now.

Marilyn didn't kill herself because of me; I was just a

rough toy-boy to fill in for Harry Gibbon. If there's a person to blame, it's him but I think she had other issues."

It was Juliet's turn to be silent. He'd managed to hit a nerve with his remark about shame. She had some of that. She kept it locked away at the back of her consciousness but it was there alright – the way she walked away from Rick when she could have stayed – or at least, shown some interest. Back then, there were far more exciting things to do than hang around while he got himself back together but yes, she looked back in shame.

She snapped out of it. "But what about the company, it collapsed because of you. Maybe she felt she had colluded. I think that might have played on her mind."

"I wouldn't concede the company collapsed because of me. If you look closely at the set up back then, you'll see they didn't have the organisation they thought they had to expand. Did she blame herself?...I couldn't say. It's all such a long time ago now and before you ask if I'd do the same all over again, the answer is obviously no…but I'm older now with all the experience a few years bring. When you're in your twenties you don't have that. So if I was in my twenties, burning with ambition, I'd probably do the same. I was sad, of course, to hear what Marilyn did to herself and I had all the same thoughts that you're having about the causes. I think it would be unfair to lay it all at my door."

Juliet was silent. He was good, very good. Maybe her article would be run-of-the-mill after all; there wasn't much she could use so far – it was mostly off the record.

Blane looked at his watch.

"I have a three thirty meeting," he said.

Juliet saw it was three fifteen. She'd better get on to company issues or she'd have wasted her time.

"I'll use the time to get some general background to the takeover. I…"

"I have a better idea. Why don't you let me take you for a drink this evening? You could fill in a few gaps then. I don't want your assessment of the company to be coloured by *my* past, it's much more than one individual. I'd like to have the chance to talk it over with you in less formal surroundings."

The man was extraordinary, she thought. I've just gone through a list of his pretty despicable actions, finally laying bare his humiliation of Marilyn Snell – in every sense – and now he's asking me for small-talk over cocktails. He'd alluded to his shame without actually admitting it; he clearly had none…about anything.

She took a moment to think about his proposition. The last forty-five minutes had been entertaining in a curious way but it hadn't pushed her article on much. She needed more.

"Okay," she said, "at my hotel – the Hilton – seven fifteen in the downstairs bar. I'm meeting friends at eight; we'll have forty-five minutes if that's alright with you."

"Perfect."

She got up from the sofa, slipped the recorder into her attaché and went to the door; wondering if she would rue her decision.

"Your disc," he called after her.

"Keep it, it's your own personal copy - seven fifteen then, in the downstairs bar."

He nodded, his smile still in place.

27

D.S. Gorman was drinking tea at the breakfast bar in Rick's kitchen. They'd been back for thirty minutes and Sophia was chatting with Rick in the main body of the room, across from the detective. Gorman's phone rang; he recognised the number.

"Yes, Boss."

"Are you alone?"

He glanced over to Rick and Sophia. Rick had picked up a satchel and was peering into it. Gorman turned away, speaking low.

"They can't hear me."

"Okay then. Hinkley's killer was in hospital under guard but he got away. Seems they had some crossed wires somewhere about how dangerous he was. The guard was from the hospital security – he was waiting for Police back-up. By the time they got there, our man was gone. Until we find him, someone has to stay with the girl. I'm sending Hargreaves to relieve you. She's on her way over to you now. Take a couple of hours and go home but I'd like you back with them for this evening."

"Understood."

"Best not mention the guy's on the loose again though."

"Of course, Boss. Anyway, they think he's either dead or

in intensive care."

"I wish," Newman came back.

"Any ideas who he is?"

"Grenard's working on it; they have a good CCTV photo but right now, they have no idea. Tell Hargreaves to check-in with me when she arrives."

Gorman closed his phone and turned back to face the room. Sophia was looking at him suspiciously.

"Have you spoken to Detective Inspector Newman yet?" she asked, as her eyes met his. She was sitting on the sofa sifting through the mail they had collected from her flat on the way to Rick's.

"Just a moment ago, actually. Someone's coming to take over from me for a few hours."

"You'll be back later, right?"

"Yes, you can't get rid of me just yet."

A few hours earlier, she had been ready to do without Gorman. It was only when he said he was going that she suddenly felt vulnerable and the need to keep him around.

"We were planning on going for a drink later with a friend of Rick's. I rather thought you would be coming along. It's at the Hilton bar – very public," she added, when she saw his scepticism.

"I'll be back by seven. Don't go anywhere before I get back. Until then, D.S. Hargreaves will be with you. She'll be here any minute."

Rick was rummaging in his satchel, searching for a text book and notes taken in his last lecture. He looked up.

"She?" he said, with surprise in his voice.

"D.S. Hargreaves is a very competent officer; you'll be quite safe with her."

The intercom buzzed.

"That'll be her now," Gorman said, as Rick pressed the 'Talk' button.

A female voice came from the speaker. "This is Detective Sergeant Hargreaves."

Rick looked across at Gorman for recognition. Gorman nodded. Rick buzzed her into the lobby and she arrived at the door of the flat moments later. Gorman made the introductions as they went through to Rick's lounge.

"I've been in the street for the last ten minutes. I watched from the bus stop; there's no-one hanging around, it's clear," Jill Hargreaves said, as she removed her coat.

"The boss wants you to check in with him – give him a call as soon as." Gorman waved as he went to the door. "Okay, I'll see you all in three hours," he called, as he went out.

From Blane's flat, Ernst Kierack had gone to his left-luggage locker at Paddington. He deposited the cash from the safe in the holdall he'd left there earlier in the day. He kept the Luger though, thinking he might put a bullet in both Blane and his new man before he set the timer for his little firework display. Ironic, he thought, Blane catching a bullet from his own gun. The effect of his pink pills was waning now and movement was laborious; there was throbbing in every joint in his body. Leaning against the bank of lockers to steady himself, he locked up and went to the taxi rank, sweat breaking on his brow as he climbed into the first cab in line.

"Bond Street," he responded to the look on the face of the driver who'd turned to him for instructions.

As the cab pulled away from the curb, he sunk into his seat and tried to imagine the variables in his plan to take his mind away from the building firestorm of pain. Blane's new man would undoubtedly be in the vicinity of his apartment building by now. I need to arrive in full view so he can see me go into the building. I'll need to know where he is beforehand. Blane, what about Blane… He never arrives home before eight so the timing needs to be right.

"We're coming up to Bond Street," the cabbie called. "Where do you want me to drop you?"

"Keep going. Cross into Brook Street and do the block."

"You're the boss. Just let me know when to stop."

The cab entered Brook Street slowly. There was a delivery van parked at an angle forcing the taxi to wait for a space in the oncoming traffic before swinging out and passing the vehicle. Kierack scanned the pavement looking for the man he'd spotted the night before and earlier at the offices of Buckley Blane. There was no sign of him. The cab hit a pothole and shot a bolt of searing pain through his torso. His head felt muzzy, his consciousness drifting into a clouded cacophony of noise and confused moments past and present. Pistol shots, muzzle flashes, running, diving, returning fire – characters from his adolescence, bad blood mixed with images of Blane and others.

Another jolt as the cab lurched to avoid a second hole in the tarmac shook him alert again. Any more and I'll be climbing the walls, he thought.

"Stop here, I've changed my mind," he instructed the driver with a tap on the dividing window. The cab pulled into the curb. He stepped out, handed the cabbie a ten pound note and left without waiting for change. The door to the lobby was fifty yards down the pavement. If he was being watched – there were no ifs – his efforts to maintain his balance and slow struggling walk, if he could call it a walk, would give ample warning to his stalker that he was home.

At the door, he spent time fumbling for his key with his right hand; his left was pushed deep into the pocket of his coat – clasped around the grip of the Luger. Slowly inserting the key into the lock then brushing sweat from his forehead, he was as ready as he could be, hoping his body would allow him to move with sufficient speed if called upon.

"Come on, now's your chance," he urged the unseen assassin under his breath, all the while studying the scene behind him reflected in the glass – but there was no-one. He pushed into the lobby.

Once inside his flat, he swallowed two pills from the dresser, foolish maybe – asking for trouble but it couldn't be avoided – he'd risk the consequences. He went to the window, closing the drapes on fading daylight and being careful not to look down at the street as he stood in full view. In the gloom of the room, he cracked the curtain an inch away from the sill and peered down to the pavement. It was busy with homeward bound commuters. Ernst let go of the drape and began to turn back to the room but suddenly hesitated. Something in the street had registered and set him gripping the curtain again. The BMW he'd seen the night before was parked in a bay at the side of the department store; the driver's face was clearly reflected in the lighted store window. How hadn't he seen the car from the cab? It was either pills or the pain from lack of them that had put him off his game. It was six pm. At six thirty he'd move and pull his tail along with him to Blane's apartment.

Jack had made the decision to take his car on his stake-out; it was too cold outside to be hanging around street corners waiting for Kierack to show. He drove by the entrance of Kierack's building and did the block before finding a perfect spot opposite a little way up the street. n his rear-view mirror he had clear sight of the entrance and the approach. There was no way Kierack would go in or out without being seen.

Jack had been sitting there since three thirty, flicking his eyes between the rear mirror and the one on the door, occasionally starting the engine to drive the heater as he listened to the radio. It was coming up to six. The pavements were busy and the last fingers of sunlight were dying in the street – still no Kierack. 'Another forty-five minutes and I'll call it a night,' he sighed inwardly.

He was beginning to question the whole idea of talking to the man about his boss when he caught sight of him, fifty yards in front, on the other side of the street – climbing out of a taxi. He seemed in some kind of pain, bent and walking with deliberate caution to avoid a fall from which he might never get up. Jack sank back in his seat, instinct telling him this might not be the time to be seen or go door-stepping.

He watched the stooped figure make it to the door and stop. Kierack was making a big deal of finding his key. He was hesitating when he drew it from his pocket as if waiting for something. After thirty seconds he appeared to overcome whatever it was that was troubling him and went in. Jack looked up at the second floor window and waited.

A few minutes passed then light spilled from it and Kierack's huge silhouette appeared in the frame before closing the drapes.

Jack's phone shrilled in its cradle on the dash – it was Juliet.

"Hi, Juliet."

"Anything going on?" she asked.

"He's just gone in. I'm not sure he'll be going out again; he looked pretty beat up."

"Oh." He detected disappointment in her voice. "I didn't get much from Sheldon Blane; I was hoping your guy there would give me something. I'm meeting Blane for a drink at seven fifteen in the downstairs bar at the hotel to try a different tack. If you get anything, call me."

Not wishing to let her down, he said, "Listen, I'll wait around for a while. If he doesn't come out, I'll ring the door."

"Okay, but be careful."

"Yeah, yeah."

"I mean it, Jack; be careful."

He hung up. *How to play it? I could wait around for say forty-five minutes – see if he goes out again – catch him at a bar maybe and talk when he's mellow,* he thought. It was by no means certain Kierack *would* go out again though – he seemed in a lot of pain and Jack didn't imagine it was from sports injuries.

Forty-five minutes – if he comes out in that time, all well and good – if he doesn't, I'll knock on the door.

There had been nights like this in Kosovo, waiting to meet an informant or a disillusioned commander for an unattributable warning of coming atrocities. The waiting was the only similarity. The luxury of a warm car in a side street was out of the question back then – a sitting target if it was a set-up. Dark doorways and frosty cobbles had made up his workplace with the fear of an infra-red spot from a sniper's telescopic sight ever present. Jack smiled; London was a walk in the park by comparison.

He snapped out of his reminiscing when he saw the door to the apartment building open and Kierack step casually into the street. He looked better, more upright, as if he'd had some miracle makeover. He wore a long coat which flapped open as he hailed a cab and climbed in. Jack pulled out to follow into Hanover Square, keeping the tail lights in view but not close enough to arouse suspicion – not that the cabbie would notice anything but he thought he saw Kierack take a backward glance through the cab's rear window. No matter; there was no possibility he would know Jack or suspect he was being followed – I've been careful.

He nearly lost the cab when he was caught at a light on Park Lane and fought through heavy traffic to catch up. They were almost at Kensington High Street before he had the tail lights again. The cab turned into Argyll Road and pulled up at a red brick building with a Deco entrance. Kierack got out and strode to the door, hesitating in the same way he had outside the building in Brook Street. What was he waiting for?

Approaching a prospective source in the street or door-stepping – was always a risky strategy. The target, if handled carefully, could be curious at first and then, after initial suspicion, a helpful mine of useful snippets.

However, accosted incorrectly, your man – or woman, could be dismissive, aggressive or in some cases, where the individual was a suspect in some misdeed, downright violent. Jack carried memories of all these eventualities. Ordinarily, he would have got to know more about his subject, giving him a chance to predict the nature of the reaction he might receive when he made his move. The situation with Kierack was different; there had been no time for homework. Juliet had pushed up the timescale for him to deliver or not.

Parked on a yellow line opposite, Jack watched Kierack swipe a card to gain entry to the lobby. Traffic prevented Jack from getting out of his car and crossing the road to catch Kierack before the lobby door slammed shut. He dodged the cars but he was too late. Kierack was inside and the door had closed.

He stood on the pavement, looking up and down the street in the hope there might be other residents returning home – no luck. Turning back to the door, he studied the bank of buttons on the entry phone – no names, only numbers.

'Sorry, Juliet – time to give up'. About to return to his car, he noticed a small piece of junk mail trapped at the base of the door preventing it from fully closing. He pushed and went in. The lobby was empty and silent; the traffic din shut out by the heavy door as this time, it snicked into a locked position. A wide staircase covered by maroon carpet fixed with polished brass stair rods, was visible through an arch. Muffled footfalls echoing in the stairwell drew him bounding up the first flight. He had no time to focus on the elbow which struck him a hammer blow as he rounded the corner on the first floor landing. There was a sensation of falling but then, blackness.

28

"Tell me about Juliet," Sophia called over her shoulder, eyes wide applying mascara in the bathroom mirror.

Rick was doing up his shirt. D.S. Hargreaves was tuned to Sky in the next room.

"What's to tell? She's a friend from back home who owes me a favour."

"There's something to tell," she said, with a wry smile. She turned and stood in the bathroom doorway, leaning on the frame in her underwear, facing him. "I noticed the way you didn't look at me when you told me about tonight. Come on, you and her were an item – am I right?"

There was a pause while Rick got his story together.

"Well, am I right," she repeated, still smiling.

"Kinda."

"You'll have to do better than that, boy."

"I met her at the interview for the job at the *Times*. I got it – she didn't. I took her out a couple of times but my accident kinda interrupted things. When I woke up, she had the job at the *Times* and I had multiple fractures. You know the rest."

"So you haven't got that whole unscratched itch thing going on then?"

"For a time," he conceded. "I was a bit sore at the way it

turned out – and sore at her for ditching me when I was out of it but…. but then I met you." He went to her and put his arms round her waist. "Now get ready or we'll be late if you're still in there when Gorman gets back."

"About that, do you think it's safe for us to be carrying on as if nothing has happened? Some guy who we don't know tried to kill me not once but a few times. When I think about it, I just want to lock the doors and hide."

"We saw him get hit by a car. We also saw him fly through the air onto another car. He wasn't moving when we left. It looked serious and he's probably dead. If he's not, he'll have more than a headache when he wakes up; he won't be going anywhere in the foreseeable future I reckon. In any case, whoever is after us…you, they're too late; you signed up to the Commissioners and Milo's Scale is going ahead. I told you on the train there might be a few more twists before we can say it's over but we've got Dave Gorman with us. So, let's hit the town and try to forget about it."

She kissed him and turned back to the mirror. "You'd better be right," she said to his reflection.

Paperwork had accumulated on Newman's desk during his absence and although he'd farmed out what he could, the shortage of personnel meant a sizeable pile remained. A temporary replacement for Hinkley, a uniformed constable not long out of the college, had been assigned to make up the numbers but he was still catching up with the methods of the squad. New cases and fielding calls throughout the day had kept Newman from making a start. It had been seven p.m. before he tackled the files. It was now seven forty-five. His mobile rang; it was Grenard.

"Daniel."

"Jim, I have some news. Not good I'm afraid."

"Go on."

"We are…. we think the man we are looking for, took the train to London. The CCTV picked up someone matching build and facial features at the Midi Station; we have someone running a program to match the known features of the suspect with the footage from the station. At a glance, it looks like him. I don't need the computer for that."

"So you're telling me he's my problem now."

"No, no, he killed one of my men. I'll be with you by lunch tomorrow with Delfic – I hope you'll let me assist."

"Okay, we'll see you tomorrow but in the meantime, give me all the details – what train he was on, your photo from the hotel and the CCTV footage. Zip it all into a file and email it to me."

"It's already on the way. Check your inbox." Grenard paused then said, "Last night – he caught the service around seven."

"That gives me something to work with. We'll check the CCTV at all the stations up to St. Pancras."

"It made no stops."

"That makes it easier. Call me when you know your arrival time.

Newman hung up then dialled Gorman.

"Are you back with the Ferretti girl?" he snapped when Gorman picked up.

"Yes, they're going to meet a reporter friend of Devan's at the Hilton; I'm following their cab."

"You couldn't persuade them to stay in?"

"I tried but they think there's no danger since the guy got

hit with the car."

"I wish it was that simple – he's in London. They've got video of him boarding the Eurostar."

"I see."

"Don't let the girl out of your sight and if you can get them to have an early night, all the better. Where's Hargreaves?"

"On her way home, I think. I took over and she left."

"Stick with the girl – I'll call you later."

"Yes, Boss."

Newman cut the line and immediately called Jill Hargreaves. She picked up on the second ring.

"Yes, Sir."

"I need you to come in right away."

"Give me twenty minutes."

When Jack came to, his first blurred sight was of his shoes. His head was lolling forward and thumped with a passion. He tried to gasp but his mouth would not open forcing him to breathe through his nose. As his eyes began to focus, he saw his calves were strapped with brown parcel tape to the legs of the chair supporting him. He realised he was gagged with the same tape that was also holding his arms at the elbow behind his back – interrogation style.

The room was the lounge of an up-market apartment; lit by table lamps and furnished with deep leather sofas set off by modern art on the walls. The chair to which he was strapped didn't seem to fit with the rest of the furniture; it was made of wood and reminded him of the chair he had at his school desk as a child. It felt rickety in the same way and loose in its joints. Maybe it came from the laundry room, if this apartment had one.

In his still unsteady vision, he saw, what at first he perceived to be a pile of clothes, stir and rise up in front of him. It was Kierack. He'd been curled fetus-like on the floor at Jack's feet but now scrambled unsteadily to his feet. Jack noticed sweat beads breaking on the big man's brow, merging into rivulets that trailed down his cheeks when he rose to his full height. As Kierack towered over him, swaying slightly, Jack got his first close-up look at the guy; sick he may be but he was one scary individual and Jack wished he'd left well alone.

"So, you're awake," the giant taunted. There was a perceptible slur to the edge of his speech, not too much but enough to notice. It wasn't clear if this was his usual accent or caused by whatever it was that ailed him. Either way, things looked bad for Jack. Juliet's words echoed in his head – 'don't get caught. I don't think he'll be a happy boy if he sees you.' She got that right!

"I checked your I.D. in your wallet – a reporter. Not a bad cover but I spotted you. I had you sussed – you and Blane." Kierack was chuckling now – walking away to a drinks cabinet by the door, steadying himself on the wall with one arm outstretched like a tightrope walker. Jack spied the contents that had been taken from his pockets scattered on the floor at his feet – wallet, phone and coins.

"No, your little plan didn't work out. How much was he paying you?" Kierack called over his shoulder to Jack. "Don't answer that," he went on, suddenly consumed by laughter. "Because you can't – I forgot." Another roar of laughter but then his cackle was cut short as he let out a gasp that creased his frame at the waist. "Anyway, I don't want to hear it," he croaked finally as he straightened, his

317

face beetroot red. "You'll have your chance to chat over old times when your friend gets here."

Jack had no idea what Kierack was talking about and he wasn't sure Kierack knew either; the man was either crazy or coming down from some kind of high he'd got on to kill the agony of his injuries. Jack wasn't sure there were injuries *or* drugs but assumed it must be so as it provided the most logical explanation for the erratic behaviour. Furthermore, he was sure Sheldon Blane would not have hired a *crazy* giant to be his personal all-over bad guy; he would have been careful. No, Mr. Kierack here was delusional about something and Jack just happened to stumble into what was clearly someone else's nightmare. He only hoped that he'd have the chance to speak before another wild notion crossed Kierack's mind – but while he was silenced with parcel tape, Jack had little chance of saying anything.

"Any moment now, I expect your friend to come through that door." Kierack was gesturing with the hand holding a brandy glass taken from the cabinet. The liquid slopping out as he spoke. "It's a real shame I won't be here to greet him; I have somewhere else to be. But first, I must set my little surprise for him before I leave."

Jack studied Kierack. He seemed to go in and out of his spasms of racking pain – one moment doubled up, the next, upright and fearsome. Alcohol was only going to make things worse. One thing which didn't change was the wild stare in his eyes – the kind Jack only associated with madness.

There was one glimmer of hope however; he had some wriggle room at his elbows taped behind him – not much, but enough to work at. The tape wasn't as tightly wrapped as it was on each of his legs. Maybe Kierack was having one of his turns when he got to the elbows. Hope there may be, but what to do if he did get his hands free. There was still the matter of freeing his legs and then dealing with Kierack who sure as hell wasn't going to stand by and watch while he made a break for it.

He worked his elbows at every moment Kierack was distracted by whatever was going on in his head. He rocked the chair from side to side to increase the play in the joints where the legs fitted into the base of the seat and hoped, when the time came, they would break away to give him mobility.

Kierack was in the centre of the room. In his hand he held a light bulb. It seemed to be part filled with liquid that swilled in the globe. Jack watched him stand unsteadily on one of the stools from the breakfast bar to reach the hallway light fitting, twisting the cover and replacing the bulb with the one he carried.

"Now I must go to the kitchen," he called to Jack as he stepped down from the stool, steadying himself against the wall as a wave of dizziness seemed to engulf him. It was only momentary. Kierack appeared to shake himself free and clear his head. "I have to prepare something – a little dish at gas mark five." He cackled again and went down out of sight behind the breakfast bar.

Jack's arms were almost free. If he was going to do something, it had to be now.

29

Juliet was worried; she hadn't heard from Jack – he wasn't picking up his phone. She was sitting in the bar at her hotel waiting for Blane at a corner table. She'd deliberately gone down early to choose a spot with a view of the entrance. She'd tried Jack's number three times while she waited but with no luck; the last attempt drew a recorded message informing her that the subscriber had turned off his phone. In the short time Juliet had known Jack, he had never turned off his phone. Something was wrong but she didn't have time to dwell on it; she'd spotted Blane – smooth and polished in his two thousand Dollar suit. He was weaving between the tables, on his way to her from the door, like an ice-hockey player dancing his moves with a puck on course to slam a goal, smile fixed in place. In other circumstances and with the benefit of ignorance, of course, she would have found him attractive, all that easy charm and innate anticipation of a woman's needs. He was right on time and she had nothing new to hit him with. Things were not turning out like she'd planned – unusual for her.

When she'd agreed to meet, she'd figured by the time seven fifteen came around, she'd have some snippet from Jack to illicit a reaction from Blane or something else to spice up her piece. There seemed little point in running the episode featuring Marilyn Snell – he'd batted that one away with his apology for being young, arrogant and inexperienced in life – hasn't everyone got something they're ashamed of? To feature the saga now would be irrelevant to the takeover and seen as a mean spirited attempt at character assassination leaving the reader wondering what Sheldon Blane had done to Juliet to warrant such hostility.

Nothing of her cross-examination had shaken anything loose from the tree, quite the contrary – Sheldon Blane had acted as if he had expected every one of her questions – even throwing some back on her. She caught a glimpse of herself in the mirrored wall across from her table, automatically examining the line of her black cocktail dress and checking it hadn't hitched anywhere as she stood to greet him. 'Jesus,' she thought, 'this is more like a date than it should be.'

"Juliet, you look stunning."

"I'm going on somewhere with some friends later – I think I mentioned it."

"Oh, yes – you did. For a moment there I thought you'd dressed for our date."

She looked at him askance. "This is not a date….. I thought we were going to talk more about your business."

"Well, that too if you like but I thought you'd done with it."

In the light of the absence of a phone call from Jack, it was hard not to agree with him.

"Yes, I suppose so but if anything comes into my head when we're talking, I may get back to it."

"Be my guest but until then, we're off the record?"

She nodded cautious agreement.

"Good," he said, looking around for a waiter. "What can I get you?"

The cab weaved through the early evening traffic in brightly lit West End streets. Rick checked Gorman was still with them through the back window. The detective's Ford was there but one car back. A stretch limo filled with raucous women waving from its windows, had squeezed in front of him at the last set of lights.

"Is he still there?" Sophia asked.

"Yes, he's still there. Now, stop worrying and try to enjoy yourself. We're meant to be on a night out."

"Okay, okay – I'm over it." She looked up into Rick's face, smiled her best party smile and tried to put the events of the last twenty-four hours – events which ran on an endless loop, out of her head.

"Okay then, let's party," he said, looking at his watch. "We'll be there in five minutes." He paused for a moment then said, "My semester finishes in a few weeks and there's a month before the next one. I'm thinking of going home for a couple of weeks. Would you like to come with me – I could show you Seattle – the sights – you know – stuff." Her eyes widened with a look of surprise.

"I'd like that…," she said hesitantly, "…very much. I'll need to find out if I can get the time off. I'm sure it'll be okay."

"When Milo's Scale hits the streets, you won't need to ask anyone's permission for anything."

"That'll be then but in the meantime, there are people depending on me; I can't just disappear without telling them. There's also the conversation I must have with Jake. He knew deep down it was over but I have to say it face-to-face; I can't just dump him by letter – he's still in the hospital. It would be heartless."

"I suppose so but all that shouldn't take too long" Rick said, studying her. She was smiling at some private thought. "And what's so amusing?"

"Bit early to be taking me home to meet Mom, isn't it?" she replied, broadening her smile.

"Very funny – I thought getting you away for a while would give you a break from the weird stuff going on here."

"I'm teasing," she said, laying her head on his shoulder. "It would be great."

The taxi slowed as it entered the turning bay in front of the Hilton then turned in a tight circle, finally pulling up at the revolving door. As Rick stepped out, he spied D.S. Gorman pulling into a parking spot fifty yards away. He paid the driver and escorted Sophia into the lobby.

"I need the Ladies," she said. "You go on down – I'll follow with Dave in a moment." She nodded in the direction of the detective who was negotiating the revolving door.

"Are you sure you don't mind."

"I'll be fine – now go; we'll be there in a few minutes."

Rick watched her as she walked away with Gorman in tow then turned and headed for the stairs which curved downwards in a wide arc to the bar. As he descended the spiral and neared the entrance arch at its base, the rise and fall of voices interspersed with peels of laughter over soft Musac, drifted up to meet him.

A manager stepped out from behind a waist-high desk as Rick entered.

"Would you like a table, sir or will you sit at the bar?"

"I'm meeting someone," he replied, looking over the man's shoulder and scanning the busy room for Juliet. He caught sight of her at a table across from the bar in conversation with a man who was rising from his chair.

The body language said this wasn't her date, so Rick reckoned it was work and their meeting was ending. As Juliet rose and stepped out to shake the hand of the mystery guy who had his back to Rick, she momentarily looked in Rick's direction, winking at him before turning back to her guest.

"She's very beautiful." Sophia's voice surprised him from behind.

"You were quick," he said, wondering if she'd caught Juliet's wink.

"I only needed a mirror – there was one in the lobby. Good thing too, now I've seen the competition."

"There's no competition – no contest as far as I'm concerned," he replied, kissing her cheek.

Gorman stood behind Sophia. "Do you plan to stay here long," he asked. They turned to face him. The three of them stood in a huddle to the side of the manager's station waiting for Juliet to free herself from her meeting.

"About an hour, I suppose – then we're going for dinner. You're welcome to join us," Rick replied for both of them.

"Er..thanks, that's very kind," he said hesitantly.

"Something bothering you, Dave?"

"No, just being cautious, I suppose."

There was a commotion behind them. They turned to face

the room. A birthday cake was being hoisted over the heads of revellers at a corner table by waiters mumbling the words to 'Happy Birthday'. Sophia opened her mouth to say something but stopped before any words could pass her lips. The colour drained from her face as she grabbed Rick's arm.

"It's him!"

"What are you talking about – who?"

"Weller – that's him."

She was indicating in the direction of Juliet's table; the man who had been with her had turned to leave – showing his face to them for the first time. He seemed distracted and brushed past them to the stairs without a glance. They made their way briskly to Juliet. She smiled as they approached. Rick spoke first.

"Juliet, who was that guy?"

"Hi, Rick, it's really nice to see you too!"

"It's important, who was that guy?"

"Sheldon Blane," she answered, slightly puzzled. "Why do you need to know?"

"No time to explain. I need to know where he's going; do you know?"

"No, could be anywhere."

"I'll follow him," he said to Gorman. "You'd better call the D.I. – I'll call when I know for sure he's somewhere he's staying put." He turned to Juliet as he was making for the exit. "Juliet, this is Sophia. Sophia this is Juliet – D.S. Gorman will explain who *he* is. I gotta go," and he was taking the stairs, two at a time.

Jack could hear the clanking of metal on metal from behind

the breakfast bar. It sounded like Kierack was using a wrench but he couldn't be sure. Now was the time – while there was noise to cover his movements.

In one great push, he heaved himself to his feet, freeing his arms simultaneously. The chair disintegrated beneath him leaving its front legs still strapped one to each of his with tape. The heavy wooden seat crashed to the floor with the backrest remaining attached. He picked it up and rushed to the breakfast bar as best he could with his taped-on extra legs and his damaged hip screaming from the contorted exertion of breaking the chair. He looked like a flailing, half-made robot that got off the table before his maker had finished bolting on its limbs.

Almost at once, Kierack's head appeared above the breakfast counter, eyes wild and sweat gleaming on his brow. Using his momentum, Jack, pressing the chair's backrest into service as the handle of a nine iron, swung the seat into Kierack's temple but then tripped on a flapping strand of tape hanging from his left leg. He caught his head on the corner of the counter-top as he fell. Kierack had also gone down but Jack could hear the giant on the other side of the bar scrabbling to his feet. Jack grabbed the edge of the breakfast bar and pulled himself up in time to catch sight of Kierack staggering out from behind. Blood trickled from the German's brow and his eyes were rolling. Jack delivered another blow and, for the third time in as many days, Kierack was bested by an amateur. He stayed down.

Spying the roll of parcel tape Kierack had likely used to bind him, Jack snatched it up and set about winding it around the unconscious giant – now was not the time to take chances. He dealt with the legs then dragged the limp body to the edge of the sofa and propped it there. Kierack's head lolled forward as Jack ran the tape around and around, binding the man's arms tight at his sides. He removed his own gag then, for good measure and partly out of an irresistible urge to hand out a bit of payback, he taped Kierack's gaping mouth shut.

He finished, cut the tape at the roll with his teeth and reached over for his phone at the centre of the room. He flipped it open intending to call Juliet. The phone was turned off. His hand hovered over the 'on' button when he realised with alarm, there was a strong smell of gas around him. Inspection of a cupboard under the sink soon revealed the cause. Kierack had removed the feed pipe before the valve and the metre. Gas hissed into the room under pressure. The pipe had been deliberately disabled at the junction and would not reconnect. Every window in the apartment had tamper-proof locks with no sign of a key and despite three heavy blows with Kierack's wrench, they refused to break.

Blane's fixer was coming round and moaning through his gag. Jack made a half hearted effort to drag him to the door but gave up at the centre of the living space; his hip was now threatening to give out completely and blood was running from a throbbing gash on his temple making him dizzy as he straightened to leave. The odour of gas filled his head as he inadvertently took a breath. It was strong and heavy, flooding every crevice of the apartment he imagined. He needed to get outside and call Juliet before a stray spark from some piece of electronics in one of the domestic appliances set it off. His muzzy head reduced his walk to a stagger for the door.

30

Rick reached the pavement outside the revolving doors of the hotel in time to catch a glimpse of Blane climbing into the first cab on the rank. It pulled away immediately. Rick boarded the next in line.

"The cab in front – can you follow it, please?" he asked the driver urgently.

"Anything you say." The driver's voice came back in a dull monotone like he'd done this a million times before but usually for women following wayward husbands or the other way around. Rick guessed this would be unusual for him though; this was a man following a man – the driver could only guess at the back-story.

Rick leaned forward in his seat, holding on to the handrail and looking over the driver's shoulder at the glimmering tail lights of the cab in front. Blane was heading through the park towards Kensington.

"Don't lose him, please."

"Relax, he can't go anywhere to shake me off."

Relax – he hadn't relaxed since…since he couldn't remember when. Finding Milo dead in the bath seemed so long ago now; a lot had happened since then and was still happening.

Blane's cab took a right as it left the park in the direction of Kensington High Street. Rick's mind wandered back to the bar at the Hilton – Sophia together with Juliet with no supervision – going over God knows what.

He'd hoped for a controlled situation – him providing the control by steering the conversation away from any uncomfortable areas – not that there was anything to be uncomfortable about – but he just felt it. He couldn't explain it…but there it was. No sense in worrying now; whatever was happening back there, was happening and there wasn't a damn thing he could do about it.

The cab in front took a right turn and stopped twenty yards up the street.

"Go past,"Rick instructed the cabbie. "Drop me just a way up."

As they went by, he saw Blane step from his cab.

"This'll be fine." He was out of his seat handing the driver the fare without waiting for change and keeping his eyes on Blane who crossed the road and disappeared into the entrance lobby of a 1930s apartment block butting up to a supermarket where the road met the High Street.

The door to the lobby was closing slowly, its speed regulated by some sort of closing device. Rick got to it just before it hit the frame. There was no sign of Blane in the lobby, so he pushed in. There was an arch leading to stairs but he guessed Blane had taken the lift set into the limestone wall to the right. The indicator lit at the third floor. He made a mental note and began to dial Dave Gorman.

As he rode the lift alone to the third floor, Blane reflected on his meetings with the infamous reporter from *The*

Seattle Times. I think I schmoozed the lovely Juliet…I got away with it! He took this moment of self congratulation to wonder why he'd harboured any thoughts of apprehension before meeting her. When it came down to it, Juliet's reputation was much greater than her bite; he'd knocked that down to a nibble at best. Not that he'd mind a nibble from her luscious lips! His grin broadened at the thought.

He was shaken back to real life as the lift reached his floor and the doors opened to a commotion. He was greeted by a fleeting glimpse of a dishevelled man, a tramp maybe, bleeding from the head and bolting for the stairs to the right of the lift. Sheldon couldn't place him but the face was vaguely familiar. It was only a glimpse but he thought the man had something taped and flapping at his legs. He stepped out of the lift and suddenly, all thoughts of the stranger, who'd been oblivious to him and whose fading steps he could hear thumping on the stairs, vanished. The door to his flat, situated at the end of the corridor and opposite the lift, was ajar.

"Son of a bitch," he shouted, as he raced to the entrance, flinging the door wide as he reached it. He peered down the hallway toward the living area and the trussed struggling body in the centre of the floor. The lighting was dim from table lamps and made it difficult to take in the scene.

"Ernst? Is that you?"

Kierack was writhing on the deep pile carpet and making urgent groans as Blane's hand hovered over the switch for the hall light.

In one compressed moment, his last instant of life, Sheldon Blane caught the pleading stare of terror in

Kierack's eyes, a thick odour of gas and a sudden realisation that came too late to halt his reflex to turn on the light.

The parking bays outside in Argyll Road were nose to tail but there were no pedestrians; the street was quiet save the whoosh of passing traffic in High Street Kensington. Rick stood on the opposite side of the road to Blane's apartment building with his phone to his ear looking up at the third floor. He was mid-sentence with Dave Gorman when the relative calm was broken by a man bursting from the lobby as if chased by demons. At the same moment, the windows at the centre section of the building on the third floor tore themselves from their frames in an erupting fireball, showering the street with a hail of glinting glass.

*****

Seattle – Mid June

Rick was in Seattle with Sophia, staying at the Four Seasons on a five day trip to see what the opportunities might be if he came back home after his course ended. It was two months since the explosion in Argyll Road. He *had* hoped to bring Sophia before this; however, Gerald Hope had needed her to be around for signatures and negotiation. He'd even persuaded her to go to Brussels on a day trip to meet the guys. Finally though, they had broken away and boarded a flight.

There seemed little point staying at the house where he

grew up as his parents were on holiday; he would take her there if there was time. The Four Seasons had been Sophia's idea – her treat in fact. He was alone in the suite adding the finishing touches to work due back with his tutor the following week. Sophia was out shopping; she'd be back soon.

There was no fixed plan, just explore the offers he'd received and show Sophia the sights. He intended to go into the *Times,* of course – Juliet had phoned three times already. Her enthusiasm curbed slightly when she'd learnt he wasn't alone – but he knew Juliet; any setback was an opportunity to her.

Juliet, she was one of a kind. He cast his mind back to that night in Argyll Road – the rush – the splinters of glass spattering on the street like crystal rain.

It had taken ten days before the full story was broken by *The Seattle Times* – the full impact only hitting home after the E.U announcement of The Milo Scale. Rick remembered being sprawled on his sofa in front of the TV running CNN on mute. An edition of *The Seattle Times* had been on his lap with a front page story by Juliet under the headline 'Reimer's Share Price Nosedives at E.U. Law Prospect'.

It had been the third piece on the takeover of BBM. Two had been Juliet's but the first to appear had been his own, two full pages – front and page two with Juliet and Jack seconding on the byline. It had given him a real charge to have Juliet's boss, the same guy who two years previously, had offered him the post Juliet now held, ask him to call around if he came back to Seattle to stay.

"There might be something here for you Rick – if you still

want it," he'd enthused down the phone when he'd read the piece.

Another memory made Rick smile – Juliet's call that day.

"Did you get it yet?" she'd gushed.

"Yeah, I got it; it's your usual great stuff." He could have read it on-line, of course, but he'd insisted she courier all of the editions in which the articles had appeared – nothing quite like having the real thing in your hand, the actual newspaper. "I guess the story's got a life of its own now; you won't need anything more from me."

"I….wouldn't say *that.* Call me if ever you're in town."

"And your husband to be? What will he have to say about that?"

There had been a pause.

"I broke up with him…..things just weren't the same when I got back from London. I guess I'd just got caught up in a swirl and when I stepped away for a moment and could see it from another place, it didn't feel right. So……call me."

Now, weeks on, he was back in Seattle. There was a click from the electronic lock to the room – Sophia was back.

That night, as Sophia lay in his arms, Rick finally felt the world returning to normal. The curtains were open and the curve of her body was silhouetted against the sheen of the moonlight on the waves in the Bay. He raised himself on one elbow to face her.

"Now that we seem to be clear of the bad guys, what do you think of the way it turned out?"

She opened her eyes and looked up at him quizzically.

"What do *you* think? I'm happy. Blane and his man have gone and Uncle Milo's scale is going into law. We have that weasel Walter Nestrom still niggling through his lawyer but that's not going anywhere…and there's the money of course – more than compensation for the niggles," she added with an impish smile.

"I wasn't meaning that particularly. I was talking about Buckley and the deal with Reimer. I know the Police cleared Buckley of any blame as far as the stuff Sheldon Blane was cooking up but nevertheless, Sam Buckley sailed off into the sunset with his pockets full from the deal. Reimer's shares have hit bedrock. I wondered what you thought about it all."

Sophia raised herself against the pillow, leaned over and kissed his forehead.

"Let me put it like this. It's a little bit like watching two people you don't like, fighting to the death……you really don't care who wins."

Epilogue

Cap d'Antibes – Southern France

From the balcony of his Deco style villa, Sam Buckley had a view of the ocean over the high wall that surrounded the property. His son and daughter, Rex and Olivia, were home from university for a few days. He watched them splashing and shrieking in the pool below. How time flies, he thought and was about to reminisce on their early years when Amanda, his wife of twenty-seven years and childhood sweetheart, stepped onto the balcony and placed the day's edition of the *International Financial Times* on the table in front of him.

"I brought your paper back with me," she announced, then kissed him on the top of his head and disappeared back into the bedroom.

Sam picked up the paper. Its tinted pages rustled in a slight breeze. There it was again, more ink perpetuating Reimer's bump along the bottom but nothing about him; there had never been anything about him. Plenty about Sheldon, of course, though he too received no blame for what was being portrayed as bad judgement by Reimer.

Sam put the paper down, took a sip from his orange juice and turned his thoughts to Sheldon. A pity about *him* really, Sam had liked Sheldon deep down…in a way. The man had a brilliant mind but always had that gangster thing going on…part of his persona…not practical though. It had made him predictable and therefore vulnerable.

Could things have worked out differently? Sam dwelled on this for a moment, mulling over the sequence of events that had led up to the fireball at Sheldon's flat.

It was the lawyer, what was his name now, Giles...Giles Edwards...the phone-call. Yes, that was the start of it.... and all by chance, as it happened. Sam had been on the way to his office when the phone had rung on Frankie's desk. She wasn't there – bathroom break, most likely. He had picked up the phone out of curiosity. There was no need to hear too many details to know that there was the potential for trouble. Sheldon should handle this little spoiler. There were only a few weeks to go before Sam's life's ambition would be realised as well as Sheldon's for that matter. Subtle pressure on Sheldon would make any threats go away.

Sam hadn't revealed his identity to Edwards, merely passing himself off as the P.A. and giving Edwards the direct extension he needed. Sheldon and his mentality would do the rest. Natu Shah, head of I.T. had been very helpful. For a private arrangement, he'd hacked Sheldon's mobiles – all three of them; so it had been easy for Sam to keep abreast of the situation. He was able to push Sheldon with a word here and a nudge there to keep the fire going if he thought things were slowing down – anything to buy time for the takeover to complete. In the event, it hadn't really mattered that much; Reimer had signed early.

Could things have been different, maybe, but no use in concerning himself now. It was still a pity though; he'd liked Sheldon...in a way.